D1616418

To Tame the Wind

Regan Walker

TO TAME THE WIND
Copyright © 2015 Regan Walker

ISBN: 978-0692401729

ACKNOWLEDGEMENTS

Many people contribute to bringing a book into the world, but some make special contributions that must be noted. For *To Tame the Wind*, this included Kalinya Parker-Pryce, a gifted artist and fellow writer who once lived in a convent in Italy and nearly took vows. Kalinya helped me to add realism to my research and to understand the internal workings of a convent. Then she stayed to give me very helpful comments on the rest of the book. As with the 3rd book in the Agents of the Crown trilogy, *Wind Raven*, my friend Dr. Chari Wessel, who donates her weekends to serving as a member of the crew of the schooner *Californian*, a period ship not unlike the *Fairwinds* in my story, made sure my ship descriptions were correct. And lastly, I must thank my beta readers whose suggestions are always invaluable.

YOUR FATHER IS A PIRATE

Though she knew he was English and a privateer, she had no idea why he had taken her, and she would wait no longer to learn the truth of it. "Why did you bring me here? Why did you take me from the convent?"

Leaning one arm against the frame of the carriage, he regarded her intently, his eyes like chips of amber.

"You have your father to thank for that, mademoiselle. As soon as he returns what is mine you will have your freedom."

Claire blinked. "My father?" Her voice sounded to her like the pleading of a feeble schoolgirl. She would not be cowed! She lifted her chin, confident in his error. "What has he to do with this… this perfidy? Papa is a man of business and letters, a man of some wealth. He has no need to steal!"

His mouth twitched up in a grin, drawing Claire's gaze to his sensual lips, reminding her of a night when she had seen him use those lips to good effect. She scowled, angry with the rogue and with herself for finding him so attractive.

He shut the door of the carriage and peered in through the open window. "Your father, mademoiselle, is a *pirate*."

Characters of Note

(Both real and fictional)

Simon Powell, captain of the *Fairwinds*
Claire Ariane Donet, daughter of Jean Donet

At the Ursuline Convent in Saint-Denis:

Sister Augustin, the *Mère Supérieure* or Mother Superior or Reverend Mother
Sister Angélique, the Mistress of Novices
Élise

On the *Fairwinds*:

Jordan Landor, first mate
Nathaniel Baker ("Nate"), cabin boy*
Elijah Hawkins, bosun and old salt
Giles Berube, sailmaker
Tom McGinnes, cook*

On the *Abundance*:

John Wingate, captain
Amos Busby, first mate, who will join the crew of the *Fairwinds*
Zeb Grant, cabin boy

On *la Reine Noire* and in Lorient:

Jean Donet, captain and younger son of the comte de Saintonge
Émile Bequel, quartermaster

In London:

Cornelia, Lady Danvers*
John Ingram, Baron Danvers, part of the British intelligence community
Higgins, the Danvers' butler*
William Eden, British spymaster
Thomas Field, American privateer captain and British prisoner

In Paris:

Dr. Benjamin Franklin, American Minister to France and Commissioner
Edward Bancroft, secretary to the American diplomatic mission in Paris
Charles Gravier, comte de Vergennes, Foreign Minister
François de Dordogne, a lawyer and Claire's betrothed

Characters with an "*" are also characters in WIND RAVEN, book 3 in the Agents of the Crown trilogy, set in 1817.

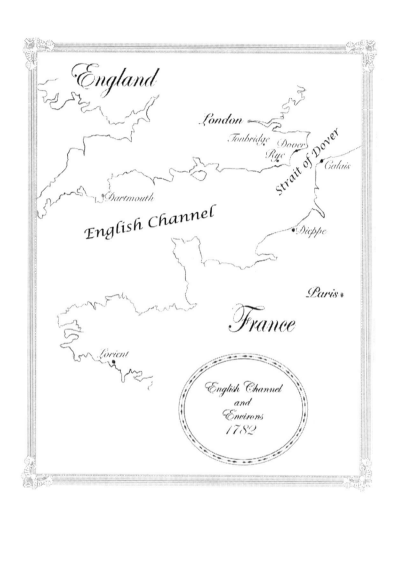

England

London
Tonbridge Dover
Rye Strait of Dover
Calais

Dartmouth

English Channel

Dieppe

Paris

France

Lorient

English Channel
and
Environs
1782

Death leaves a heartache no one can heal,
love leaves a memory no one can steal.

--From a headstone in Ireland

Chapter 1

Saint-Denis, a town north of Paris 1780

A small scraping sound exploded in the still night like a pistol shot setting Claire's every nerve on end. Flattening herself against the cold stone wall, she peered back the way she had come, her eyes searching the darkness. Someone was following her. A small form, instantly recognizable by its frailty and pale blonde hair, crept from the shadows.

Élise.

Claire bit back a groan. Her friend had followed her once again. This was not good. Not good at all. She waited until Élise was almost level with her, and then stepped away from the wall, into the girl's path.

Élise gasped.

"What are you doing here, Élise? You should be home in bed. Your family will be worried if they discover you are gone."

The younger girl seemed torn between triumph and defensiveness. "I knew it! I knew you would defy Mother Superior and sneak out again. I have been watching the convent, waiting, and here you are." She leaned closer, her excitement almost tangible. "Where are you going? What is your adventure tonight?"

Claire scowled. "Go home, Élise."

The girl persisted. "Non, I will not. Where are you going?"

Claire let out a sigh. "To see a masquerade." The relief she had felt at being free of the confines of the convent disappeared with the responsibility for her unwanted companion. Élise might want to be a part of Claire's adventures but she really lacked the fortitude.

Élise's eyes widened. "The one the sisters spoke of?"

"Oui, if you must know. But you should not follow me this night." Claire lifted her gaze to scan the canopy above her. Dark clouds marched across the sky, and where they parted, the moon cast its pale rays on the streets. A cold wind blew her hair across her face. "There is rain in the air and you will catch a chill."

"Deny me this and I will tell Mother Superior of your… your escapade." Élise's spurt of defiance was so uncharacteristic it rendered Claire momentarily speechless.

"Then you had better keep up, for I am in a hurry and will not slow down for you." Claire shrugged out of her woolen cloak. "Here." She thrust it around the other girl's shoulders covering her dark blue convent school dress. "It might help ward off the chill." The cloak fell to the ground on the shorter girl, but it could not be helped.

Claire set a brisk pace through the empty streets, hugging the shadows until she reached the broad expanse of manicured lawn surrounding the château where the bal masqué was being held. Moonlight, thin and weak, shed light on their path, but not enough to reveal Élise and herself to those inside the château.

Behind her, Élise's labored breath had become an audible rasp. The sound pricked Claire's scalp. Élise was all but wheezing. Claire paused, worry warring with impatience.

When Élise reached her, Claire caught the younger girl's cold hand in her own and drew her close. "Are you certain you do not wish to return home?"

Élise nodded.

"Then we must hurry for we cannot risk being seen." Or

being caught in the rain. Perhaps they could be gone before it descended. Hearing a distant rumble of thunder, Claire suffered a pang of guilt, but with no time to waste and no wish to turn back, she let go of Élise's hand and darted toward the terrace. Glancing over her shoulder, she was relieved to see the frail blonde was keeping up.

Élise should not be out on a night such as this. Claire shrugged off the nagging thought, anxious to observe the masquerade she had looked forward to all day. Her excitement had grown ever since that morning when she'd heard the younger nuns describing the fête one of the convent's benefactors was hosting.

She reached the stone balustrade surrounding the terrace. Élise joined her scant seconds later, gasping for breath.

Lively music wafting through the tall doors that stood open to the stone terrace drew Claire's attention from Élise's labored breathing to the colorful characters that populated the magnificent ballroom. Lighted by ornate crystal chandeliers and candles in gilded sconces, the rich costumes of red, gold, green and orange silks and satins sparkled on the twirling couples. The brilliant flashes of color, so different from the black and white of the nuns' habits, took her breath away.

The dancing men and women were costumed in what she could only assume they had a mind to be, and not what they otherwise were. Though she was certain all were from the aristocracy, they were dressed as milkmaids, shepherdesses, jesters, pirates and a few Persian kings. It was as if the characters in the fantastic stories her mother read to her as a child had come alive.

To one side of the dancers, a devil dressed in black conversed with a cardinal in scarlet and a woman attired as a trousered hussar. The red pelisse with its gold braid worn over blue trousers might have been tailored for the woman's curves, but Claire recognized the uniform all the same.

Many wore masks, from simple black to those more elaborate, some even bejeweled and adorned with feathers.

Her heart raced at the pageantry of it. If only she could join them. If only she could dance to the wonderful music. "Oh, Élise… is it not the grandest sight you have ever seen?"

Élise drew the cloak more tightly around her. "It is cold."

So why did you follow me? Claire bit back the question. She had to remember Élise was a day student, one of those to whom the nuns gave charity, who lived at home and looked to the older Claire for adventure. But tonight was not a good time for her to do so. "Your parents will not be pleased you left home without their permission to follow me."

"If you did not sneak away from the convent, I would have no cause to be out and about."

"Oh, pish! So now it is my fault you are here?" Instantly, her traitorous memory reminded her of the scolding she'd received after her last nocturnal outing. You, Mademoiselle Donet, the Reverend Mother had scolded, are a trial. A wild child your father expected me to educate and keep until you marry, a challenge that, on some days, seems beyond all endurance.

Claire knew her papa did not share that opinion. He was proud of her and had told her so on his many visits. If only he had not chosen to send her away to the convent school when Maman had died. Surely a governess would have sufficed. And their housekeeper in Lorient could have seen to her needs while he was away on business. But he had insisted she stay with the sisters even after she was of an age to return home.

She sighed remembering the day her papa had sent her to the Ursuline Convent. She had just turned seven. She remembered the teary scene as if it were yesterday. She missed him so. To please him, she had worked hard to become proficient at her subjects. But now, at sixteen, her restless spirit drove her to escape the convent walls whenever she could.

And she was determined not to miss the most elegant ball in Saint-Denis—perhaps in all of Paris!

"Quickly, Élise." Claire gestured toward the bushy tree, its branches reaching over one side of the terrace. "We must climb that tree so we can better see into the ballroom."

"You go," said Élise, her huge, brown eyes looked up at the tree and then back to the stone balustrade. "I can see all I want to from here. I do not like to climb trees."

"Oh, all right," Claire said, annoyed. "I will only be a moment. Stay close to the balustrade, away from the wind." Leaving Élise in the shadows of the terrace, she hurried toward the tree, impatient for a better look at the dazzling array of costumes.

Using a rock as a stepping-stone, she scaled the lower limbs. A hawthorn tree! Its nasty thorns warned her of the pain they could inflict, but she was determined. As she ascended higher, a branch with sharp thorns caught her dark blue dress. She tugged it free and heard the fabric tear. Sister Angélique would not be pleased, but it was a small price to pay for a glimpse of Paris' nobility attired in their costumed finery.

Avoiding the thorns, she balanced on one of the limbs, holding aside a leafy branch, and turned her attention to the glimmering ballroom. The music slowed as the dancers assembled for the Menuet de la Cour Papa had described to her, but which she had never seen.

It was then she spotted him.

A flash of shimmering gold cape swirled around broad shoulders. A gilded mask of an eagle barely concealed long, blond hair tied back at his nape. At his side hung a sword in a golden sheath. His was the brilliance of the sun compared to everyone else's candle, a mythical creature condescending to join the parade of mortals now moving in slow cadence. Tall and well-muscled, he moved with sinuous grace through the steps of the dance as his lips curved in a brilliant smile.

For the first time, her heart sped at the presence of a man, the sensation so unfamiliar her hand flew to her breast to rub the pounding spot. Oh, he was handsome, this golden one.

Who could he be?

The minuet ended. The golden one took his partner by

the hand and led her to the terrace. It was then Claire's gaze shifted to his partner. The female hussar! The woman wore a gilded blue mask over brown hair swept up into a nest of curls. Not a very good disguise, Claire thought.

Her gaze followed the striking pair as they descended the terrace steps. Claire released her grip on the branch and shifted slightly while avoiding the thorns, so she could keep in sight the couple coming closer. And closer. Her breath froze in her chest when, a moment later, they stopped at the base of her tree. From where she was perched she had a clear view of them. Her heart beat so fast she worried it might leap from her chest. Mon Dieu, do not let them look up!

The man stood back, his eyes roving over the woman's costume, down to her trousers and then back up, pausing at her breasts bulging into view from the short, red pelisse she wore open at the neck. "So, you would wear the trousers tonight, ma petite chérie?"

The woman inched closer to him, her breasts brushing against his chest. Slowly she removed her mask. "If you—an English privateer—are brave enough to risk detection by attending a masquerade in France, I would not presume to act the man, my eagle." The woman's voice was low and husky as if she had something caught in her throat. The mask slipped from her hand to the ground.

English? The golden one is English and a privateer? Claire would never have guessed. His French was impeccable, his speech that of an aristocrat. The news of his origin took her aback. From the whispered tales she had heard at the convent, she would have expected an Englishman to have horns and breathe brimstone, but this one was so handsome she could not tear her eyes from him.

He smiled at his partner, a long, leisurely smile that caused Claire's pulse to speed. If he smiled at me like that...

He ripped off his mask and flung it to the ground. "I could hardly resist the opportunity." Then in a more serious voice, "Besides, I had business here tonight."

"Your only business now is me," said the woman in a sensual voice.

The golden one smiled, backing her against the tree, then bent his head to kiss her.

Claire had never seen a man kiss a woman like that. The woman seemed to enjoy his kiss, running her hands through his hair. She hung on to his shoulders as if to keep from falling. Silly woman. She was wedged between the man and the tree and in no danger of falling... Perhaps the woman was weak?

Transfixed by the couple, Claire's eyes widened as the man's mouth moved to the woman's neck while his hands were busy elsewhere. Mon Dieu! Is he unfastening her trousers? The woman's hands moved to assist his efforts. Oh my, oh my! Claire's heart leaped into her throat.

Sliding down his partner's trousers, the golden one freed one of the woman's legs from her boot and ran his hand up her bare thigh as he lifted it to his hip. The woman's moan covered Claire's gasp. Before Claire could think what would come next, he lifted the hussar to his waist where she wrapped her legs around him, encouraging him with whispered words.

Claire's heart raced. She could only wonder what they would do. What she was about to witness.

"Oh Simon," sighed the hussar. "You make me want you so."

Want him for what? Claire wondered.

The golden one's mouth moved to the woman's neck as he pressed her more firmly against the tree with his chest while undoing his breeches.

"Hurry," the woman urged.

Why is the woman in a hurry? Their ragged breathing, the woman's sighs. Oh my. Claire bit down on her knuckles, nearly drawing blood. She must look away. If I do not, I will go straight to Hell when I die. But her eyes would not oblige.

Another rumble of thunder sounded above her, louder this time. A streak of lightning coursed through the sky, lighting the grounds around the château.

Claire lurched back, nearly falling, and felt a thorn pierce her back. With a gasp, she jerked away as a loud crack sounded and her branch gave way.

She shrieked as she started to fall, grabbing at branches whose thorns ripped into her hands and her arms. She landed with a high-pitched grunt as her breath was knocked out of her.

Not far away, an oath spewed forth in the man's deep voice.

Struggling to breathe, Claire crawled behind a bush while looking about for Élise. They must flee!

Before Claire could run, she heard the sound of heavy footfalls crunching the leaves near the bush where she cowered.

"You are not well hidden, whoever you are," he said in a stern voice.

With reluctance, she rose, brushing off her dress and ignoring the pain from her many scratches. Her face was suddenly bathed in light from the ballroom.

The golden one stood before her, his cape thrown back over his shoulders, his arms crossed over his chest and his breeches restored to their prior condition but there was a decided bulge in the front of them where before there had been none.

Horrified she had been discovered, Claire backed away, thankful the bush was between them. Lightning lit the sky, illuminating his amber eyes glistening above the gold of his costume. He was even more handsome without the mask, and younger than she had thought, perhaps only in his early twenties.

"What have we here?" He sounded amused. "A maiden masquerading as a novice? Where is your mask, pretty one?"

She might have asked him the same question, but Claire did not speak. She was too mesmerized by his presence to utter a word.

Coming up behind him, his partner gave Claire a long,

studying perusal while adjusting her costume. She whispered something into his ear and turned to walk toward the terrace. But the golden one never took his eyes from Claire.

"Such a dull costume for those beautiful, azure eyes." His voice, now a purr, reminded her of the convent cat. The similarity was reinforced when he prowled toward her with his hand outstretched. "You watched from the tree. Were you spying? Or, did you wish to be next?"

Shocked, Claire thought to explain, then decided against it. It was clear from his expression he was toying with her, she a mouse to his cat. And she had just interrupted this cat's evening meal!

He must have seen the fright in her eyes because he paused, his gaze examining her more closely, lingering on the torn dress, the scratches on her face and her long, black hair hanging disheveled about her shoulders. He withdrew his extended hand to rub his fingers over his chin.

"I see now. You are but an innocent. And a young one at that." He shrugged. "Out for a frolic? A little spying on your elders? Hmm?" When she didn't answer, he said, "You'd best be gone, pretty one, before some frog-eater in his cups takes you for a courtesan playing the novice."

Claire needed no further urging to act upon his advice. Seeing Élise edging toward her from the shadows, she gave him a parting glance, then turned and ran, grabbing the other girl's hand without stopping.

Behind her, his deep laughter echoed across the lawn.

With another clap of thunder, the clouds unleashed their fury, pelting them with rain that soon became a torrent.

What more could happen this night?

Chapter 2

Sister Augustin placed the letter on her desk and strolled to the window overlooking the garden where the young woman crouched, weeding. Despite the stone walls, her office was overwarm this summer's day and her woolen habit weighed heavier than usual. It had to be oppressive toiling in the soil in the afternoon sun.

A deep sigh escaped her.

How long had it been? Two years? *Oui*, nearly two years since Élise had died. It had changed Claire Donet. Gone was the rebellious young adventuress and, in her place, was an obedient student who had announced only last week she wanted to enter the novitiate to join the Order.

"What has you so troubled, Reverend Mother?" Sister Angélique's familiar voice asked from behind her. Sister Augustin looked over her shoulder to see the Mistress of Novices, her closest friend, enter the office and pause by the large globe near the reading nook. With a deft flick of her wrist, she set the ball spinning.

Acknowledging her friend with a smile, Sister Augustin returned her gaze to the young woman. "It's Claire Donet. I've received a letter from her father."

"Oh?" Sister Angélique asked.

She gestured to the girl bent to her weeding. "He has

11

arranged a marriage for her to a prominent, young lawyer from a good family in Paris. It is time that she should be leaving us."

Sister Angélique joined her at the window to watch the solitary figure working in the garden. "She will not willingly agree, I think."

"I suspect you are right."

"She has changed much in these last few years. I have been amazed at the transformation," observed Sister Angélique.

"*Oui*, but for some time now I have wondered."

"What is it?"

Sister Augustin did not hesitate to share what had been on her mind. "Can we believe what we see? Has the hoyden who defied me at every turn truly become the humble postulant?"

The knowing smile that lit her friend's face eased some of her anxiety.

"It would be a minor miracle, I grant you," said Sister Angélique.

Sister Augustin was tempted to smile herself. "When I look into those innocent eyes, I see a deep sadness. It's as if she is doing—"

"Penance?"

"Exactly. But for a lifetime?" Sister Augustin's spirit was, indeed, troubled, for though she would be pleased to have a young woman with Claire's spirit and determination in the Order, she doubted it would suit in the end. Perhaps God's better plan had given rise to her niggling doubts.

Shaking her head, Sister Angélique turned to face her. "Claire blames herself for Élise's death. I tried to tell her at the time it was Élise's own decision to follow her that led to the pneumonia that took her life, but Claire would not listen."

Sister Augustin well remembered Claire Donet's tear-stained cheeks and the hollow eyes that had persisted for weeks after the younger girl's death. If only she had perceived the deeper wound beneath them. "I feel it is more than guilt

To Tame the Wind

on Claire's part," she said thoughtfully. "I sense a determination in her. It's as if she has applied the same stubbornness that once led her to defy our rules to her new goal to be a member of the Order. But in my heart, though it may sound strange to you, I long to see again the fire in her eyes when she defied me. She seemed so much more alive then."

"What do you propose?"

"I will meet with her, of course. And then, we will see. If she remains adamant, I will have no choice but to present her wishes to her father. Perhaps M'sieur Donet will have some influence where I do not."

Sister Angélique's gaze rested upon the young woman. "Do you remember that moonstone ring her father gave her last year?"

Sister Augustin searched her memory, then shook her head. "I have only a vague recollection. I seem to remember him saying the stone matched her eyes."

"I am not surprised your memory of it is vague. Though Claire smiled sweetly for her father as she accepted the gift, when he left, she put the ring away and has not worn it since. I took it as a sign."

Sadness settled heavily in Sister Augustin's soul. "If that is so, then it would seem she has shut out even her 'beloved papa' in the pursuit of her goal to become one of us."

୧ ୬୧୧ ୨

Claire forced the trowel deeper into the dirt, only vaguely aware of the persistent moisture dampening her brow and running down her cheeks. Once again, she tried to extract the weed's tenacious roots that desperately clung to the soil. She must dig them out or the insidious plant would return to spoil the garden. Much as her old character and her memories of a man dressed as a golden eagle might shoot up one day after a thunderstorm to spoil her plans to become a nun. It could not be. She was no longer that girl!

The night of the torrential downpour was still fresh in her mind. And Élise's every horrible wheeze and hard draw of breath in the days that followed. Claire vividly recalled the girl's gray face, her sunken eyes, the blueness around her lips as, days later, she fought for breath, coughing out her last words.

And Claire remembered, too, her promise, a promise made when the young girl, brought to the convent for care, lay dying.

Hearing the nuns say in hushed tones that Élise was nearing the end, Claire had stolen into the girl's room when the sisters were at Compline, to sit at her bedside, sponging her heated forehead, trying to bring her some relief.

"My only regret at leaving this world," Élise had said in a weak voice, "is not seeing my…" She had coughed then and gasped for air, panting hard with the effort of breathing. "…my dream come true, to become an Ursuline." Gasping for breath, she had whispered, "To teach young girls as the nuns taught me."

Élise had tried to rise off the pillow soaked with her sweat.

Claire gently eased her down and sponged her forehead with cool water. "Rest now, you have exhausted yourself."

"No." The girl fought to speak. "I must… continue." She had paused only for a moment and then, with uncharacteristic determination, began again. "My family is not wealthy, as is yours." The girl's large brown eyes, sunken in her face, had looked intently into Claire's, and at that moment, Claire felt ashamed of the wealth her father had amassed in recent years.

"If it hadn't been for the kindness of the sisters… " Élise's words faded to a whisper, and Claire had to lean in to hear them. "I would never have learned to read."

Élise's eyes had closed for a moment. Claire inhaled sharply.

At the sound, her young friend opened her eyes, now

glassy, and stared up at her.

Claire had known then what she must do, and sensing the time was short, did not hesitate. With tears filling her eyes, she had vowed, "I will live your dream, Élise. I will be that Ursuline sister for you. I will teach the young girls."

"You? But… "

"Yes, me. It is right that I do this."

And with that, Élise smiled, closed her eyes and drifted into unconsciousness. Her breathing continued to be shallow and after a few breaths she had gasped and slipped back into shallow breathing.

Claire had fallen asleep in the chair next to the bed, listening to Élise's ragged breathing.

She awakened with a start when suddenly there was silence. The nuns' singing had ceased. Élise's small hand was still in hers, but there were no awkward breaths coming from the bed, no gasping for air.

And she knew… Élise had left this world for the next.

The memory brought with it tears that streamed down Claire's cheeks to mingle with the perspiration already there. There had been nothing she could do to save her young friend. She was left with only the guilt of her own misdeed that had led her friend into a sickness unto death.

Sweeping the tears away with the back of her hand, she reached for the main root of the weed. With one hard pull, she yanked it free of the ground, satisfied it would never grow again.

꩜ ꩜ ꩜

The following day, try as she might, Sister Augustin could not concentrate on the correspondence scattered on her desk. A sound on the wooden steps outside her office drew her gaze to the open doorway. Scant moments later, Claire Donet stepped into the opening.

"Reverend Mother, you asked to see me?"

She rose. "Come in, Claire." Indicating one of the chairs on the other side of the desk, she said, "You may be seated."

Without a word, the young woman settled into one of the two tapestry chairs. Though faded with long use, they were still elegant. Along with her precious books and the globe, they were the only material things Sister Augustin treasured.

"Would you care for some water?" She gestured toward the pitcher of water and glasses sitting beside a bowl of fruit on the front of her desk, before resuming her seat.

Claire sat stiffly. "No, thank you, Reverend Mother."

Sister Augustin's gaze strayed briefly to the image of Saint Ursula that hung on the opposite wall and to the crucifix beside it. *Please*, she silently prayed. She needed God's help for the difficult conversation looming before her.

Looking back to where Claire sat, the light from the window casting its rays on the young woman's dark hair and fair skin, Sister Augustin was struck once again what a beautiful young woman in both outward appearance and character Claire had become. But would she accept without argument what she had to say?

Sister Augustin's fingers curled around her rosary beads she had taken from her desk and placed in her lap.

"Claire, you know your father asked me to allow you to stay beyond the age most girls leave us?" At the young woman's nod, she continued. "He wanted you to remain in our care with the additional education we could provide until you were of an age to marry. The time has arrived. He has sent me a letter." Seeing the girl's sudden interest, Sister Augustin elaborated. "He has selected a husband for you."

A look of consternation crossed the young woman's face. "I cannot marry."

Sister Augustin let out a breath. "I thought you might say that."

Claire's chin rose. "I intend to enter the novitiate and become one of you. I am going to teach the children."

The inflexible tone was alien to the compliant young

woman Claire had become in the last two years. But she had to be made to see reason. "Claire, our Order is dedicated to teaching girls that femininity is inextricable from their piety. But we also teach that holiness is achieved not by retreating from an imperfect world, but by joining the world, equipped with the things you have learned here. We are committed to changing the world by changing the young women who will nurture that world. Only a rare few are meant to join the Order."

Claire stared back defiantly. "And I am one of them."

The time had come to address the issue directly. Sister Augustin let go of her rosary, placed her folded hands on her desk and regarded the young woman before her. "You knew that Élise wished to join the Order when she was of age?"

Claire dropped her gaze to her hands, folded in her lap. "Yes."

"We cannot live others' lives for them, Claire. We can only tread the path God has set before us. Your own path, Claire, not another's."

Clear, blue eyes met hers and, in them, Sister Augustin saw a protest. She held up one hand. "You have a strong will, Claire. And courage." She could not resist a smile. "On my better days, I pictured you one day taking your place at the side of a man intended for greatness in the eyes of God, bearing him children who would do much good. I have never imagined you in the cloistered life."

"But—"

"If Élise had lived, there is no certainty she would have been accepted into the Order."

Claire frowned. "But her dream was to become a teaching sister."

As gently as she could, Sister Augustin said, "Wanting something is not the same as getting it, Claire." Her nerves tightened a little as something like disapproval clouded Claire's face.

"Surely you would not have refused her because she was

not from a noble family?"

The question was not unexpected so Sister Augustin took no offense. "Of course not." Claire's expression eased a little. "It had occurred to me that Élise might have entertained the hope of joining us. Sadly, she did not broach the subject with me or the sisters, so we had no opportunity to counsel her." She hesitated. "The truth of the matter is her health alone would have made it impossible. She would not have been physically able to endure the convent's routine. Nor did she have the inner strength for this life."

Claire lifted her chin. For a moment, Sister Augustin thought she saw a flicker of the old defiance.

"Unlike *me*?"

Refusing to be drawn into an argument, Sister Augustin placed her rosary on the desk and rose from her chair. The young woman also rose.

"Think about it, Claire. In your evening prayers tonight, ask God what he would have you do. Tomorrow morning, after Lauds, come and see me. If, after prayer and contemplation, you are still of this mind, I will write to your father. But I cannot predict his thoughts on the matter."

Claire bowed her head, then turned and left the room.

Sister Augustin stared after her. *That young woman is special.* She was tempted to tell Claire's father the girl should be allowed to join the Order, but she hesitated, and then dismissed the thought, knowing in her heart it was not the right thing. Claire would be a fierce defender of the downtrodden and an intelligent and creative teacher, yet Sister Augustin could not escape her inner conviction that Claire Donet was meant for something a world away from the convent in Saint-Denis.

She settled into her chair and stared out the window, fearing the answer she would receive the next morning would not be the one she hoped to hear.

Chapter 3

Rye Harbor, England

A pounding on his cabin door interrupted Simon Powell's examination of the chart of the English Channel spread upon his desk. "Enter!"

The door burst open and Amos Busby, the burly first mate on Simon's second ship, the *Abundance*, erupted into the cabin, his wiry brown hair clinging to the sweat on his forehead. "Captain," he rasped. His chest heaved as he hunched over, hands on his knees, wheezing.

Surprised to see Amos in Rye, Simon snapped his fingers at his cabin boy who stood open-mouthed beside the desk. "Pour the man some ale, Nate."

"Yes, sir." The lad snatched up the pewter flagon, splashed some of the amber liquid into a mug and pushed it toward the first mate's outstretched hand.

Amos straightened, took a long swig and wiped his mouth with the back of his hand. "Aye, that's better." He stepped forward and set the mug on the desk. "'Twas this morning before dawn, sir. The damned Frenchie Donet seized the *Abundance*."

Simon surged out of his chair, the legs screeching across the timbered deck in protest, as his mind tried to take in the words. "*What?*" Fury raced like a firestorm throughhis veins. "That heathen frog has my ship?"

19

Amos backed away from the desk in the face of Simon's wrath. "We were anchored off Dover in heavy fog, sir. I had just come on shore with some of the crew, fixing to arrange for supplies when, bold as brass, a sloop flying the red ensign of one of our merchantmen crept up in the fog, and its crew slithered over the rail with knives between their teeth."

"You saw this?"

"No. 'Twas Zeb, the cabin boy. He was the only one to escape. Jumped overboard and swam to shore"

Simon let out a breath and raked his fingers through his hair. "Bloody hell." His brows drew together in a puzzled frown. "How did you know it was Donet? He captains a brig-sloop with that Frenchified Jolly Roger of his."

Amos held up his hand. "A minute, sir." He disappeared out the cabin door, immediately returning with a young lad in tow. Simon recognized Zeb Grant, the cabin boy on the *Abundance*. Soon after he was hired on, the sandy-haired lad had become a favorite of John Wingate, captain of the *Abundance*.

"Here's the lad, Captain," the first mate said, shoving the boy forward.

Zeb quaked before Simon's intense gaze.

"I understand you were there, Zeb. Did the ship fly a Jolly Roger on a blue field?"

"Nay, sir. She flew a British flag." That news did not surprise Simon. Pirates and privateers carried many flags.

"Did the men who attacked you speak French? Did they talk of Donet?"

The lad stood at attention, obviously proud of the knowledge he alone possessed. "They did, sir. They spoke the Frenchie tongue. I understood some. One of 'em dropped Donet's name and reminded his men of their orders."

Busby interjected, "The crew would've been suspicious of any ship, Captain, even an English one coming so close, but the fog hid them."

"'Twas as dense as pease porridge, Cap'n, with nary a

light on deck," said Zeb. "Made the Frenchies near invisible till they were 'longside."

Simon fixed his gaze on the cabin boy. He needed answers, not excuses. "And the crew?" he demanded, concern for his men settling into his gut like a heavy weight.

"The Frenchies said their orders were not to kill 'em, but one of ours took a knife in the chest and a few suffered slashes before I jumped. We was outnumbered, sir, 'twas at least two to one."

"It's not like Donet to attack a privateer," said Simon. "His usual fare is English supply ships." *What the devil is he up to?*

"I'm thinking it was the crew and the ship he was after," suggested the first mate.

"They talked of capture," Zeb cut in.

"Did they say nothing of cargo?" Simon asked.

"No, sir," Zeb replied in earnest.

"'Twas an odd affair, Captain," said Amos. "It's not like the bloodthirsty Donet to be so—"

"Gracious?" Simon raised his brows. "No, I should say not. Damn scurvy corsair!" For years, the French pirate had been the bane of their existence, attacking English merchantmen and supply ships for the cargo bound for the Colonies. But from his contacts in Paris, Simon had recently learned that the American commissioner, Dr. Franklin, had been enlisting privateers in his cause to gain prisoners to exchange for Americans held by the British. "Seems like Donet has a new mission."

"Aye, sir," Busby replied. "And maybe a new letter of marque."

"Pirate scum." Simon clenched his teeth and his eyes fastened on the *Abundance*'s cabin boy. "What of Captain Wingate?"

"It were him that took the knife in the chest," said Zeb, sadness and worry etched on his young face.

Simon sank into his chair, resting his forehead in his hand.

Wingate was a good captain and more. He was a friend from their boyhood days in Dartmouth who'd signed on as a seaman the same day as Simon.

After a moment, Simon raised his head. The *Abundance*'s first mate looked dead on his feet. "Sit down Mr. Busby."

The man eagerly reached for a chair.

"Nate, fetch Mr. Landor and Mr. Hawkins," ordered Simon.

"Aye, sir." The boy darted through the door.

Simon turned his attention back to Zeb. "Do you know if Captain Wingate's wound was fatal?"

"I didn't stay long enough to find out, sir. The knife was stuck high in his chest near his shoulder, so mebbe not. 'Twas him who yelled at me to jump just after he took the blade."

Simon turned to the windows, casting his gaze on the harbor and the sun glistening off the water. The river mouth formed a huge marsh, a labyrinth for any pursuers, the perfect port for a privateer, which is why he had selected it as the home port for his two schooners. He let out an exasperated sigh. If the *Abundance* had been anchored here, he would still have a second ship, and he would still have his friend.

At the sound of boots coming toward him, Simon shifted his attention to the cabin doorway where his curly-haired first mate, Jordan Landor, appeared. Behind him was Elijah Hawkins, the wizened old bos'n of the *Fairwinds*. The old salt wore his usual dark blue knit cap pulled down over his ears where it met his short gray beard.

"Captain?" said Jordan, his green eyes casting an anxious glance at the first mate from the *Abundance*.

"Come in, Jordan. You, too, Elijah. We have a most unpleasant business to deal with."

With a nod and a mumbled "Amos" to the first mate from the *Abundance*, the two men claimed the remaining chairs in front of his desk. Young Nate and Zeb took a stand in front of his shelf bed.

Simon allowed his gaze to drift out the window, this time

stretching beyond the harbor toward the coastline of France. In a somber mood, his jaw set in firm resolve, he turned to face the two men who had joined them.

"Donet has struck again and this time he has taken the *Abundance.*"

❧ ❧

Simon studied the faces of the men who were gathered a few days later around a table in the common room of the Mermaid Inn in Rye, key members of his crew from the *Fairwinds*, and several from the *Abundance* who had been ashore when it was seized. Good men and true, some former Royal Navy, some who'd crewed with him on his first ship and some from Dartmouth, all now together as one, having fought enough battles in the last several years to bind them together.

From their faces, he could see his men still seethed at the Frenchman's effrontery. For his own part, Simon was more than a little embarrassed that one of his ships had been so easily taken. If his friend John Wingate had survived the knife wound, he would be giving himself a scathing rebuke about now.

"We must retake her and regain the crew," Simon said, not bothering to hide his anger. "I will not lose them to that heathen, God-cursed Frenchman."

Sally arrived at their table just then to hand out mugs of ale. "Can I get you and your men some food, Captain Powell?" The blonde innkeeper's daughter waited for a response while glancing at the others, but their gazes were fixed on Simon.

"Not just now, lass, we've a problem to solve," he said. "Perhaps later."

"Just give a shout when you're ready." She smiled and left, swaying her hips flirtatiously as she walked away. Simon watched her wend her way through the empty tables to the one by the front window where two men conversed over their food. It was only afternoon and the tavern had yet to fill for

23

the evening, which suited his purpose well.

"It can be done," said Jordan Landor, in a low voice, his green eyes staring off into the distance. "Donet can't stay in Lorient forever and I reckon that's where he's holed up with the *Abundance*." Then turning to Simon, "He'll be expecting trouble and prepared to sink us right quick. 'Twill call for stealth."

"Aye," said Simon. He'd had experience at stealth, going in and out of France for the last several years collecting messages and gathering information for his superiors in London.

Undaunted, he was about to set forth his plans for the hazardous mission when Amos Busby spoke up. "I'll go, Captain. It's my crew, too."

Simon nodded. "We'll include you in the plans, Amos."

Elijah Hawkins pulled his pipe from his mouth. "I've a thought ye might want to consider, Cap'n."

All eyes turned to the old bos'n whose advice, though rarely given, was seldom ignored.

"And that would be?" Simon raised a brow.

Elijah took a draw on his pipe, then blew out the smoke. "I'd heard tell Donet had turned to privateerin', so I did some sniffin' around, askin' about 'im on the quiet like. Knew it was only a matter o' time before he tangled with us." He laid the stem of his pipe along the side of his nose, a sly grin deepening the multitude of wrinkles carved into his face. "Last time we slipped into Paris to see the Scribe, I learned somethin' I reckon will be right useful now."

Elijah's reference to "the Scribe" stirred Simon's interest. It was their name for the British spy who worked as a secretary for the American mission in Paris. "And?" he asked impatiently.

Speaking out of one side of his mouth, holding his pipe in the other, Elijah leaned forward and lowered his voice. "Seems Donet has somethin' he prizes more than his ship." The old seaman sat back in his chair, a satisfied smile on his face as he puffed on his pipe.

Simon narrowed his gaze. "Enough mystery, Elijah. What could he possibly prize more than *la Reine Noire*?"

A gleam came into Elijah's pale blue eyes. "A daughter, Cap'n—"

"He has a daughter?" Jordan blurted out, his brows rising. "I didn't even know he had a wife."

"He's not had a wife fer many a year," said Elijah. He turned the stem of his pipe toward them, stabbing the air as he spoke. "That's why he keeps the daughter in a convent near Paris." He scratched the side of his nose with the end of his pipe. "Must be young if she's there, I should think." Then to Simon, "If ye had her, I 'spect ye'd soon have yer ship."

"Hmm," murmured Simon, thinking of the possibilities. They could sail to Dieppe, the closest port to Paris, and after a days' carriage ride, take the girl from the convent.

"You know where this convent is?" he asked Elijah.

The old bosun sat back in his chair, his pipe resting on his chest and a smug look on his face. "It just so happens I do."

"It might work," said Simon, letting his gaze drift over his men to judge their reaction. "If there are no objections, gentlemen, we'll set our course for Dieppe, not Lorient."

Every head at the table nodded.

In less than an hour, Simon and his men were back on the *Fairwinds* gathered round a map of the area surrounding Paris, planning the raid that would gain them a treasure for ransom.

"We need some intelligence," insisted Simon after they'd agreed on the plan. "I'd not want to grab the wrong girl in the dead of night."

"I'll do the scoutin', Cap'n," offered Elijah. "I can take Mr. Berube with me. The sailmaker speaks the Frenchie tongue as well as ye an' me. Once in France, we can travel by horse. If all goes well, we'll be back in a little over a week."

Simon thought Giles Berube a good choice for the mission. He'd spent his youth in France before coming to England to live with his uncle who was a sailmaker in

Dartmouth where Simon had first met him. Simon nodded to Elijah. "Aye, and while you are there, see if the Scribe has left any messages for me. This business with Donet has delayed my return."

"Aye, aye, Cap'n," said the trusted old seaman.

Simon turned to his first mate. "Mr. Landor, see to the transport for Mr. Hawkins and Mr. Berube to the port of Dieppe."

☙ ❧ ☙

True to his word, a little more than a week later, Elijah and Giles stumbled into Simon's cabin where the *Fairwinds* was anchored in Rye. The wide grin on the old seaman's face and Giles' eyes twinkling with mirth told Simon the two had been successful.

"Well?" Simon asked, eager to hear the news. "Sit down and tell me."

"Before I ferget," said Elijah, "here are the messages I retrieved from the Scribe's tree." The seaman shoved a packet of paper toward him on his desk, then took his pipe out of his waistcoat pocket and packed it with tobacco. The two men sat in the chairs facing his desk.

"And the other item of business that has you smiling?"

"Aye, we got lucky there, Cap'n," said Elijah, looking to Giles to explain.

Giles was prepared. "Seems the villagers in Saint-Denis remember well a convent student whose father, Jean Donet de Saintonge, the son of the comte de Saintonge"—he paused and raised his brows—"is a wealthy benefactor of the convent."

Though Simon was aware Donet had turned pirate some years ago, he had no idea the Frenchman possessed noble blood. The why of it made the man all the more intriguing. "That is most interesting. I can only wonder why a comte's

26

son would deny his heritage to become a pirate."

"Perhaps he was bored," suggested Giles.

"Must be more than that," Simon conjectured. But the subject was not his primary concern. "Did you get a description of the girl?"

"Aye, we did," said Elijah. "Had a chat with the butcher in Saint-Denis. Man rambled on about an older girl, one who stayed on when others left. Talked about her hair as black as the nuns' habits. Said she often accompanies the sisters when they come to the village on errands. The butcher couldn't leave off talkin' about her strikin' blue eyes. 'A clever girl' he said."

"And that's not all, Cap'n," said Giles. "Once I learned that the nuns were customers of the butcher, in the guise of delivering fresh meat to the convent, I gained entry. Took no time at all to learn the layout of the place and the location of the students' sleeping chambers and the one Donet's daughter shares with some older girls. I marked their window that leads from the garden."

"You have a knack for intrigue, Giles." Simon smiled, satisfied he now had all he needed. Rising, he strode through the open cabin door, followed by the two men, and ascended the ladder to the weather deck. There, he announced to his first mate and his assembled crew, "We leave with the tide for Dieppe and thence to Paris." To Jordan he handed the packet from the Scribe. "See that these messages get to London."

Much to Simon's satisfaction, the wind and the tide were with them. Not long after, he set a southerly course and they sailed that evening. The long summer days gave them light for many hours.

The pale light of dawn saw them anchored off the port of Dieppe, the *Fairwinds* now flying the flag of an American privateer.

Though the wind had favored them, the weather on the north coast of France was less than agreeable. The scattered rain had not impaired their progress as they dropped anchor and let down the skiff, but it was enough to concern him for the mission ahead and the carriage ride to Paris. He did not look forward to muddy roads that would slow their progress south.

Wasting no time, Simon departed the ship, climbing down the Jacob's ladder to where four of his men waited in the skiff. He sat in the stern with his tricorne hat pulled down over his forehead to ward off the rain while the crew he'd handpicked for the mission pulled at the oars bringing them ashore.

The cliffs of Dieppe loomed ahead in brooding shades of black and ochre flecked with occasional patches of rust, made more somber by the rain. Hundreds of feet high, they hemmed in the port like a setting for a dark jewel, a forbidding wall that urged caution. It was familiar ground to Simon. He'd anchored off Dieppe many times whilst on missions for England to retrieve messages from the Scribe and pay calls on his contacts for news of French supply ships. He smiled to himself, remembering the masquerade he'd attended two years before to spy on one of his targets. There had been the diversion of his amour dressed as a trousered hussar. And the young chit he'd mistaken for a costumed courtesan. Not all of his assignments were unpleasant.

Elijah raised his head and the wind whipped stray, gray hairs around his face. "Smilin' at the rain, Cap'n?"

"No, 'twas just a memory. What of the arrangements on shore?"

"I knew ye'd be anxious to be off, Cap'n, so before we left France fer Rye, we arranged for a post chaise and team to be waitin' fer ye. Giles can see to those while I secure the skiff."

The thin sailmaker nodded. His tricorne, beaded with rain, shadowed his features, save for his stubbled jaw. "Aye, Cap'n, 'tis all organized."

In short order, they reached the shore and the skiff was stowed. Soon, they were in the carriage and hurtling down the road to Paris, mud flying in all directions.

By the time they reached Saint-Denis, it was evening. Encouraged by extra coin, the coachman had driven hard, stopping only to change horses. The sleep they'd managed was much disturbed by the rutted road, but it was enough. And they'd have hot food before it was time to seek out their prey.

Chapter 4

Saint-Denis

Exhausted, Claire finished the letter to her papa, set the paper on the bedside table and blew out the candle.

The half-dozen older students in her chamber were already asleep on their narrow beds. One of the most senior of the convent's boarding students, she enjoyed her role as a *dizainière*, a pupil-teacher, with younger students to look after. It meant her days were full and they left her with little enthusiasm for conversation when she sought her bed after Vespers.

Claire undressed in the dark room. Echoing through the walls, Claire could hear the soft voices of the nuns singing at Compline in the chapel. It was a soothing, familiar sound. One day soon, she would join them.

Would she be a good nun? In the past two years she had tried hard to repress her secret longings so that she might become an acceptable postulant. She had not always succeeded. The memory of a golden man and the craving for a life beyond the convent's walls and a home where she could put to use all the nuns had taught her still lurked, hidden in the recesses of her mind. When the cravings taunted her, she would remember her vow to a dying girl.

Would Élise, looking down from Heaven, be pleased?

And what of Papa's plans? If he knew his only daughter intended to join the Order, would he agree? Or might he still insist she wed? She had wondered whom her papa had selected. Since her meeting with the Reverend Mother, Sister Angélique had told her the man was a lawyer in Paris. She shoved aside the curiosity it roused. Like her secret longings, it was not to be.

She rubbed her eyes. Worry over her conversation with the Reverend Mother and the nightmares that came often had robbed her of sleep for days. And this day had been full. After her classes, she had accompanied Sister Angélique to the village for shopping. Upon her return, she had sought a quiet place to rest for a few minutes, but her mind was filled with what she must tell her papa in the letter she knew she must write. Surely he would understand why she could not marry.

When the afternoon began to wane, she had drawn on what little patience she'd had left and helped the younger girls with their work before joining the others to set the table for the evening meal. Afterwards, she was so weary she had to pinch herself twice during Vespers to stay awake. But she had not allowed herself to pursue her rest until she had composed the letter to her papa.

Weariness crept over her like a heavy cloak, dragging her down. She was too tired to think more about her future this night. The solace of her bed called to her. Perhaps tonight the nightmares—the wretched dreams of Élise gasping out her last breaths—would not come.

She reached for her nightgown, a pale swath lying across the foot of her bed, illuminated by the moonlight shining through the glass panes of the only window in the room. In the mornings, the window allowed her a glimpse of the sun's first rays. That and the waking birds called her to Matins each day.

Pulling the modest nightgown over her head, she plaited her long hair and peeled back the cover of her bed. She stepped out of her slippers and slipped into the welcome coolness of the clean sheets.

A noise outside the window disturbed her thoughts, but too bleary-eyed to care about an owl out for its evening meal, she rolled over, said a quick prayer for her papa, and succumbed to sleep.

❧ ❧ ❧

Giles eased the window open and Simon, using his arms, soundlessly lifted his body onto the sill and then into the room. The sailmaker followed closely behind. Simon stepped to one side and gestured Giles away from the window where the moonlight would most assuredly reveal him in silhouette should one of the girls awaken.

Simon surveyed the sleeping students. Several with dark hair rested their heads on white pillows. *Damn.* How was he to find the one with blue eyes without waking them all? And what if more than one had blue eyes? A moment's anxiety gripped him. He had no time for this. Forcing himself to remain calm, he gazed about the room in the faint light afforded him, seeing what appeared to be workbooks and papers stacked on the small tables paired with each bed. From the table closest to him—next to the bed where a girl with dark hair slept—he picked up a letter, still unsealed. Tilting it toward the moonlight, he studied the elegant script.

M. Jean Donet, Lorient.

He grinned. Luck was with him. He'd found the girl. He gazed down at her. Her head lay to the side, her black plait resting over her shoulder. In the moonlight her skin looked like fine porcelain.

Gesturing to Giles, Simon pulled a handkerchief and a strip of cloth from his pocket, then gently rolled the girl onto her back. She moaned, but before she could rouse, he stuffed the handkerchief into her mouth and wrapped the strip of cloth around her mouth, securing it with a knot at the back of her head.

33

Her eyes flew open, her fear stark and tangible. She tried to sit up, her hands reaching for the cloth around her mouth.

He grabbed her hands. "*Ça suffit!*" he whispered in French as he bound her wrists with a strip of cloth. "I will not harm you."

Even in the dim light her eyes flashed her disbelief.

She twisted on her bed, straining against the binding cloths and kicking out her feet. Her muffled grunts were starting to worry him for fear one of the other girls might hear.

He pulled the blanket from her bed and wrapped it around her against the night chill.

Giles grabbed her ankles and bound them, then stepped to the window and jumped to the ground.

Simon scooped up the squirming girl and passed her through the window into the sailmaker's outstretched arms.

He was about to depart when he remembered the note tucked into his breeches. Lifting the paper from its hiding place, he laid it on the girl's pillow. A last scan of the room told him the other girls still slept. Satisfied, he jumped through the open window to the ground, turned and eased the window closed. Reclaiming the girl from Giles, he and the sailmaker crept from the convent grounds and to the carriage where his men waited.

❦

Trussed up like a cat in a bag, fear and anger warred within Claire as she was awkwardly jostled in the arms of her abductor. Now starkly awake, questions swirled in her head. Though the cloth rudely stuffed into her mouth prevented her from demanding answers, she uttered a muffled oath that would have shocked the Reverend Mother.

Who are these men? The man who carried her had not been overly rough. He could have thrown her over his shoulder like a bag of stolen goods but oddly, he carried her like something that he valued, something precious.

Racking her brain, Claire tried to recall an incident or anything that might provide a clue as to the source of her abduction, but she could think of nothing. Her life at the convent was simple, uncomplicated, absent of discord, particularly in the last two years.

Why have they taken me?

Perhaps they knew her papa was a man of means? Would they hold her for ransom? But there were other girls of the nobility at the convent whose fathers were wealthy men with lands and titles. Why had these bandits taken her?

She shivered with fear at the thought of what might lie ahead.

Robbed of her sight for the moment and unable to speak, her other senses rose to the fore. The sound of the men's boots crushing plants as they strode through the gardens, the tight bindings that chaffed her hands and ankles and the warmth of the man's shoulder where her head rested, albeit unwillingly. She was angry now, more angry than afraid.

Who are these men? When her eyes had first opened, she had glimpsed only a masculine form and fair hair. His face had been shadowed. Unlike the other one who had carried her for a brief moment, the one who held her now did not smell of unwashed clothes. His scent was of soap and salt, like the smell of the sea.

When speaking to the others, even in hushed tones, his voice was somehow vaguely familiar. It was also the voice of command. *He must be their leader.*

Though he had initially spoken to her in whispered French, he now conversed with his men in English. And the deep timbre of his voice stirred her memory. *Had she heard it before?*

She understood some of their whispered English since her papa had long used the language in his business and her mother had taught her to speak and read it as a child. Still, years had passed since she had spoken the language. But she understood their words saying they were headed to a ship, the

Fairwinds.

Where they pirates then? Would they sail to England with her as their captive? Could it have something to do with their American war?

But why take me?

❧ ✦ ☙

At the crack of the coachman's whip, the horses leapt ahead, speeding the carriage northwest toward Dieppe. Simon relaxed for the first time in hours.

Elijah and Giles rode on top with the coachman; two more of Simon's men followed on horseback as guards, leaving him alone in the carriage with the girl. Long after she had ceased struggling, he could feel her anger rolling off her in waves. He had said nothing, knowing enough about women to allow her anger to cool before he tried to reason with her. Not wishing to hear her angry invective, he left the gag in place.

Sometime later, the girl's moan roused Simon from sleep. Even in the dim light with part of her face covered by the gag and blindfold, he could see she was pale and her face was twisted in what appeared to be pain as she dreamed, slumped awkwardly against the back of the seat. He gently removed her gag and blindfold, taking care not to wake her. Her hands and feet he left bound. The face that was revealed took his breath away. She was beautiful with an oval face, dark, crescent brows and delicate, bow-shaped lips. No child, this one, but a woman full grown.

On impulse, he lifted her into his lap to make her more comfortable in the swaying carriage, and to try and calm her. As his chin brushed her cheek, he caught a whiff of fresh lavender.

Her skin was as soft and smooth as a baby's. Cradling her head against his shoulder, he reveled in the feel of her warmth. Gathering the curl at the end of her long plait between his fingers, he noticed it, too, was soft. And as black as a raven's wing. Everything about her was feminine, alluring.

She ceased moaning and curled into his chest like a kitten seeking his warmth.

Her beautiful, bow-shaped lips tempted him. For a moment he considered stealing a kiss. But she was his enemy's innocent daughter. And he her abductor.

No kiss of his would be welcomed and none was given.

ᘐ ᘐᘒ ᘐ

Claire stirred as the rays of the sun warmed her face, but instead of the gentle sound of the songbirds that woke her each morning, she heard raucous shrieking. *What is that noise? Am I late for Matins?* The cacophony of sound suddenly reminded her of her childhood in Lorient before she'd gone to live at the convent.

Gulls.

Eyes still closed, she frowned. *Non. It cannot be gulls.* She inhaled, deeply, cautiously, smelling fish, and the unforgettable briny smell of the sea.

She opened her eyes and the memory of the night returned. *Mon Dieu!* Had all that really happened? She looked around the carriage, realizing she'd been left alone. Her captor had removed the blindfold and the cloth that had been stuffed in her mouth. *Dieu merci!* She swallowed and licked her dry lips, her dazed brain trying to make sense of her predicament. *Where am I?*

Realizing she was still wearing only her nightgown and wrapped in the blanket her captor had thrown over her the night before, a wave of shame rippled through her at the thought he and his men had seen her in such a state.

Not that she had been given any choice in the matter! Anger surged through her veins at the memory of her abduction. *English pirates!*

She drew the blanket more tightly around her and pushed herself into a sitting position. Through the open carriage window, she glimpsed the sun glinting off the ocean, so bright she winced. White, puffy clouds floated idly in the blue sky. A ship with sails furled was anchored just off shore. On the beach, men loaded crates into a small boat. It wasn't Lorient but it might still be France. The nearby cliffs looking out on *la Manche*, what these men would call the English Channel, told her it was.

Had she been left without a guard? Might she escape? A shout for help would only gain the attention of her kidnappers, but perhaps she could work loose the bindings on her hands and ankles and sneak away before they were aware. She reached toward the cloth around her ankles.

The door of the carriage swung open, a gown was tossed into her lap and a broad-shouldered man filled the opening.

Claire's jaw went slack while her heart kicked into a gallop as if responding of its own accord to the first man to stir it from slumber.

"*Bonjour*, Mademoiselle Donet," he said in French. "Captain Simon Powell." He bowed in a grand gesture. "Your humble servant with something for you to wear."

The golden one. It had been nearly two years since she had seen him, but she had never forgotten the night of the masquerade. She had never forgotten him. Though the linen shirt stretched tight across his broad chest and the leather breeches and boots he wore now were a far cry from the shimmering costume he'd worn then, his amber eyes were the same. Impossibly, he was even more handsome than in her faded memory. In the last two years, he had never been far from her thoughts, for the night she'd first seen him—and imagined a man's pleasure—was the night Claire's girlish dreams had ended forever.

And now he'd returned to France and abducted her.

He leaned into the carriage and untied her feet, then her wrists. The touch of his rough hands on her skin sent odd chills rippling through her. She bit her lip, shamed by her body's reaction to this stranger. Her living temptation turned away for a moment, then faced her, a cup in his outstretched hand. "'Tis only water," he said when she was reluctant to take it.

Too grateful to complain, she hastily brought the fresh water to her dry lips and drank her fill.

"I'll give you some time to dress," he said not unkindly. His eyes shifted to her blanket-covered nightclothes. "I wouldn't want my men to see you as you are."

Claire felt her cheeks burn at the thought.

"The gown is modest enough to please even your nuns," he said. "Call me if you need... ah, assistance. I will be just outside."

She fumed at his insolence, at his actions that had placed her at his mercy. Though she knew he was English and a privateer, she had no idea why he had taken her, and she would wait no longer to learn the truth of it. "Why did you bring me here? Why did you take me from the convent?"

Leaning one arm against the frame of the carriage, he regarded her intently, his eyes like chips of amber.

"You have your father to thank for that, mademoiselle. As soon as he returns what is mine you will have your freedom."

Claire blinked. "My father?" Her voice sounded to her like the pleading of a feeble schoolgirl. She would not be cowed! She lifted her chin, confident in his error. "What has he to do with this... this perfidy? Papa is a man of business and letters, a man of some wealth. He has no need to steal!"

His mouth twitched up in a grin, drawing Claire's gaze to his sensual lips, reminding her of a night when she had seen him use those lips to good effect. She scowled, angry with the rogue and with herself for finding him so attractive.

He shut the door of the carriage and peered in through the open window. "Your father, mademoiselle, is a *pirate*."

❧ ⚜ ❧

Simon left the stunned girl and walked a short distance toward the shore to watch his men loading supplies into the skiff. Damn but she had beautiful eyes, like the blue of the open sea on a cloudless day. The Saint-Denis butcher had been right about that. But her beauty only complicated matters. His men would take an interest.

He supposed he should not be surprised she was unaware of her father's surreptitious dealings. After all, Donet had hidden her away in a convent where she'd been isolated from the world. She had no knowledge of her father's piracy or his part in a war that would determine if America would have its independence. It seemed to Simon that despite England's desires, such was inevitable. Had not the Commons voted to end the war just a few months ago, following the defeat at Yorktown? Yet the battles continued, and so did Simon's work on the sea and in Paris.

In London, they called it the American War, but Simon thought it was more appropriately dubbed the French War. After all, the American victory at Yorktown had only been possible with the aid of the French fleet. The American army, too, was fed, clothed and paid by England's enemy. And France's privateers, like Donet, had wreaked havoc on British shipping.

Jordan strode toward him across the sand, interrupting his thoughts. "Soon as this load of supplies is on board, Captain, we'll be ready to sail."

Simon was gratified to feel the wind rising. "The girl is just getting dressed. I'll bring her in the last boat."

Jordan shot a glance toward the carriage. "How is she faring this morning?"

"None too happy, but she'll come—willingly or unwillingly."

Jordan chuckled, his disheveled brown hair blowing about his face. "Unwillingly, most likely." At his signal, the skiff, now loaded with the last of their supplies, shoved off.

Turning back to Simon, Jordan asked, "How will Donet

know we have his daughter?"

"I left a message for him on the girl's pillow. I expect I'll soon have a reaction."

"Like poking a stick at a shark, more like. But at least your note will ensure the continued health of the *Abundance*'s crew."

"My thought exactly. I imagine the good sisters will be in a panic when they realize they've misplaced one of their students. The note will at least tell them she is with me, though I doubt that will be of much comfort."

Simon heard the carriage door open. He wheeled around to see the French girl's long, black plait falling over her shoulder as she bent forward to step down. He hurried up the beach to help her.

Not unexpectedly, she refused his hand.

The blue gown his men had procured from the local seamstress in Rye fit her well, hugging tightly to her small waist. He'd guessed right that if she was an older student, at seventeen or eighteen she would be taller than the young girls and slim, and she was. The shift and the dress were enough to render her decent even without a corset. But he'd not counted on her bosom filling the bodice, which it certainly did. Casting his gaze over her slender form, he suddenly noticed her bare feet peeking out from beneath the gown.

Damn. He'd forgotten shoes.

"I expect you'd like some private time, mademoiselle, but do not think to escape. One of my men will be watching where you go." He raised his brows in amusement. "They are probably hoping you will give them reason to follow."

Her only response was a frown as she turned and stalked off in the direction of a dense cluster of bushes to one side of the carriage.

He strolled down to the water's edge to watch the return of the skiff, determined to keep his mind focused on the task set before him. Gulls scavenging along the waterline took to the air at his approach, wheeling and screeching in protest. They quickly settled higher up the beach behind him.

A few minutes later, the flurry of screeching gulls alerted him to the girl's return. He turned to watch her. Bare-footed, she gingerly picked her way through the shells left scattered in the sand by the outgoing tide. He strode up the beach.

"I must apologize for your lack of shoes," he said when he reached her. "I'll see you get a pair as soon as we anchor in Rye."

"Rye?"

"'Tis the *Fairwinds'* home port." He did not mind her knowing this. Even if Donet learned of it upon her return, the Frenchman could not intrude there with any success.

Though she'd refused his hand, she now walked beside him as he strolled toward the water. Shielding her eyes with her hand, tendrils of her ebony hair blowing around her face, she looked toward his ship where his men were scurrying up the rigging as they prepared to sail.

"You fly the American flag, yet you are British and would speak to me of an English port?"

He couldn't help the smile despite her haughty tone. How little she knew of privateers. She held his gaze, waiting for an answer. *By God, she is lovely.* "A necessary ruse when we are in French waters."

A frown crossed her face. "I see." She mumbled words in French he was certain were not ones the nuns had taught her.

"These are perilous times, mademoiselle, particularly in the Channel. One must be cautious."

"Especially when one is kidnapping another man's daughter," came her impudent reply. "You deserve to be hung, sir."

His lips twitched, fighting a smile. "Notwithstanding how you came to be among us, I will endeavor to make you comfortable while you are my *guest.*"

"*Oui,* but even if you act the gentleman, Captain—"

"Powell," he reminded her.

Her eyes, like deep pools of crystalline water, fastened on him. "Even if you act the gentleman, Captain Powell"—giving him a look that told him she very much doubted he would—"you will have ruined my good reputation. Your ship is hardly a fitting abode for a future nun."

His brows drew together involuntarily. *Nun? She expected to become a nun?* "You will have to excuse me, mademoiselle, but you hardly look the nun." His eyes raked over her very feminine curves. *Definitely not a nun.* "No matter your future, you need have no worry for your safety. I left a message for your father assuring him you will be well-treated." Inwardly he corrected himself. In fact, his message to Donet had been rather vague on that point. He wanted the Frenchman to be concerned enough about his daughter to promptly surrender the *Abundance* and her crew.

The skiff returned and his men jumped out and hauled the small boat onto the sand. He gestured her toward it. "Will you accompany me to the ship?"

She balked. "No. I will not. I have no intention of leaving France."

"Well, then, allow me." In one quick movement, he hefted her over his shoulder.

She gave out a harsh shriek. "Stop! Put me down, you beast!" This she shouted in English while pounding his back with her small fists.

His men laughed at the sight of their captain carrying the French wildcat.

"You speak English quite well, mademoiselle!" Simon remarked as he strode towards the skiff ignoring her attempts to injure him. "I'm delighted."

He drew near the skiff, his men looking on with avid interest. It wouldn't be the first time they had seen their captain carry a woman so, though on prior occasions it had been for an entirely different reason. Still, with her beauty, perhaps it was not a bad thing for his crew to think he had claimed her as his.

He set the angry girl in the skiff, keeping his eyes on her as his men shoved off and began rowing to the ship. The fiery rebellion in her eyes told him if he but looked away for a moment, she would jump overboard in a useless attempt to swim ashore.

He spoke to her in English. "Do not think to try it, mademoiselle. I am a very good swimmer."

Her plan thwarted, she crossed her arms over her chest, shot him a frown and looked away, obviously seething.

No matter her resentment, she would soon learn that while he could be polite, he would have his way, particularly when it meant recovering his men and his ship.

Chapter 5

Jean Donet strode confidently across the deck of his ship to stand at the rail. Gazing into the sunset, he pulled his cocked hat low over his forehead. His hair was neatly queued at his nape. Though quite different than how he dressed as the captain of a privateer, it was his usual attire when contemplating a visit to his daughter—a bunch of lace at his chin, a waistcoat of burgundy velvet, and breeches of black satin above white stockings and silver-buckled shoes.

Beyond the port of Lorient, where his ship was anchored, the sky drew his attention where it met the sea in a flame of deep orange melting into a band of dark red. Above the fiery colors, streaks of yellow and gold cut large swaths across the celestial canvas. A more spectacular sunset he had never seen. Claire would have thought so, too. But she would never see the sunset from the deck of his ship. He could never tell her of his former smuggling and subsequent piracy, or the sixteen-gun brig-sloop they had gained him, named after the black-hearted queen of France herself, wife of the king who oppressed the French people. Claire could never know that her papa was now a privateer sailing under an American letter of marque—and an American flag. He had happily retired the one with the skull and crossbones set against a blue field of fleurs-de-lis he had used as a pirate.

45

Claire and the good sisters of the Ursuline Convent in Saint-Denis knew him only as the wealthy son of the comte de Saintonge. And, in truth, he was that, though there was so much more to know. Had they known the whole of it, they would have been dismayed.

As a younger son, he had known if he married outside his noble father's wishes, he would have few prospects and fewer coins. But despite that, he had married the beautiful Ariane Moline when he was twenty and she but seventeen. The estrangement from his father that followed mattered little compared to the desperate passion he'd had for Ariane, a passion that had not abated in the years God gave them.

He thought of his daughter, born soon after his marriage, and rubbed the thin mustache on his upper lip as he pondered. Claire had his black hair and Ariane's blue eyes, the same eyes that haunted his dreams. Now that she was of age he would fulfill his promise to Ariane and ensure their daughter's future.

And, afterwards? He had no idea. His country had defied England, with whom they were not actually at war, in order to help create an American republic that many feared might one day devour Europe. He hoped that would never be and that France—and he—had made the right choice. He had reason to believe they had. The unpleasantness with England was showing signs of ending. America would soon be free and the connections he had made in the government would assist whatever future course he chose.

"*Capitaine?*" The rough voice of his quartermaster roused him from his meandering thoughts.

He turned to face the man who had sailed with him for the last nine years. "*Oui?*" Of uncertain origins, Émile Bequel was in his late thirties, the same as Jean, though he looked older. The quartermaster's swarthy face was all hard planes, his dark eyes disclosing little. Yet he'd faithfully discharged every task Jean had ever assigned him. Since the first day his quartermaster had glimpsed Claire at the convent six years ago, the tough seaman had loved her as if she were his own child.

"The *Abundance* is anchored in port," said Émile.

"Ah, *c'est bien*. And the English prisoners?"

"In the warehouse where M'sieur Bouchet sees to their wounds."

"None were killed?"

"No, the men were careful to take them alive, though one tried some foolish heroics and was wounded worse than the others."

Jean pictured the old physician they had relied upon since he began sailing. Pierre Bouchet was a man of small stature and thinning gray hair, but with fine features behind his spectacles. Even now, he would be bent over the injured captives and soundly cursing Jean under his breath. Perhaps Bouchet had cause. Over the years, the physician had cleaned up more blood from the wounds of his men than Jean cared to remember.

He turned to his quartermaster. "See that Bouchet is rewarded."

"Already done," Émile confidently replied.

"Excellent." Concern for his crew made him ask, "Any lost?"

"Not one. Lucien tells me it was easier than he'd expected. Sailed that English sloop we captured last week into Dover unnoticed. *La chance* was with him. Just as he arrived, a large number of the crew on the *Abundance* went ashore. Lucien was able to board her in the fog, surprising the captain who was still on board."

Jean couldn't resist a smile. Capturing the English sloop had proven fortuitous, indeed. He rested his hands on the polished wood rail and looked back to the fading sunset. "First we will go to the convent to see Claire, then to Paris to call upon M'sieur Franklin."

"The commissioner will be pleased to learn we have another load of prisoners for him to barter for his precious Americans," said Émile.

"I will let him have the English sloop and both crews.

You can sail the sloop and the prisoners to Dieppe, but I intend to keep Powell's fine schooner. I want it for Claire's dowry. The *Abundance* is a proper name for such a purpose, no?"

Émile chuckled. "Have you told the little one of her coming marriage?"

"I wrote of it to the Mother Superior in my last letter, so perhaps Claire knows."

"Do you think she will be pleased with your choice?"

"I will know soon enough."

ᔦ ᔔᔶᔉ ᔧ

Rye Harbor

Claire sat on the edge of the bed where Captain Powell had rudely dropped her only moments before, leaving both her thoughts and her gown in a jumble.

The infernal privateer claimed her papa was a pirate. *Absurde! Could he have Papa confused with another man?* Surely a comte's son would have no dealings with an English sea captain. But then she recalled the night she had first encountered the golden one. He was attending a ball. In France. With members of the nobility. The possibility the English captain knew more about her papa than she did made her stomach clench. *It could not be!*

Without warning, the ship lurched. She leapt up to go to the window, nearly falling to the deck as she tried unsuccessfully to walk while the ship rolled and the world shifted beneath her feet. Grabbing on to the captain's desk, she steadied herself and gazed out the window to see the cliffs fading into the horizon. The nuns had taught her geography, so she knew the coastline of France. And she knew the location of Rye, where he'd said they were headed. It was one of the Cinque Ports on the southeast coast of England. But knowing that brought no comfort. She felt only a deep sense of loss and a foreboding for what lay ahead. Would she ever see the cliffs of France again?

Still holding on to the desk, she maneuvered herself into the chair and studied the cabin. Its location in the ship and its size told her it must be the captain's. *Who is this man who has taken me captive?* She knew nothing of him save for what she'd learned the night of the masquerade when she'd seen him with the female hussar. Her cheeks heated at the memory of the two lovers trysting beneath the tree. A future nun should never have witnessed such a sight. But she had. And she had wondered even then if it had changed her forever, awakening a part of her that would never be silenced.

His cabin was larger and better appointed than she would have imagined. The windows on the sides allowed light to stream through the panes of glass framed by dark blue curtains. The bed where he had thrown her so unceremoniously a short while ago was covered with the same dark blue cloth. That he had dropped her in his bed did not escape her notice. With a deep breath, she continued her survey. Four chairs surrounded an oak pedestal table in the center of the cabin. On the table sat a fenced tray that held four round bowl glasses and a flat-bottomed decanter of what she assumed—with his forays into Paris—was French brandy.

A bookcase, built into the side of the cabin, contained shelves crowded with well-used volumes secured by wooden strips. At least she'd have something to read to occupy her time.

Her searching eyes found no weapons. She had yet to examine the content of his chests but somehow she was certain he'd removed the sword, a pistol and a knife a privateer would be expected to have. Not that she'd been trained in the use of any of them. Panic rose in her chest. Would she need a weapon? If he was holding her as hostage, as he had said, would he harm her? Would he allow his men to do so? She shuddered at the possibility.

A glance around the cabin told her someone took good

care of Captain Powell, or he insisted on order. Everything was in its place and spoke of a discipline she would not have imagined when she'd first seen the flamboyant golden one at the masquerade. There was obviously more to this English captain than she had thought at first.

The cabin door swung open and a boy of perhaps twelve entered carrying a wooden tray. With an easy stride, he reached the desk as if the deck wasn't reeling beneath his feet and set down his burden.

Doffing his dark brown tricorne, he bowed. "Good day, mistress." Straightening, he smiled. "Cap'n says ye speak English. I'm to see to yer needs." The boy, who was a handsome lad with sun-bleached, brown hair, ruddy cheeks and brown eyes, a shade lighter than his hat, seemed elated to have her as a new responsibility. "I brought ye some food, though I can't vouch fer its taste. We've a new cook."

She looked down at the plate of mangled eggs. "Hmm."

The boy pursed his lips as if unsure what more to say about the master of their galley. "New cook's name's McGinnes. Tom McGinnes. Ye'll be meetin' 'im soon, I 'spect. Hails from Ireland. He's young fer a cook. Me belly tells me he ain't been cookin' long neither, but the cap'n likes 'im."

"And who might you be?" she asked, fixing a pleasant smile on her face. If he was going to tend to her needs, she wanted his favor. He might become an ally and help her escape.

He stared at her as if he hadn't heard the question. Then shaking his head like he was coming out of a trance, he said, "Oh, did I ferget to say, miss? I'm Cap'n Powell's cabin boy. Me name's Nathaniel Baker, but everyone calls me Nate… well unless the cap'n's issuin' orders or angry. Then I'm Mr. Baker." His brown eyes twinkled.

She shared a smile with him. "Does he get angry very often?" Despite the captain's assurances he would treat her well, and she had seen him at his most charming, she wondered.

"Not often, miss."

Her gaze returned to the tray. In addition to the eggs, there were fresh berries, brioche, butter and a pot of jam. *Brioche?* "Does the ship's crew often dine on our sweetened French bread?"

"The cap'n has a fondness for it, so whenever he's in France, one of the crew picks up a supply."

"Most civilized."

"Best part is 'twas not made by McGinnes." The boy grinned. "He tried to make rolls a few days ago, but they were as hard as rocks. The cap'n ferbade 'im from doin' it again."

She liked the lad. "My name is Claire Donet, but then I suppose you know that."

"Aye, mistress, I do." The boy tipped his hat and started toward the door. "I'll bring ye some water. Oh, and the cap'n's asked me to get ye some shoes when we anchor in Rye." He stole a glance at her bare feet as if trying to fix the size.

"Thank you, Nate. You are most kind."

"The cap'n's done right by me, miss. When he got this ship, he took me with 'im. I've been here ever since."

Well at least he can be generous with small boys. "I would take it as a favor, Nate, if you would tell the captain I'd like to speak with him."

Looking doubtful, the boy nevertheless agreed. "Aye, miss, I'll tell 'im. What should I say 'tis about?"

"He must return me to the convent, Nate."

With that, the lad shrugged and retreated to the door leaving her alone. She turned to her food, suddenly ravenous. Captain Powell must be made to see reason.

Sainte Mère, he cannot keep me here!

༄ ༄ ༄

At the sound of the topsail's luffing, Simon tilted his head back and gazed skyward. "Trim that sail!" he shouted to the crewmember working aloft. The wind had risen and was now blowing fiercely in a southeast direction. He would use it to his advantage as they sailed to Rye. He was eager to leave the shores of France.

"Cap'n," Nate said, coming toward him from the aft hatch, "Mistress Donet would like a word with ye."

"Oh she would, would she? And what does she want now?"

Suddenly finding interest in his shoes, Nate said, "She's of a mind to go back to the convent, sir."

"Not likely," Simon mumbled under his breath, the wind stealing away his words.

"Sir?"

"I said 'tis not likely."

"But she looked so pitiful when she begged me to ask ye."

Begged? Somehow he could not picture it in his mind. Moreover, she had to know he could not grant her request no matter if she did. Seeing the anxious look on his cabin boy's face, Simon let out an exasperated sigh. "All right. I'll see her." Spotting his first mate amidships he called out, "Mr. Landor, you have the ship. I'm going below."

At Jordan's nod, Simon quickly descended the aft ladder leading to his cabin. He suspected she'd want more than a word. Even though she had reason enough to object to being kidnapped, he had hoped she would not be much trouble. But remembering the fire in her eyes when he'd dropped her onto his bed, he resigned himself to the confrontation his gut told him was coming.

He knocked once, unlatched the door and ducked his head as he entered his cabin, his eyes focusing on the spot where he'd left her. The bed was empty. A movement at his desk drew his gaze to where she sat in his chair behind an empty tray. "I trust breakfast was satisfactory?"

"Quite satisfactory," she replied. "We seem to share a fondness for brioche, Captain." Her tone was short, as if the concession was grudgingly made.

The sun coming through the window cast a halo around

her dark hair though he was certain it was no angel he'd captured. "If not the food, what is it that has you summoning me from the deck?" He knew, of course, but he would hear it from her lips.

"We must discuss my… situation, Captain Powell. Before the ship goes any farther, you must reconsider your plan and return me to the convent. There has to have been some mistake."

Apparently she had not understood him, or his resolve. Once committed, he rarely altered course. Besides, in this case he had no choice. "Alas, I cannot do that, mademoiselle, at least not until your father returns my ship and my men."

"Your ship?"

"My second ship, the *Abundance*. Along with it, your father seized a large number of the crew. He now holds them prisoner, I suspect to exchange for Americans."

"What?" She shook her head in denial. "That is ridiculous. Papa would not do such a thing! And he has no ship with which to capture another."

Simon chuckled to himself. She really knew nothing of the man's deeds. "I'm afraid he would and he does. It seems he's told you little of his life. I suppose you do not know of his brig-sloop *la Reine Noire*?"

"Papa has a ship?"

Remorse swept over him. In her bewilderment, his captive suddenly appeared as vulnerable as a newborn lamb. He regretted being the one to shatter the image of her "papa" but it could not be helped. "I could remain silent and allow you to think what you will, but I believe it might help you to know that I was telling the truth when I said your father is a pirate. Or, rather, he was. I believe he now sails as a privateer under an American flag." Simon hesitated, regarding her curiously. The bewildered look in her blue eyes told him she knew nothing of any of this. *Just how far removed from the world was that convent of hers?*

Perhaps he should start at the beginning. "Surely you

know of the American war with England and France's support on the American side?"

"Of course I know of the war," she snapped. "And I am aware that France is aligned with America in its desire for independence." With a glare in his direction, she added, "At the moment England is friend to neither country."

He needed no reminder of the rivalry between his country and France. "Your request to return to France is denied, mademoiselle, at least for the present. And I'd ask you to stay in my cabin." He turned on his heel and departed. He did not want the girl wandering about his decks, parading her beauty in front of his men. With that thought, he reminded himself to post a guard as night fell.

Once he was topside, he went to the rail and stared into the dark waters of the Channel. He couldn't blame the girl for wanting her freedom. She was a hostage in a dangerous game that had only begun.

He looked to his left and saw Elijah had joined him at the rail. Despite the wind, the old seaman neatly patted tobacco into his pipe and lit the bowl while strands of his gray hair, freed from his cap, whipped around his face.

"Ye look a might disturbed, Cap'n," he said letting out a puff of smoke.

"The French girl is none too pleased to be my guest," said Simon. "And she's all too free with her tongue." His brow furrowed. "I thought convent schools raised young women to be demure and well-mannered."

Elijah chuckled and blew a ring of smoke into the clear air only to have it swept away by the wind. "Not this one, Cap'n."

Simon snorted. "She thinks she has the makings of a nun."

Elijah took his pipe out of his mouth, leaned his arms against the rail and smiled. It was the look of a man who had lived long enough to have an opinion on almost everything. "Nay. I'm thinkin' Claire Donet takes after her father. Can't see her makin' a nun. More like she's as wild as the wind, that one."

"Aye, I'm quickly coming to see that. But still I must deal with her. She'll be with us for a while."

"There's an art to catchin' the wind to set a vessel on the right course, Cap'n. Yer a master at it. I'm thinkin' if anyone can tame Donet's daughter, 'tis ye."

⟡ ⟡ ⟡

Claire could feel her anger simmering just below the surface as Simon Powell's words came back to her. Could her beloved papa really be all the English captain had said? *Surely not!* A privateer was not so bad, perhaps, but a *pirate*? Pirates did horrible things, like murder and rape. Papa would never do that.

It was just an excuse for the English captain to hold her prisoner for as long as it took to get what he wanted. The stark realization that she was the pawn of a man to whom she had felt an attraction since the first night she'd seen him had her biting her lower lip. For two years, she had thought of him, longing to see him again while forcing his handsome face from her mind. Now, here she was—his hostage!

Her anger boiled over. *Mon Dieu*, the audacity of the man! Seeing a book on the edge of his desk, she had the sudden urge to hurl it through the air. The urge grew. Perhaps if she was a thorn in his side, he'd want to return her to the convent. With a swift reach of her arm, she lifted the book and hurled it across the cabin. It struck the cabin door with a satisfying thud. Throwing his book felt so good, it was worth the penance she would suffer later.

Carefully making her way to the shelving, she freed the strip that held the books and began tossing them to the deck. They cascaded down in a waterfall of paper and bindings, and with each one that hit the deck, Claire began to feel free, the spirit inside her, bound for so long, suddenly released.

Once she began the destruction, she did not stop. A pot clanged to the deck. A brass spyglass joined the pile of books.

Crashes echoed around the cabin as, with a vengeance, she tossed more of his things onto the spreading mass of objects around her. The ship pitched and rolled and she had to hang on to the bookcase to keep her footing but even that did not dampen the exhilaration she felt at her effort to let the man know in no uncertain terms she was not happy with her abduction. He would take her back or regret it!

The cabin door opened and young Nate peeked in, his eyes widening as he looked around.

Claire straightened her shoulders and set her mouth in a tight expression that she hoped would tell the boy, "*So there!*"

He slammed the cabin door shut, the sound of his feet scampering down the deck toward the companionway fading as she lifted a wooden box and thrust it into the midst of the debris.

❦ ❦ ❦

"Cap'n!" shouted Nate.

Simon covered his ear. "Not so loud, lad. I'm right here." He turned from the rigging he'd been examining to his cabin boy. "What's the matter?"

"'Tis the French girl, Cap'n." The boy's face was flushed as he took a deep breath. "She's wreckin' yer cabin!"

Simon frowned.

Nate's face bore an expression of panic. "She's thrown all yer books to the deck."

Simon's frown deepened. "I'll have no schoolgirl tempest on my ship." Stalking to the hatch, he took the ladder in three steps and flung open his cabin door. It banged against the bulkhead as a brandy glass flew past his face and crashed, shattering into a hundred pieces.

"What the hell is going on here?" he roared.

She stood speechless in the center of his cabin next to the table, his books forming an untidy heap around her topped by his spyglass and his chronometer. On her face was a crazed expression. Her black hair was in violent disarray about her shoulders. She looked like a witch in the midst of a storm unleashing her fury, nothing like the future nun she pretended to be.

He seethed at the unnecessary destruction before him. Narrowing his eyes, he stomped toward her, shoving the debris aside with his boot. Lifting his spyglass and chronometer to the table, he stepped closer to her and grabbed her upper arms. Tightening his grip till she grimaced, he demanded, "Well? Answer me!"

She squirmed and twisted. "I do not wish to be your prisoner."

"Do I look like your fairy godmother?" he asked in a cold voice. "I care naught for your wishes!"

Jerking one arm free, she swung her fist at him, connecting with his jaw. He seized her arm and twisted it behind her bringing her slamming into his chest.

"I am not one of your crew to obey your every whim," she raged. "I am a *lady,* and I will be treated as such, even by a common sailor like you!"

"A lady?" Still steaming, he looked down at her bow-shaped lips, which in his anger tempted him beyond reason. If this was the only way he could dominate the girl he would see to it.

He took her lips in a harsh, demanding kiss.

He expected her to fight all the more, which he would have enjoyed given what she had done, but to his surprise, she softened. When her mouth opened on a sigh, he took full advantage, plunging his tongue in to probe her softness. Letting go of her hand, he wrapped his arms around her waist and drew her tightly into the hard planes of his body. She moaned as the kiss deepened, sending a message straight to his groin.

God, the taste of her is sweet.

Moments later, when he finally lifted his mouth from hers, they were both breathing hard and his heart was racing. Her blue eyes were glazed and her lips swollen with his kiss.

Remembering Elijah's words, he whispered, "It seems I have found a way to tame the wind after all."

～ ✠ ～

The cabin door closed with a thump, the sound jarring Claire back to the present. What had just happened? Her heart still pounding in her chest, with trembling fingers she explored her pulsing, sensitive lips. A deep sigh escaped her as she carefully stepped to the bed and collapsed upon its edge. *Damn the arrogant man! Tame the wind, indeed.*

To her shame, she had responded to him like one of the tavern wenches she'd seen in the village of Saint-Denis. *Sainte Mère!* She had no barrier that was effective against his hot, seeking mouth. Instead, she had clung to him like the trousered hussar that night in the château's gardens. Were all women turned into pudding by his impassioned kisses? Even now, her body tingled in an unfamiliar way and she felt his absence like a tangible thing.

Did she now have to fear her own desire for him would put her virtue in danger? *It cannot be. I cannot want my abductor. I am to be a nun!*

The words floated in her mind like so much chaff on the wind, making her wonder if she was worthy of the vows she had hoped to one day take. In some way she did not fully understand, he had marked her, as surely as he had marked his ship the *Fairwinds.*

She gazed at the objects she'd tossed to the deck in her fit of pique and froze. To her utter horror, sliding down the pile was a Holy Bible, some of its pages now torn. Snatching it from the heap, she fell to her knees and clasped the sacred volume to her breast. *Mon Dieu, forgive me.*

A soft knock snapped her out of her prayer. *Had the captain returned?* No, he would never knock. It was young Nate who slowly opened the cabin door, stuck his head in and looked about, his brown tricorne askew.

"Gads, mistress. Why'd ye do this?"

Guilt assailed her. "I lost my temper."

The boy smiled encouragingly, as if she could do no wrong, and stepped into the cabin. "Don't worry. I'll soon have the cabin set to rights."

"But it's my fault entirely," she protested, feeling more guilty by the moment. The boy was not the one who deserved her anger and she had been taught to be polite, controlled. "I'm not usually so undisciplined, but your captain seems to stir my wrath."

"Aye, I see he has. But I'm here at his command to set all in order."

She rose and carefully set the Bible on the table, regretting the loss of control for which she would surely have to do penance. "Then I will help you, Nate." Reaching for an intricate brass pot encrusted with jewels, she held onto the table and then to the bookcase where she returned the pot to the shelf where she'd found it.

Together the two of them worked to put all the books and other things back into their proper places. Claire experienced a pang of remorse when she realized she had broken one of his fine brandy glasses. She gathered the pieces into her hand and Nate held out a bucket to catch the glass shards. "This one is beyond repair, I fear."

"Not to worry, mistress," the cabin boy said with a winning smile. "The cap'n has a hoard of 'em squirreled away in the hold. 'Twouldn't be the first that fell to the deck."

"You are very kind to me, Nate, and serve your master well."

The boy beamed and, to Claire, it seemed she had found a friend.

Chapter 6

Turning away from the Mother Superior, Jean Donet crumpled the note in his hands and gritted his teeth, as outrage rose in his chest. Merde! He had expected Powell to strike, but in Lorient, where the Abundance was guarded night and day, not in Saint-Denis where he hid his most valuable treasure. Where he believed Claire was safe with the sisters behind convent walls. Where his own misdeeds could not touch her. Never had he expected the English privateer to kidnap Claire. But he'd been wrong. Powell was more wily than he'd imagined and more well informed.

His dark brows drew together. "I will have my revenge and my daughter!" he hissed to Émile. The first mate's dark gaze echoed his own rage.

Jean faced Sister Augustin, who backed away with an anxious look. "I am most sorry, M'sieur Donet. We had no idea Claire was in danger."

Coming to his senses, he shot a glance at Émile, who wisely remained silent in the face of his captain's anger. "No, of course not. I will handle this, Reverend Mother. I do not hold you responsible." The danger to Claire had always been there but he'd grown complacent after so many years.

From her habit the Mother Superior withdrew an unsealed letter, which she handed to him. "Claire must have written this the night she was taken. It concerns her desires for her future. Knowing her wishes, I had also sent you a letter, but it may not have arrived before you left."

Something he had heard in the tone of the nun's voice puzzled him as he unfolded the letter. "What were her desires? Surely you told her I wish her to wed, that I'd arranged a marriage?"

"*Oui*, Claire was aware of your plans, but she had developed a strong commitment to the Order and hoped to one day take vows to join us. I, for one, did not encourage her, but since I was unable to dissuade her, I told her I would pass along her request to you, which I did."

He looked up from the paper. "No, that is not the path I have in mind for my daughter."

"I thought as much, m'sieur."

"Please have her things packed, *s'il vous plaît*, Reverend Mother. I have a meeting in Paris this afternoon I must attend and I would take them with me."

The Reverend Mother nodded, then hesitated. "There is something I have held for her, knowing it was among the things she prized." The nun walked to her desk and opened a drawer. Lifting out an item, she dropped it into his open palm. He turned it over with his thumb. The blue moonstone shimmered in the ring he had given Claire for her birthday a year ago.

He studied the stone that he'd purchased because it reminded him of her eyes... her mother's eyes. "It was not on her hand when she was taken?"

"No, she kept it safe among her things. But I am certain she will be grateful to have it again."

A short while later, he and his quartermaster departed. The horses pulled in their traces as the coachman's whip cracked over their heads. Jean stared out the window at the ever-changing landscape as the carriage sped on its way through the city. "If he harms one hair of her head," he hissed to his quartermaster sitting across from him, "or fails to return her, I will kill his crew." He clenched his teeth. "All of them."

"*Oui*, I will see to it myself," came the grim reply from Émile, his harsh voice sounding as deadly as Jean's thoughts.

He pulled the crumpled parchment from the pocket of his waistcoat, flattened it out and handed it across the space. "Send Powell a message to the address in Dartmouth he gives in the note. Offer to meet with him in Paris to arrange an exchange—his men for Claire. Warn him if he harms her, the bodies of his men will soon be washing up on the coast of England."

Not long after, the carriage pulled up in front of the imposing gray stone of the Valentinois château in Passy, a village just west of Paris. Though his thoughts were consumed by Claire and what indignities she might be enduring at the hands of the English privateer, he would not disappoint the American commissioner.

M'sieur Franklin was respected by all in Paris, a man wise in his words. He cared little for the trappings of nobility while careful to observe its niceties, the importance of which Jean well understood having once been a part of that world. Beyond that, Franklin had a wit Jean admired. Aligned as France was with America, Jean had been pleased to accept the letter of marque Franklin had issued him.

He and Émile arrived at the door and a servant graciously escorted them into the large sitting room where Franklin greeted his guests.

"It is good to see you, as ever," said the aging American as he extended his hand.

"And you, m'sieur," said Jean. He shook the man's hand and re-introduced him to Émile.

"Welcome again," Franklin said to Émile.

Jean recognized the two men standing behind Franklin. The one with the prominent nose, gray hair and dark brows, Edward Bancroft, was secretary to the American mission in Paris. Standing next to him was Charles Gravier, comte de Vergennes, the French Foreign Minister. Jean was quick to acknowledge both.

He respected Vergennes, for it was he who had convinced the king to support America in the hope it would weaken Britain. Having secured the king's agreement to aid the young republic, Vergennes then worked tirelessly to bring the Spanish and Dutch into the fold. But Jean believed the alliance now in place owed as much to England's vanity, ignorance and pride as it did to the efforts of the French minister.

"I have persuaded le comte to stay for tea," said Franklin. "He and I have been discussing the American situation and I know he will welcome any news you have."

"Of course," Jean replied. After all, he served both America and France.

At Franklin's gesture, the four men took their seats on the two brocade-covered sofas facing each other over a small oval table, where tea was served. Jean marveled, as he always did, that the American commissioner seemed so vital though he was now in his mid-seventies. His hair, which fell thinly to his shoulders, was more dark brown than gray. The commissioner's waist had expanded since the last time Jean had been to Passy, but he was not surprised. Franklin's love of French food and wine was well known.

Franklin took a sip of his tea and set down his cup. "I trust you have brought me good tidings, M'sieur Donet. Something with which to bargain for my Americans languishing in British prisons? Those who have escaped tell me horrible stories of their confinements."

"*Oui*, I bring you an English sloop and her thirty crew. I had thought to bring you the crew of another ship, but at the moment my efforts have been thwarted."

"You would be mysterious, my friend?"

"I have no choice. Something I hold dear to my heart is involved. But I promise you more British seamen and soon."

"I suppose I cannot complain," said Franklin, "you have brought me hundreds of English seamen and more than twenty prizes in the last year."

Bancroft lifted his pen from the tablet on which he'd been scribbling as if the figure had surprised him. As secretary to the American mission, he had to know Jean had secured British ships and their crews for Franklin's prisoner exchange, but perhaps the secretary had not kept an account of the number.

Desiring to steer the conversation away from his reasons for withholding the crew of the second ship, Jean asked, "How go the negotiations for peace? Is there aught I can do to help?"

Franklin shared a knowing look with Vergennes. "There has been much talk, but little progress, I'm afraid. The British representative insists it should be sufficient they give America its independence. I informed him in no uncertain terms we will not bargain for that which is already ours, that which we have purchased at the expense of so much blood and treasure."

Jean nodded. "I believe the English are exhausted by the war but too proud to make peace."

Franklin nodded.

Vergennes interjected, "We do not lose hope, however. Paris is crawling with English emissaries these days, so perhaps an accord will be reached. France has little interest in prolonging what has become a very expensive war."

Franklin gave his colleague a kind look. "We are not unmindful of the generosity of our French friends." Then looking at Jean, "And your efforts, M'sieur Donet."

Throughout the conversation, Bancroft said nothing but continued to scratch upon his pad. Jean slipped him a side-glance, recalling the rumors that spies surrounded Franklin, both British and French. Bancroft was in a prime position to gather useful information, and while he might be an American, Jean had heard he once made his home in London.

As such meetings had gone in the past, after Franklin told Jean of his needs for ships and the numbers of British seamen he hoped to have with which to bargain, their conversation turned to those men who were helping or hurting the American cause. Jean wanted to inquire about the man to whom he had promised his daughter. When he reclaimed her, the marriage would be his first priority.

"Have you encountered François de Dordogne in the negotiations?" he asked the two men sitting across from him.

"Ah, the young lawyer," said Vergennes. "Why, yes. He has drafted several papers for me. Very good work, too."

Jean shared a look of understanding with his quartermaster and inwardly breathed a sigh of relief. He had selected Dordogne for his well-respected family and his reputation as a rising star in legal circles, often advocating the ideals of reason and individualism rather than tradition, which would appeal to Claire. But the lawyer was still in his mid-twenties and, as yet, untested. It comforted Jean to know that Vergennes was aware of the young man and had used his services with good results. It was important that Claire's husband be respected in society. The dowry Jean would provide her would set Dordogne on firm ground to care for Claire and their children.

No doubt it was one reason the lawyer had eagerly agreed to the match and asked no questions asked about Jean's recent business dealings.

The brief meeting concluded with Jean explaining the location of the ship and the captured British seamen and promising more bounty and soon, which put a smile on Franklin's lined face. Plying the Channel for English ships had become a profitable pastime and Jean did not intend to disappoint.

࿐ ༚ ࿐

Rye Harbor

Alone in his cabin on the *Fairwinds*, now anchored in Rye, Simon looked up from the ship's log to see the man who had been guarding Claire Donet's door at night standing before him. "You wanted to see me, Anderson?"

"Aye, Cap'n. 'Tis the French girl."

Simon set down his quill and gestured for the man to sit.

The burly Anderson, who often assisted the ship's carpenter, dropped into the chair on the other side of the desk.

Seeing the look on his crewmember's face, he spoke his thought aloud. "What new mischief has she gotten into now?" To allow her privacy, Simon had given her his cabin while he shared the first mate's. Each night, he posted a guard at her door, often it was Anderson. It wasn't just to keep her from trying to escape while they were in port, but to make sure none of his crew, who might happen to return from the Mermaid Inn with too much ale in their bellies, disobeyed his orders to leave her alone.

"'Tis no mischief, sir. 'Tis her dreams."

He sat back and crossed his arms. "Tell me more."

"Well, at first I thought it were just an odd dream. I've had 'em meself. But this tweren't no single dream. She's had more than one in the nights I've stood guard. Some would call 'em night terrors. She moans and screams in her sleep like she's bein' chased by one of McGinnes' banshees. The sounds die down after a time."

"Have you asked her about this?"

"Aye, once. After the first time, the next morn I ask if she slept well. All she said was 'Not altogether, Mr. Anderson'. I thought ye should know, Cap'n."

"You were right in telling me. I hope she's not troubled by her captivity."

"Don't think that were it, Cap'n. I heard her call out a woman's name... Elsie, Lisee...somethin' like that. It were slurred, ye see."

"Thank you, Anderson, that will be all."

As the big man rose and left, Simon picked up his quill, dipped it in the ink and then hesitated. *What would cause her to have such dreams?*

He had lingered in Rye, now well over a week, to await a reply from Donet and to see to the needs of his hostage, her clothes, shoes and other things a young woman might need. Elijah had taken her to Sally at the Mermaid Inn who had more knowledge of a young woman's clothing. All Simon knew of feminine attire was how to remove it.

There'd been no word from Dartmouth or Donet. With a fast coach from Paris and a faster ship across the Channel, he thought he might have heard something by now, unless Donet had not yet received the missive he'd left on the girl's pillow in Saint-Denis.

An hour later, he had turned to his charts of the Channel when his first mate stepped over the threshold. Jordan's dark eyes, usually full of mirth, carried a grave look. It raised the hair on the back of Simon's neck.

"You have news?"

Jordan stepped into the cabin. "I do. Donet received your note. You won't be surprised to learn he's sent a nasty reply."

"I expected as much. After all, we have his daughter. What does he say?"

"You might as well read it." He walked to the desk and dropped the letter on top of the ship's log. The blue wax seal was already broken. "The short answer is he agrees to the exchange and threatens the crew with death if she's harmed."

Simon unfolded the single sheet, quickly confirming the message, and raised his head. "He says nothing of the *Abundance*?"

"I noted that as well. Expect the pirate intends to keep her."

Simon sat back, wondering if he should go himself. But the note said Donet was sending his quartermaster. And he'd need Jordan in London. "Send Elijah and Giles to Paris for the meeting Donet wants. Whitehall has enough of its representatives in France right now, they'll be in good company. Tell Elijah to demand the return of the *Abundance* as well as her crew."

"I'll see to it, Captain," Jordan said and turned to leave.

Before his first mate had stepped through the cabin door,

Simon asked, "Where's the girl now?"

Jordan paused, looked over his shoulder and smiled. "She's in the galley with Nate listening to tales from our new cook. Safe enough, I think. And one of the crew stands guard as you ordered."

He nodded and Jordan departed. *So she's discovered McGinnes.*

During the day when he had work to do at his desk, Elijah often escorted her to the weather deck. The galley was a new venue for her, but he'd known she'd eventually find her way there. His Irish cook was only a few years older than she and quite a charmer. Educated in one of the Ursuline schools for the poor in Cork, they would have many stories to exchange. Simon had no bias against Catholics, as many in London did, and knew the Ursulines to do much good. That his captive was Catholic concerned him not at all. That she was French nobility and the daughter of his enemy concerned him more.

Since Simon had kissed Donet's daughter, they'd arrived at an uneasy truce. He was polite and she was cool and remote, though from the way she had responded to his kiss, he suspected a core of molten liquid simmered beneath the surface. He was certain she feared her response should he kiss her again. No future nun would have responded so. How would she explain *that* to the sisters in Saint-Denis? Lord knew he wanted to kiss her again. No woman had captured his attention like the wild Claire Donet. He still remembered the taste of her lips, the feel of her soft breasts pressed against him and the way she had kissed him back, notwithstanding her innocence. In his mind's eye, he could still see the look of wonder in her passion-glazed eyes when he'd left her in his cabin that day.

She was a tasty tidbit he dare not touch again.

Simon looked about his cabin, noting the feminine things piled neatly on top of his sea chest at the foot of his bed. Oddly, he did not resent the intrusion into his domain. And he liked the lavender fragrance her presence left in his cabin.

But he had more to worry about than her dreams or his attraction to the French beauty. Yesterday's messages from London had included a summons from his superiors, William Eden and Lord Danvers. He must sail to London. The night they had taken the girl from the convent, one of his men had retrieved additional messages from the Scribe in Paris that he must place in their hands.

Once they were anchored in the Thames, he would leave Jordan in command, but what was he to do with the French girl? He did not want her to remain on the ship. Nor did he want to leave her in Rye. The Mermaid Inn was not a safe place for a fetching young innocent who must be watched at all times. And because of the note he had left him, Donet was now aware of Simon's connection to Dartmouth, so that was not an option. Not that he wanted to let her out of his sight. There was no help for it. She would have to go with him. He smiled to himself. She would enjoy Cornelia, Lady Danvers. After all, the baroness, only six years older, was an American.

Chapter 7

Claire sat in the galley listening to the cook weave stories of Irish fairies, her mind wandering. She had been on the ship over a sennight and anxious to escape. Once they had anchored in Rye, seeing land so close, she had begun to devise a way to get a message to her papa. A friend would be needed as she had no coins to bribe someone motivated only by greed. To a man, the captain's crew appeared loyal to him. Though she still held out some hope young Nate could be persuaded to help her, she knew she would feel guilty for making use of the growing affection between them.

Elijah Hawkins had introduced her to Sally at the Mermaid Inn, who'd offered to find Claire another gown and proper underclothes. Claire was happy for the chance to be alone with the woman, thinking the innkeeper's daughter might be enlisted to help. But Sally had been more interested in why a woman was aboard the handsome captain's ship. After listening to her prattle on about the gallant captain of the *Fairwinds*, Claire determined the woman was too enamored of Simon Powell to be of any assistance in her cause. The woman's affection for the English privateer annoyed Claire more than she wanted to admit. Had they been lovers? Shrugging off the nagging thought, she admitted any help she might find for an escape would have to come from another source. And since the captain never left her unguarded, it would not be an easy task.

Claire had been reluctant to accept the captain's generosity in providing her clothes, but she reminded herself that none of the expense would have been necessary had he not kidnapped her in the first instance. So, reluctantly, she had accepted the clothing she so desperately needed.

One advantage of being in port was that she was able to walk about the ship without holding on to the rail for balance. But that did not mean she was comfortable. When Mr. Hawkins escorted her on deck, she could feel the eyes of the crew ogling her. The only woman on the ship, she stood out like a raven in a flock of white gulls.

Nearly all her life she had lived in the world of women. Now she was immersed in the world of men. Even the ship's cat, a lean, black feline that stalked the decks for its dinner, was a male.

Sometimes the change from the convent to the ship was jarring. The crude language and ungentlemanly habits of the crew often startled her. Sister Angélique would have been horrified. But at those times, Claire would suddenly become interested in the large numbers of beach-nesting terns flying low over the harbor, their black heads and striking white plumage catching her eye. When he was on deck, she would beg Mr. Landor to lend her his spyglass so that she could watch the birds up close. Soon, her feigned fascination became real as she watched the elegant birds take flight over the rocky shore. Behind them was the hill town of Rye, a glittering topaz rising out of a setting of blue-green water.

After a few days of strolling the deck with Mr. Hawkins, Claire had noticed a change in the men. They cursed less and smiled more.

"'Tis yer doin'," said Mr. Hawkins. "The men know'd ye were in a convent. They're not wantin' to offend a woman who talks to the Almighty."

"But Mr. Hawkins, I am no closer to God than is any God-fearing man on this ship."

"But there be few of those, lass."

Her memory of her fit of temper in the captain's cabin suddenly returned with a pang of remorse. Her actions had hardly seemed godly. Though she was an unwilling prisoner on the ship, they had treated her as the guest Captain Powell had claimed she would be. In such circumstances, would not the Reverend Mother expect her to be civil? If the privateer's crew could change, perhaps so could she. "I am grateful for the crew's courtesy."

"Aye, I 'spect they know that, too, mistress." The old seaman drew on his pipe sending a puff of smoke into the clear morning air, a pale cloud against a sky of blue.

Because she wasn't so preoccupied with keeping her balance now that the ship was anchored in calm waters, she noticed more about the schooner. It was a sleek vessel, black-hulled with two fine masts and a well maintained deck. Even now the crew was scrubbing it clean as they did most mornings.

When she remarked on it, Elijah explained, "'Tis the cap'n's baby, this one. He coddles it like a lass. Handpicked the crew, he did, from those who'd sailed with him fer years."

"And you are one of those?"

"Aye, been with him since he sailed as first mate under another cap'n. Even then it was clear how good a cap'n he'd make."

To her relief, Elijah had assured her that while the crew might gawk at her and occasionally engage in course talk, she was in no danger from the captain's men. None would defy his orders to treat her as the lady she was. The captain, she feared, was another matter. It was her own weakness for him that placed her in peril. Even knowing the man was her papa's enemy did not nullify the fascination she had for him, one she'd had from that first night she'd seen him at the masquerade. So she took the coward's way out and avoided him as much as she could.

When she was not with Elijah, a member of the crew dogged her every step. Captain Powell, it seemed, did not trust her, which was probably wise on his part, for escape was ever on her mind. But with no coins and no friend to aid her, she had yet to arrive at a plan.

She had discovered the ship's galley was a safe, cozy place to while away a few hours. There was a stool or two to sit upon and Tom McGinnes, the Irish cook, working away at his table or stirring something on the black stove, made her laugh with his stories of the Ursuline sisters in Cork. His escapades rivaled hers in Saint-Denis and must have caused the nuns many sleepless nights. When he'd finished recounting one of his stories, he would tell her and Nate, who often joined her, of the Irish legends. This morning was no different.

"When the Gaels first came to Ireland," the cook began as he slapped a mound of dough, sending a cloud of flour into the air, some of it lodging in his long copper hair he reined in with a ribbon, "they banished the natives to the underground where they became the fairy folk. 'Twere the *Sidhe*, don't ye know. 'Tis said they live in the hawthorn tree."

"Truly?" asked Nate, his eyes wide.

"Sure an' the tree is a door to the fairy realm, best left undisturbed if'n ye ask me," he counseled while he continued to knead the mound of dough.

Claire rubbed her arm, feeling once again the thorns slicing into her skin as they had two years ago when she had plunged to the ground from her perch in the tree. It had been a hawthorn tree, and for a long while after, the cuts had pained her. "What happens if one disturbs such a tree?"

"Now that'd depend on yer intent, lass," he said with a gleam in his green eyes, looking from her to Nate and then to the silent crewmember, standing in the corner. "The hawthorn fairy can enchant yer life and bring ye love if'n she's of a mind to. They say she protects the unwary, but if the one who disturbs her tree means ill, she can bring great misfortune."

Nate stared at the cook, enraptured.

"Well I never meant… " she mumbled under her breath as a shudder came over her. Was all that had happened the result of her climbing that hawthorn tree? *Holy Mother, no!* Sister Angélique would call the Irish cook's stories heathen foolishness. "Surely you don't believe such tales?"

"I ain't sayin' if'n I do or I don't," McGinnes replied. "But I seen things I can't explain, strange things, both in Cork and since I been at sea."

"Careful, McGinnes, or you'll have these two believing we've mermaids off the stern," said the amused voice of the captain behind her.

Claire turned on her stool to see him leaning indolently against the bulkhead. The small galley seemed to shrink with his tall form and the masculine energy he gave off. Amidst the smell of stew cooking, she detected the smell of the sea and the man himself. His golden hair hung loosely to his shoulders as he stood there smiling, his arms crossed over his chest. The muscles of his forearms, browned from the sun, flexed, reminding her of the strength he had used to hold her to him just before he'd kissed her. A shudder, not unpleasant, coursed through her.

When his amber eyes turned on her, she sat up straighter on her stool. "Good day, Captain Powell."

"And to you, mademoiselle." He made a small bow. She was certain the gesture was done to further his amusement. Then turning to McGinnes, he said in a serious tone, "Much as I enjoy my time in Rye, I'd have you set an early dinner, and feed the crew early. We sail for London on the evening tide."

"Aye, aye, Skipper."

"London? You are sailing to *London*?" she asked, hardly believing he intended to take her there.

"Aye, I am." Bidding the others good day, he turned to her. "Would you accompany me, mademoiselle? There is something I would like to ask you."

She rose from her stool, unable to imagine what the captain had in mind and keenly aware they had not been alone together since he'd kissed her. As they walked to his cabin, she asked, "How can you take me to London? What about returning me to Saint-Denis?"

"That will have to wait."

Inwardly she fumed. Much as she'd like to see London, she had hoped her captivity would soon end. Reluctantly, she entered his cabin, where he held out a chair for her. "I'd offer you sherry but we do not keep it on board."

"I do not require sherry, Captain. What was it you wanted to ask me?"

"I'm told you suffer from bad dreams."

"I would have no knowledge of that," she said shortly. Did the guard he had posted at her door report to him about even her sleep? She was well aware of her nightmares but she could not bring herself to bare her soul to him, to tell him of the girl who still haunted her dreams. And it was none of his business anyway.

"I see." He watched her for a moment.

"Is there anything else, Captain?"

"Not at the moment. You may go."

She rose and left, determined not to let the man get any closer to her than he already had.

༛ ༄༅ ༓

Simon watched the young woman march from his cabin, her head held high, hearing in his mind the sound of a door slamming in his face. So she would tell him nothing of the nightmares that plagued her. He had seen the faint, blue circles under her eyes and wondered at their cause even before Anderson had spoken of her troubled dreams. But he could not pry her secrets from her.

She was not the first to shut him out, only the most recent. His father had been the first, then his mother's family. Despite them all, he had succeeded. So why should it leave him feeling unsettled that a mere slip of a French girl was unwilling to share her burdens with him?

Perhaps it was a matter of trust. Their attraction to each

other notwithstanding, they were still enemies. Moreover, while he was bastard born, she was French nobility. But he had trouble seeing her in those terms. She did not act like the members of the aristocracy he had known in England, Lord Danvers being a notable exception. She was more like the baron's wife, Cornelia. Even though she could be stubborn and had a temper that, at times, defied reason, he liked Claire Donet. She was intelligent as well as beautiful. And he wanted her as a woman. He wanted to share her confidences, to share her fears. Foolish desires, all.

What Claire Donet did with her life was her own affair. Hadn't she told him it was none of his business when he'd inquired of her reasons for wanting to join the Ursulines? What bad dreams she had and their cause were also her affair. She would be gone soon.

He had a war to see to its end, his men to recover and a shipping enterprise to build. He must focus on those things.

Focus, he told himself.

◌ ◌◌ ◌

The first thing Simon noticed when he returned to his cabin after conferring with the ship's carpenter on some needed repairs was the setting of his table. Typically the table would remain bare, save for his brandy and glasses, until Nate delivered the meal. Then the stack of pewter plates would be passed out. But today there was a white linen tablecloth on which was set blue and white porcelain dishes. In the center was a decanter of claret wine. All was laid out with careful attention. Scurrying around the table was Nate, checking the placement of the silver.

"What's all this?" Simon inquired, baffled.

"Mistress Donet has been teachin' me how to set a table. I thought as it's our last dinner in Rye before we sail for London, I'd show ye what I've learned."

"And the tableware?"

"Ye probably forgot, sir, but it was the extra we had in the hold from that time ye bought Lady Danvers all those dishes."

"Aye, it does look familiar."

Most days his French captive joined him for dinner along with his two first mates, Amos Busby from the *Abundance* having joined the *Fairwinds*' crew. So he expected she would share the early meal today. Sure enough, before long the two first mates strolled into his cabin along with Claire Donet. Her ebony hair was twisted into a knot at her nape, which was how she often wore it. The blue gown was still lovely on her despite its daily wear. He reminded himself to ask Nate to fetch the ones she'd ordered in Rye.

Jordan's eyes widened when he glimpsed the table. "Ah, what a difference the lady has made!"

To Simon, she appeared pleased, possibly smug. Shooting him a glance, she said, "I don't suppose you like the change, do you?"

"It's an improvement," he admitted. She seemed mildly pleased by his response which after their afternoon, was encouraging. While her English had improved since she'd been with them, she still had a deep French accent, which was so sensual it often left him staring at her mouth when he had no intention of doing so.

In uncharacteristic fashion, Amos Busby pulled out a chair and gestured her to it. "Well, I like it," he said. "'Tisn't often I've dined in so civilized a manner aboard ship."

"We don't often have the time or calm waters," Simon reminded him.

"I'll be back with the food," said Nate as he straightened a last knife and left.

Simon poured the claret and handed each person a glass of the dark red wine. He lifted his own in toast. "To a fair sailing to London."

"To a fair sailing!" the three echoed.

A few moments later, Nate returned with McGinnes and

two trays laden with food.

"I thought to make somethin' special for ye," said the Irish cook in his lilting brogue as he set the dishes on the table.

Inwardly Simon groaned. What new cuisine horror was about to befall them? It was better when his new cook relegated himself to simple stews. While in port they always had fresh meat and vegetables. "What is it?" he asked with dubious interest, peering at the dishes set before them.

"A soup to start, Skipper." He began ladling out an orange liquid into small bowls.

"Soup?" They rarely had soup, only stews.

"Gingered carrot, Captain," Claire Donet said, winking at the cook. Some collusion was going on, he was now certain. "Perhaps you are new to the dish?"

"Sure an' Mistress Donet gave me the idea."

"I see." And Simon did.

"And for the main dish?" inquired Jordan.

McGinnes lifted a lid to reveal slices of beef covered in a dark sauce. "'Tis a bit of beef in red wine. And vegetables."

"I'm starved," said Amos.

"I'm overwhelmed," said Simon. He only hoped the food tasted better than McGinnes' last venture into the unknown.

McGinnes stood back, beaming his pleasure at the array of food he'd set before them. Nate collected the lids and trays. "As I've had a bit of time," the cook said, "Mistress Donet's been teachin' me to plan meals. Oh an' before I ferget, dessert will be sugared fruits," he said pointing to a plate he had set on the desk.

"Smells wonderful," said Jordan.

"I'm sure it's splendid," said Claire Donet with an encouraging smile directed at the cook. From McGinnes' response, Simon was certain she and the Irishman were now partners in some culinary plot.

Resigned to sample the orange broth set before him, Simon raised his spoon of steaming liquid to his mouth just as the girl bowed her head and said a prayer of thanks. Remnants of her convent life, he assumed. With his spoon suspended in front of his face, he and the two first mates watched in silence. As soon as she finished, they dove into the food.

His captive shot him a look of disapproval.

Simon ignored her. But he had to admit the soup was quite tasty and the beef was better than McGinnes' usual fare. Perhaps the Irishman was learning to cook. Or God was answering the French girl's prayers.

She ate with delicacy, her manners those of a lady. The afternoon sunlight filtering in through the windows cast a warm glow over her pale skin. He wasn't the only one who stole glances at her. Jordan and Amos had taken a new interest in their reluctant guest. He suspected she had no idea of her effect on men. Half his crew was drooling over her yet she appeared to remain ignorant of their lustful glances.

When several minutes had gone by and a shadow crossed her face, he asked, "Why so brooding, mademoiselle?"

"I was just wondering what the sisters and my friends at the convent were doing. Dinner is the one time when we can gather to share not only a meal but the events of the day and, oft times, the news of the village."

Simon had not thought much about her schooling at the convent. "What did they teach you at the convent besides how to pray?"

"All manner of things," she replied in a somewhat defensive tone. "To read and write, of course. But also mathematics, Latin and the things a lady of society must know, like the planning of meals, needlework, art and music. Because my papa chose to have me stay longer, I was able to learn things the younger girls did not."

Simon *was* impressed.

"I had no idea," said Jordan.

"I don't suppose they taught you how to cook?" Simon inquired. "McGinnes could use some help."

"No. That was not one of our subjects. It was expected I would one day take my place as the mistress of my own home where I would have servants, including a cook. But being French, I know something about food." This she said with a superior tone he supposed was the purview of the French when it came to culinary matters. "And being as I'm your prisoner," she added petulantly, "I needed something to do while on your ship."

Ignoring the question of her status, he said, "Well, you have my thanks for whatever you have done to inspire McGinnes. The food is a genuine improvement."

Between bites of beef, Amos and Jordan chimed in their agreement.

His captive smiled, seemingly satisfied at what she'd accomplished.

༄ ༔ ༄

When dinner was concluded, Claire ascended the ladder to the deck above, her guard following. But even his presence and the captain's many questions could not dampen her spirits. Though she resented the captain's thinking he could haul her around like a crate full of goods wherever he sailed, the more she thought about it, the more she was delighted with the news they were sailing to London, a city she'd never seen.

London!

A captive she might be but they had not mistreated her and now she was to see a place she'd never been. Surely she could see it once before taking her vows?

The captain had told her he would allow her to remain on deck as they sailed if she stayed out of the way. As if she would be a burden! *Insufferable, handsome lout.*

Taking care so as not to fall in a crumpled heap to the deck when they sailed, she accepted the arm of Amos Busby, as he led her to the rail. Despite who her father was, the first mate from the captain's other ship had been kind to her and for that she was grateful.

Shielding her eyes from the sun with one hand, she

gripped the polished wood of the rail with the other in anticipation of the lurch that would come as the sails filled with wind.

"All hands on deck to weigh anchor!" shouted Mr. Landor. He stood on the quarterdeck with his hands clasped behind him and his legs planted firmly on what she knew would soon become a rolling deck.

Some of the crew scurried into the rigging. Nate had told her all that would take place in preparation to sail, but this was the first time she'd be experiencing it for herself.

"Hands to the capstan! Set the capstan bars! Heave around now!" Mr. Busby yelled out.

At his words, a part of the crew hastened to circle a wooden cylinder with bars pointing out at right angles like spokes of a wheel. *That must be the capstan.* Each man took hold of one bar, pushing on it as they circled around. With their effort, a rope as thick as the spread of a man's hand was dragged from the water and coiled around the wooden structure.

Suddenly one of the men broke out in song.
> *Our packet is the Island Lass*

The other men, joining him, sang a refrain.
> *Low lands lowlands lowlands low*

And so it continued,
> *There's a laddie howlin' at the main topmast*
> *Low lands lowlands lowlands low*
>
> *The old man he's from Barbados*
> *Low lands lowlands lowlands low*
>
> *He's got the name of Hammer Toes*
> *Low lands lowlands lowlands low*
>
> *He gives us bread as hard as brass*
> *Low lands lowlands lowlands low*

Nate took his place next to her at the rail. "Ye like the

crew's song, miss?"

"Very much. Seeing them work together like that is exhilarating."

The song soon became a loud chorus of deep male voices singing in perfect harmony. Her foot began tapping in time with their song and her heart sped as she joined them in spirit. It was exciting to feel the energy rise as they readied the ship to sail. Their singing was different from the soft, high voices of the nuns at Saint-Denis and she loved it. There was a power in the crew's deep voices she had never experienced before.

"Up and down! Up and down," bawled Mr. Busby, and the singing trailed off. "Vast heaving, there!"

Claire had no idea what his words meant, so she watched to see what the crew did in response. Immediately, the men at the capstan stopped their work and stood by with sweat running down their faces and their chests heaving as they shook out their hands and arms.

Mr. Landor moved to the rail, checked the wind and craned back to look at the thin, red pennant streaming from the top of the mainmast. He looked toward the helm and with a nod from the captain, shouted, "Hands to make sail! Man the topsail gear! Man the foresail gear! Man the mainsail gear! All halyards, haul away! Haul away smartly!"

Crewmembers hauled the heavy lines hand-over-hand. In response, three tall squares of canvas billowed out above like sheets on a laundry line caught in the wind. With a sharp tug, like a horse jerking free of its tether, the ship surged forward. Claire gripped the rail with both hands and held on.

"Heave away, you men!" cried Mr. Busby. "Stamp and go! Stamp and go!"

Claire waited, anxious to see what the strange commands would produce. The men at the capstan leaned in and strained, their muscles bulging with the effort as they pushed at the bars. There was no singing now, only low grunts and growls as they slowly, slowly pushed around the capstan, bringing in the final length of the huge rope and hauling the massive anchor up to the large wooden beam on the side of the bow.

Quick as a monkey, one of the crew scrambled over the bow to secure the anchor to the ship.

Mr. Landor turned his gaze toward the stern. Claire's eyes followed. The captain stood at the ship's wheel, smiling with apparent pleasure at the brisk teamwork of his crew.

Claire couldn't take her eyes off him. *He was made for the sea. Here he rules as surely as a king on his throne.* Though his crew had shouted the orders, it had been the captain who had directed all with a nod of his head, a look in his eye. Subtle commands to his first mate that were instantly carried out.

He held his head proudly as the wind billowed his white shirt, his strong hands on the wheel, strands of his golden hair, glistening in the sun, blowing around his face. He looked every inch the fierce bird of prey he appeared that night in Saint-Denis… *l'aigle royal*, the golden eagle. She could not look away from his strong face and his powerful form. He was magnificent. How she envied him the freedom to chart his own course, to sail the seas to places she'd never been. *How I would love to sail with him.*

Disturbed by her thought and afraid he might catch her staring, Claire quickly turned to watch the men at the anchor finish their work. The ones who had manned the capstan were removing and stowing the bars, all the while exchanging friendly insults.

The thick anchor rope was now splayed on deck. It was dripping water and covered with mud, muck, slime—and to her horror—sea creatures! The muck had fallen onto the legs and hands of the crew, though they did not seem to notice. The creatures flopped, flailed and scuttled about the deck obviously trying to get away. She saw starfish and slimy things she could not identify slithering toward her. In a matter of minutes, they began to dry out in the warm air and a sickening smell rose in her nostrils. With a grimace, she stepped from the rail, backing away from the creatures.

Nate followed her, asking with a grin, "Are ye bothered by a wee sample of the sea, miss?"

"Not entirely," she said truthfully. "But I am glad they are over there and I am now over here."

The cabin boy laughed, drawing the attention of the captain. For a moment her gaze met his where he stood at the helm. She looked away, embarrassed that she was staring once again at his powerful form.

"Do they always sing with their work?" she asked Nate in an attempt to cover her lapse.

"Most times. It makes the work go easier."

The ship rolled beneath her feet leaving Claire unsteady. She looked toward the rail, a short distance away. Observing her plight, Nate offered his arm, which she gratefully accepted. "Thank you, Nate. I'm still a bit awkward on deck."

He tipped his tricorne to her. "Any time, mistress."

Chapter 8

Simon was pleased at their progress. Their course was steady, heading south by southeast, taking advantage of the favorable winds at their back as they headed into the Channel. It was a warm summer's day without clouds or rain on the horizon. The waters, though never placid, were not white capping.

He exalted in having his hands on the wheel, feeling the *Fairwinds* respond to his urgings. Like a woman she was, though easier to tame than some. He might have no family but he had his crew, and his ships, or he would as soon as he returned the girl.

He shot a glance at his captive and smiled at the thought of the convent-raised girl moving her foot in time to his men's work song. She had more spirit than even she was aware of. He recalled their earlier dinner where she had acted the lady, but he also knew there was fire in her belly and he liked it when she could not contain it, no matter it might be anger that spilled forth. He liked her kissing him back when she was angry even more.

She had apologized for making a mess of his cabin. Likely her convent training made her feel guilty for the incident. It prompted the thought that had been rumbling around in his head since he'd first taken her from Saint-Denis. How could such a woman become a nun? He was not mistaken about her. She had a fiery temper like no nun he'd ever met. And he'd seen her pleasure at their sailing, her face lifting to the wind with a look of intense joy as the ship glided out of the harbor. She had a desire for adventure and the sea much like his own. It had been that same love of the sea that first led him to join the crew of a merchant ship.

He was a son ignored by a father who only wanted to forget his bastard's inconvenient existence. But on his deathbed, the Earl of Montmorency had left Simon ten thousand pounds, more than enough to purchase and outfit his first ship, the *Abundance*, named after a legacy bestowed by a guilty conscience.

When the request came from Lord Danvers in London to meet with William Eden to discuss helping the government retrieve messages from their spies in Paris, he had quickly agreed. He might be a patriot, but he was no fool. Coming to England's aid now, as a spy and a privateer, would serve him well in the future. He had dreams of building a merchant shipping enterprise the likes of which England had never seen. And for that he needed his country at peace.

They reached the open Channel and he set a course heading northeast toward the Strait of Dover when he heard the lookout's cry.

"Sail ho!"

"Where away?" shouted Jordan from amidships.

"Dead ahead!" came the reply on the wind.

His first mate strode toward him wearing a serious expression and holding out a spyglass. "Captain, you'd best have a look."

Simon gestured for Jordan to take the wheel and accepted the spyglass, extending it to its full length as he studied the sails on the horizon. The ship was a fair distance away, but he caught a flicker of red, white and blue flying off the stern of what looked to be a brig-sloop. If Donet had an American letter of marque he might fly that flag. A sudden dread came over him. "*La Reine Noire?*"

"Aye, could be. A brig-sloop to be sure. Might be coming from Calais."

Casting his gaze about the deck, he spotted the French girl still standing at the rail with his cabin boy. The lad was so absorbed in their conversation, he'd likely missed the threat. "Mr. Baker!"

The boy turned. "Sir?" he yelled back.

"See our passenger to my cabin—now!"

Nate took her by the elbow and hustled her toward the aft hatch. As they drew closer to where Simon stood on the quarterdeck, she gave him a puzzled look.

"It seems your father intends to pay us a visit, mademoiselle."

"Papa?" she asked, concern showing in her beautiful blue eyes. Tendrils of her ebony hair whipped about her face causing something to settle in his chest, a longing he'd not experienced before. Produced as it was by Donet's daughter, it was most unwelcome.

Ignoring her question, with a jerk of his head he signaled to Nate that haste was in order. The lad urged her through the hatch to the deck below.

"Will he attack?" Jordan asked, staring eastward toward the sails growing larger on the horizon.

"Aye, he will for a certainty, but he won't be looking to sink us. He'll not risk his daughter. I expect he'll try to do enough damage to leave us limping so he can board. Donet would have his daughter and keep his spoils, if he could."

Simon raised the spyglass. The brig-sloop was beating against the wind, heading toward them through the rough waters of the Channel. As he watched, the ship veered off slightly. He handed the glass back to Jordan and took control of the wheel. "He's moving to attack from the south. If I'm right, he'll try and rake our starboard."

"Your plan?" asked his first mate.

"To escape, of course. I'll not risk my ship against so many guns. And, like Donet, I'll not risk the lady." Simon felt protective of her, even possessive, but he knew his feelings for her were not worth a button on his waistcoat. He must think only of his men. "Neither will I fail to engage."

He bellowed to his crew, "Run out the guns!" His men, watching the other ship closing, were swift to move.

The French ship, as Simon had predicted, was preparing to bear in passing with its guns rolled out, ready to blow holes in the *Fairwinds*.

"Hold fire!" Simon shouted, gritting his teeth. To allow Donet to fire his guns while his own men did nothing was asking a lot. But for his plan to work, he needed them to forebear.

Turning to Jordan, he barked, "Give me all the sail you can!"

His first mate shouted the orders aloft. The square-sails filled with a "thump" and the yards creaked as the *Fairwinds* picked up speed, lunging ahead like a racehorse hearing the starting shot.

A moment later, Donet's guns blazed away. A crash, followed by a crunching noise, told him the French guns had hit wood. But as the *Fairwinds* sailed clear of the cloud of smoke, Simon let out the breath he'd been holding. From what he could see, only the fancywork on the stern's transom had been clipped. His smaller, lighter, faster schooner had managed to fling itself out of the reach of most of the Frenchman's guns. Below decks, his captive would be frightened, but it could not be helped. He would comfort her later.

Grinding the wheel hard to port, Simon deliberately turned across the wind, a tactic he knew might lose him the forward drive he needed. The sails shivered and flapped, but then caught the wind with a crack like a whip. The main boom swept across the deck, and the schooner was through the wind and away on her new tack, running a circle around the slower, larger ship.

When the schooner turned across the bow of the Frenchman, he bellowed, "Fire!"

The *Fairwinds'* guns belched smoke sending shot into the

French ship from stem to stern, destroying, Simon hoped, at least some of their gunnery posts. He was rewarded with the sound of a smash, the splintering of wood and shouts coming from the brig-sloop as the French crew scrambled to deal with the damage.

He turned the wheel again, this time hard to starboard, bringing the wind to their back. With *la Reine Noire* crippled, unable to fire its guns, Simon set a course for the Strait of Dover, and to the cheers of his crew, sped away.

૭ ༩ஂ ૭

When the cabin door opened, Claire was still shaking, shocked at all she had endured.

"Are you all right?" said the captain, his brows drawn together. His white shirt stretched across his muscled chest, he appeared a strong tower in a swirling world of chaos.

Without thinking, she ran into his arms and held on to the one man she'd wanted in the midst of the battle.

No, I am not all right.

Minutes before, her heart in her throat, she had stared into the mouths of eight threatening guns, too stunned to move and not knowing where to flee. The moment had been suspended in time, her agony endless, as the ships passed close in front of each other. Then, to her amazement, her papa appeared, standing on the deck of the other ship, shouting orders to the crew. His long black hair wild and loose about his shoulders, his dark eyes crazed with fury, he looked every bit the pirate Captain Powell had claimed he was. When he had shouted the command "Fire!" the guns had spit forth white smoke laced with crimson flames. She crossed herself, thinking her life was over. But to her surprise, the schooner seemed to fly through the inferno. Then a loud crack had sounded nearby sending a shudder through the deck. Pieces of wood had flown past the windows. She had feared the ship was breaking up and gripped the edge of the captain's

91

desk. But as she braced herself, the schooner shook off the bonds of the sea and glided over the water as if it had wings.

The danger had passed, but she was still shaking. She needed his strength. He was a lifeline in a raging sea. In his arms she felt safe.

He held her tightly and kissed the top of her head, a gesture so tender it nearly made her weep.

"And here I'd thought to send you below decks to keep you safe. Instead, it seems I sent you to the only place your father aimed his guns."

With sudden clarity, Claire understood it all. Her papa did have a ship. And this man, this English captain—her golden one—was her papa's enemy, on the opposite side of America's war. How could she find comfort in his arms if that were true? Anger welled up inside her, anger at him and at herself for her attraction to him. Rearing back, she sent her fist into his chest. "You! You fired on my papa! How dare you!"

His amber eyes flashed as he clenched his jaw and lifted his chin, but he did not let her go. "Did you happen to notice, mademoiselle, that your beloved papa fired on my ship *first?*"

She raised her hand to slap the impudent smirk off his face but he grabbed it, twisting it behind her. "This time I claim a prize for a victory won."

His lips crushed hers in a demanding kiss.

She fought his embrace, but even enraged at his confrontation with her father, she warmed to his touch, the fight in her melting away as his kiss became tender. Reaching her free hand to the nape of his neck, she held him to her, her heart pounding a fierce rhythm as she entwined her tongue with his.

He let go of her hand and, gripping her hips, drew her tightly into his heat as he continued to kiss her.

Moments later he pulled away, the loss of his warmth leaving her feeling bereft. She was panting and so was he.

"Sweetheart," he said, looking into her eyes, his voice husky, "whatever compelled a woman with your passion to seek the veil?"

She raised her chin and frowned her displeasure at the sarcastic tone of his voice. "It is none of your concern." She pulled away and he let her go. It was bad enough he had fired upon her papa's ship and scared her half to death, turning her into a ninny, vulnerable to his masculinity and his kiss. Never would she tell him of the consequences of her foolish behavior the night she'd first encountered him. How could such a man understand her promise to Élise?

"Well, you will never make a nun."

She stiffened. "And what makes you think that, sir?"

Tossing her a wry smile, he said, "I'd be happy to show you, mademoiselle, but I fear the display would be too sinful for you, and might cost me the men your father holds." And with that, he turned and abruptly departed.

Staring at the closed cabin door, Claire felt her cheeks warm. *Incorrigible rake!* Was he suggesting he would do to her what he had nearly done with that female hussar?

Surprisingly, the thought was not altogether unpleasant. And that made her wonder. Was he right when he told her she would never make a nun?

☙ ⁂ ❧

Back on deck, Simon proceeded to the bow and raised his spyglass looking eastward, but his mind was not on the Channel ahead. It was on the French beauty who stirred a craving in him like no other woman.

Why had he kissed her again?

To want her was to court disaster. Claire Donet must be returned to her father as she had come—innocent. Yet, even now, she was hardly the innocent she had been, responding as she had to his kisses. She was fire in his arms and a flame now growing in his heart. It had taken all his control not to carry her to his bed and make her his. She would not have resisted, he was certain, for the passion he had felt in her would rise to

93

meet his own. Given who she was, that would be sailing into dangerous waters.

A flock of birds flew across his line of sight, recalling him to the task at hand. The Channel was clear as far as he could see, but as they neared Dover, he knew the number of ships would increase. He and his countrymen faced the French, Spanish and Dutch aligned against them. Despite the Royal Navy's plying the waters of the Strait intercepting merchant ships, hoping to seize war supplies, they had not captured all.

La Reine Noire continually eluded them.

After the shot he'd sent into the Frenchman's brig-sloop, it would be a while before Donet could transport war supplies. Limping back to port, as he must have done, he would have to make significant repairs, allowing Simon time for his trip to London. He thought of his captured crew and worry furrowed his brow. He could only hope Donet would keep them in good health knowing Simon held the one thing the pirate prized above all.

Chapter 9

London

Claire held on to the rail, staring transfixed at the hundreds of boats and ships crowding the River Thames. The afternoon sun bathed the sky in golden hues etching the clouds in brilliant light and sending a myriad of colors rippling through the water.

All around her ships were tied up to a tall mooring post, to the wharf or to each other, some with their sails hanging loosely from the crossbeams like so much neglected laundry left out in the rain. Her blood surged with excitement at seeing such a sight.

They had sailed up the Thames, the captain at the wheel, navigating the river from its mouth through a dozen treacherous bends to where they were anchored in the area of the river Nate called the Pool of London.

She had marveled at the captain's skill sailing in changing winds and the river clogged with so many ships moving in both directions. At the most difficult place in the river, he had taken the wheel and, with his brow furrowed in concentration, deftly maneuvered the schooner away from the other ships while steadily maintaining their course. The memory of those same powerful hands holding her sent tiny shivers down her spine.

Would he keep her with him in London? She could not deny that she looked forward to more time with him.

Nate joined her where she stood on the foredeck of the ship and tipped his brown tricorne to her, his eyes quickly taking in her new gown. "Yer a picture this mornin', mistress!"

Claire warmed to the cabin boy's compliment, glad she'd taken the extra time to dress her hair. "Thank you, Nate."

The cabin boy gestured to the other ships tied up to the wharf. To Claire, he appeared as excited as she was to be in the busy port. "See the men movin' on the decks, mistress?"

Directing her gaze to the laborers hefting cargo from the ships to the wharf, she remarked, "They are certainly working hard."

"Aye, and soon we'll be seein' the same thing on the *Fairwinds.*"

She shifted her gaze to the water and watched as men and women richly attired in colorful cloaks, jackets and hats were being ferried in small boats to the ships. "Are those passengers?"

"Some, but might be a ship owner or a king's man among 'em."

Claire let her mind wander to the faraway places those passengers might travel. Places she had read about, places she had dreamed of in her days at the convent. Places Simon Powell had no doubt been.

Ahead of them loomed a tall, arched bridge spanning the river, the golden sky behind it. Majestic stone buildings whose spires reached toward the clouds stood as sentinels on either side. "What bridge is that?" she asked Nate.

"London Bridge."

She knew from her lessons that London was the largest city in Europe and its port the busiest. The number of ships anchored in the Thames attested to its importance in matters of trade. The bustle excited her, it was so different from the quiet village of Saint-Denis, or even Paris with its meandering Seine River.

Warm, muggy air carried the stench of the river to her nostrils, but beneath it were the exotic scents of ginger and sandalwood, spices from the West Indies, and the faint odor of hemp and tea that spoke of the faraway places she'd only imagined. What must it be like to sail to those ports? Her spirits rose with the thought. If only she could sail to them on a ship... *his* ship. When she thought of sailing to faraway places now, she thought only of the golden one, his sure hands at the wheel, his eyes upon her.

Hearing boots on the deck, she glanced behind her to see him striding toward her. Despite her resolve to treat him with formal politeness, her heart beat faster when their eyes met. There was a twinkle in his eyes today.

He nodded to Nate, then paused to survey her appearance. "Beautiful as ever, mademoiselle." She detected a hint of amusement in his voice. Did he find it surprising she could look the lady?

"Thank you for the gown, Captain." She ignored the voice of her conscience telling her it was highly improper to have accepted it; a hostage had little choice if she were to be properly clothed.

"As soon as the customs men depart, and our cargo is unloaded, we can leave."

"Where will we be going?" she asked him, suddenly anxious to know. Would he hide her away in some dark abode like a caged animal?

"I've friends in London with whom we will stay until your future is more certain."

Inwardly, she breathed a sigh of relief. He would keep her with him. But the fact he could just drag her around like one of his shipping crates was disturbing. "I suppose I have no choice in the matter?"

"None." He handed a letter to Nate. "Take this to Lady Danvers. She will be expecting it."

"Aye, Cap'n. I remember the place."

Claire felt a twinge of jealousy. Was this Lady Danvers his

maîtresse, his paramour? She would ask Nate. He would tell her.

❧ ❦ ☙

A few hours later, Simon guided his captive to the waiting carriage that would take them to the London home of Lord and Lady Danvers. He had an open invitation from Cornelia and her husband, John Ingram, Baron Danvers, to be their guest whenever he was in town. He and Cornelia were of an age and Danvers only a few years older. They had become good friends in recent years. That the baron worked closely with Simon's superior, former Under Secretary of State, William Eden, who was the head of England's spy network in Europe, made the arrangement all the more convenient.

For the occasion of her meeting his friends, he had given his captive a new gown, one Sally had procured for him in Rye, one he'd been saving for this moment. He wanted the French girl to feel comfortable meeting their hosts. And for some reason he'd not pondered overlong, he liked to see her in gowns that befitted her beauty. When he'd first seen her on deck, she was a sight to behold in pale green brocade. The gown hugged her slim waist and revealed just enough of her pale breasts to entice him to want to see more. He could look at other women with no reaction at all. Why did this one stir him so? She'd managed to pin the sides of her hair up. On her head was a jaunty hat that matched the gold flowers on her gown. The innocent, French convent student was suddenly a very exciting woman.

He intended to ask Cornelia to see that his hostage had a wardrobe befitting the granddaughter of a French comte. Knowing the baroness loved to shop for female frippery, he thought it a task she would relish, especially at his expense. He had in mind, too, that Cornelia could chaperone his reluctant charge and keep her occupied while he went about his business. Donet's daughter might not try to escape in London, but he would not leave her to her own devices, or unprotected.

While the baroness always traveled with footmen, he would send one of his own men to watch the French girl lest she try anything foolish.

Sitting across from him, she gazed wide-eyed out the open carriage window as they drove away from the Thames. He was not surprised at her excitement. London had many sights to fascinate a young woman just out of the convent.

"You and Lady Danvers will have much in common."

She turned her clear, blue gaze on him, a look of surprise on her face. The faint circles still lingered under her eyes, making him wonder again about her disturbing dreams.

"Nate told me Lady Danvers is the wife of an English baron. How can we have anything in common?" There was a note of defiance in her voice, reminding him that every inch of ground he gained with her was ground she only grudgingly surrendered.

"Ah, but Lady Danvers is an American, mademoiselle." It amused him to spar with her. She had a quick mind. But it was not her mind that had drawn his attention when he'd first seen her in the gown. He squeezed his fist, forcing himself to rein in his thoughts. They would only lead to frustration.

"An American married to an English nobleman?"

"I imagine it's been awkward for her since the war," he conceded. "She met Lord Danvers before the war began, when she came to London for a Season. They fell in love and she never returned to her family in the Maryland Colony. Her brother is the captain of a schooner, as am I." Then he added with a grin, "Only on the other side."

"He fights for America's independence?"

"He does. Just like France. Now do you see how much you have in common with Lady Danvers?"

She looked out the window as if reluctant to admit his point, stubborn as always. "They shall have their independence, I am certain."

He chuckled. "Yes, mademoiselle. I do believe you are right, owing much to France, of course. Though as yet no

Regan Walker

agreement for peace has been reached, there can be little doubt America will soon be her own country."

She turned her face to look at him. "Does it not bother you?"

"Not at all," he said sincerely. "I only want peace. A strong America will mean more trade." Then with his mouth twitching up in a grin, he added, "I do not intend to always be a privateer." Why it was important that she know he had ambitions for the future, he did not ponder.

"Probably wise," she said. "It would seem to be a hazardous profession."

"As is piracy," he said with a grin. She did not rise to the bait but gazed out the window at the government buildings they were passing.

The coachman had taken a route that led past St. James Park on their way to Mayfair where the Danvers' London house was located. They had just passed Westminster. Seeing it brought back memories that anywhere else he could forget, memories of seeing his father, the Earl of Montmorency, leaving Parliament, indifferent to a son he had never claimed.

Wanting her son to know of his noble heritage, despite the earl's deserting her to wed a woman of his own rank, Simon's mother had told him of his father when he was fourteen. She must have known she was dying.

Simon had been too proud to be shamed by his status, but he had been curious. And that was what led him to come that day eleven years ago to watch the Lords leaving Westminster and to inquire which was Montmorency. He would have recognized him had those he'd asked not been able to point out the earl. His father was tall and fair, not unlike Simon in appearance. He had watched as the earl greeted his countess. She'd had his younger half-brother and sister in tow. Unlike Simon, the earl's other children were dark-haired, apparently taking after their mother.

But if his father did not want to know Simon, then Simon cared not to know him. So, on that day, he had turned away, vowing to wear his bastardy like a glorious cloak.

He would show them all.

That the money for his first ship had come to him as a result of his father's guilt did not alter Simon's views. He had taken the money but would have rejected the name had it been offered. To Simon, the father he never knew was a distant mountain, cold and aloof and only seen from afar.

His mother, who had carried her noble lover in her heart until her death, had been his inspiration. She believed in her only child and sacrificed much for him. Because of her, Simon could read, write and speak French. He deeply regretted she had suffered, for most of her own family had disowned her. Only the kindness of a caring aunt had seen they were not without funds.

His mother had once told him the world would eventually come to his door. He had doubted the words when she'd first said them, but now he believed it would happen. He would prove himself to a doubting world and make his mother proud.

The carriage rolled to a gentle stop in front of the tall, stone edifice that was the home of Lord and Lady Danvers. Simon shrugged off his melancholy, stepped down and turned to offer Claire his hand.

She took it, gazing up at the looming structure. "It is quite grand, isn't it?"

"'Tis," he said, unable to resist a smile. "A bit more than they need, perhaps, but then the nobility likes their houses large. Besides, Lord and Lady Danvers often have guests."

༄ ༄༄ ༄

Claire stepped down from the carriage, glancing at the captain and then to the grand home before her. She had seen châteaux in France that were more impressive than this London house but this one was still imposing. A gray, stone structure, it rose three stories into the air with eight tall, Doric pillars gracing the front.

The captain's touch as he helped her from the carriage had been warm, even through her gloves, but all too brief. Much to her dismay, the attraction she felt for him had grown. Today he had shed the costume of a sea captain and donned the attire of a gentleman, handsome in his nut-brown coat over a saffron silk waistcoat and white shirt with an artfully tied cravat. Brown doeskin breeches clung to his muscular thighs.

She sighed realizing the longer she stayed with him the more difficult it would be to see herself as one of the Ursuline sisters. Even now, she had little desire to return to the simple clothing of the convent. Her times of prayer had grown less frequent, too, as the days passed and the rituals of her former days were cast aside. Most troubling were her recent fantasies of Simon Powell that lay in an entirely different direction than Saint-Denis. She let out a resigned sigh, realizing she would have to add those sinful thoughts to the list of sins for which she must eventually do penance.

The captain accepted a large package the coachman handed down to him, tucked it under one arm, and escorted her toward the footman holding open the front door. The white marble entry hall was two stories high. A butler standing to one side accepted the captain's tricorne.

"Higgins," Captain Powell addressed the butler, "how orderly the world seems when you are in it."

The drab, diminutive butler in gray breeches and morning coat, who managed to seem old though he couldn't be more than thirty, did not alter his morose expression when he saw the captain's smile. "Thank you, Captain Powell."

Claire was surprised by the exchange. It was not the French way for a servant to be so indifferent to his master's guest, particularly one paying a compliment, but Claire supposed such coolness was very English.

The captain handed the butler the package he had carried in from the carriage. "Will you give this to Lady Danvers at some opportune time?"

"Of course. Her ladyship is awaiting you and Mademoiselle Donet in the parlor."

They entered a large, elegant room with cream-colored walls decorated in raised relief where it joined the ceiling. A sand-colored carpet with floral designs in rose and dark blue covered nearly the entire floor. Rose silk curtains with gold embroidery framed the tall windows that cast light onto the white brocade sofa and armchairs facing the fireplace.

Over the white marble mantel of the fireplace hung a large portrait of an older man. Judging by what he was wearing and his white powdered wig, Claire thought it must have been painted sometime in the past. An ornate crystal chandelier was suspended from the center of the ceiling.

For all its opulence, the most elegant thing in the room to Claire's mind was the woman who stood in the midst of it.

"Lady Danvers, may I present to you Mademoiselle Claire Donet, granddaughter of the comte de Saintonge?"

Claire curtsied before the young baroness whose face bore a winsome smile. She was a vision in soft blue silk, the bodice of her gown covered in lace with peach bows at her elbows, complementing her auburn hair and unusual russet-colored eyes.

"Lady Danvers," the captain said when Claire rose. "May I introduce Mademoiselle Claire Donet, granddaughter of the comte de Saintonge." Claire noted his impeccable manners and not for the first time thought there was more to him than a sea captain.

Lady Danvers smiled. "I am delighted to meet you and have been looking forward to having you as my guest since I received Simon's note."

"Mademoiselle Donet," he turned to Claire, "allow me to present my good friend, Cornelia, Lady Danvers."

Looking askance at Captain Powell, the baroness said, "Simon, whatever have you been telling her? Does she think me given to formalities observed by the *ton*? You know better." Then facing Claire, "We shall have no formality between us, no curtsies, no 'Lady Danvers'. I'm Simon's age so only a half dozen years older than you, Claire. We shall become the best of friends, beginning now. You may call me Cornelia."

Claire immediately liked the American whose accent and manner were not at all English. "You honor me."

"Not at all. It is my preference," the baroness said with a saucy wink.

"I am so happy to meet an American here in London," said Claire. "Though you are farther from home than I, unlike me, I understand you chose to be here." She shot a glance at the captain.

He rolled his eyes.

"It is true," said the baroness with a warm smile, "we may be different in that respect. Simon explained a little of the situation in his letter to me, but I cannot wait to hear the story from you. Men tell tales so differently than us women. But that can wait. It is late, so first, we shall have tea. Then I will show you to your rooms."

As if summoned, the butler, Higgins, stepped into the room accompanied by a maid carrying a silver tray laden with tea and a plate of small, triangular-shaped sandwiches and fruit tarts. Claire was suddenly famished.

ᔕ ᓂᙓ ᓂ

Accepting the tea Cornelia poured for him, Simon sat back, remembering the dinners in his cabin with his captive. From the way she spoke, the way she held her teacup, even the way she exchanged pleasantries with the baroness, it was apparent the young mademoiselle was raised to one day take her place in the upper ranks of society. French society, he reminded himself. Her father might choose to hide his noble heritage, but it was here for all the world to see in his daughter.

Lord and Lady Danvers knew of Simon's parentage, of course. All the peerage knew of the Earl of Montmorency's bastard. The nobility had few secrets, at least amongst themselves.

Perhaps because the baron and his wife were nearly his age, and he worked with Danvers, he was accepted into their circle. To the *ton*, he had been a nonentity. A bastard did not ask to be acknowledged. Only in recent years, when he had become a successful privateer, an agent of the Crown and a friend of Lord and Lady Danvers, did he gain even a little standing in society. Though his dealings could be surreptitious when need be, London Society saw him as a novelty. And the *ton* approved of novelties.

Claire and Cornelia were getting along famously, barely noticing him. It pleased him to know the two would be friends. When tea was concluded, the baroness rose. "Come. I'll show you to your rooms and you can be off, Simon. Leave Claire to me. We have much to discuss and, based upon your letter, much to arrange. Oh, and Danvers is waiting for you in the usual place, or so he said, as he hurried out of here a few hours ago."

Simon was happy to accommodate the baroness. He felt pressed to see Eden and Danvers as soon as possible.

He followed the women up the wide staircase. At the top, Lady Danvers turned to the right. "I have put you both in the east wing. It's rarely used these days."

Their rooms, Simon was surprised to discover, were across the corridor from each other. While perhaps a bit too close to be entirely proper, he would certainly not object.

The women hurried into what would be Claire's bedchamber. He was happy to leave them to their chatter. He turned to his own chamber, the same one he'd stayed in the last time he was in London. There, he found his sea chest sitting at the foot of the tall, four-poster bed. Higgins, efficient as always, had no doubt seen to it.

He fingered the messages in his coat pocket, anxious to see them delivered

Chapter 10

Simon sat back in the carriage, vaguely aware of the sound of the horses' hooves on the cobblestones, as he thought about the meeting looming ahead.

He had carried many messages to Eden over the last few years, all gathered by prearrangement from the same grove of trees in Paris. He didn't bother reading the ones he carried in his pocket. They would tell him little. Some of the missives he'd transported to London had been blank pages, at least until the heat from a flame was applied, and then words magically appeared. But there had been others, like the ones he carried today, innocuous bits of correspondence from one Edward Edward to a Mr. Richards, detailing the author's exploits with a certain member of the female sex. Simon knew they were more, much more. When Eden applied a chemical he kept behind his desk, lines of text describing French activities in Paris and shipments of war supplies destined for America would suddenly appear between the lines of the original letter.

The Scribe was nothing if not careful.

In a part of Whitehall that gave no hint of its purpose, Simon was shown into an office where Lord Danvers and William Eden rose from their chairs to greet him. Danvers, ever the properly attired nobleman, wore a coat and waistcoat of blue-gray silk over black breeches. The baron's light brown hair was confined to a queue. Eden, as was his want, was more subtly attired, each article of clothing a different shade of brown. The three men were all of an age and enjoyed each other's company though they came from vastly different walks of life.

"Ah, Powell, at last you have come," said the baron extending his hand. And then with a smirk, "You are weeks late."

"I had a bit of a trouble or I would have been here a fortnight ago." Simon reached out and shook the baron's hand, then Eden's.

"Something we should be concerned about?" asked Eden as he poured brandy from a decanter into three glasses.

Simon decided to give them at least part of the story. Danvers would soon know the truth of it in any event. He took a sip from the glass offered him. "The French privateer, Jean Donet—you will recall the nuisance he's become to our shipping—seized the *Abundance* off Dover along with a large number of her crew." At their raised brows, he said, "I believe it may have something to do with Dr. Franklin's campaign to gain British seamen to barter for American prisoners. According to the cabin boy who escaped, Donet was careful not to kill any of my men." Simon did not mention Wingate's wound, hoping his prayers had been answered and his friend had recovered.

Handing a glass of brandy to Danvers, Eden shrugged. "The American commissioner is behind several recent captures of our vessels. It seems he gives letters of marque to any ship's captain he can enlist in his cause. I have no doubt Donet is one of them. 'Twill do Franklin no good. We've no interest in releasing the prisoners until an agreement's been reached ending the war."

"I cannot wait that long for my ship and her crew," said Simon. "To encourage Donet to return what is mine, I took his daughter as hostage."

"You did *what*?" asked Eden, incredulous.

"I kidnapped his daughter," said Simon coolly.

"I did not know the Frenchman had a daughter," said Danvers, looking puzzled.

"Nor did I," said Eden. As head of their spy network in Europe, Simon supposed there was little he did not know and must find this new information frustrating.

"He does, as it turns out," said Simon.

"You have Donet's daughter here in London?" Danvers asked.

"As a matter of fact, at this very moment," Simon replied, "I believe she is planning a shopping trip to Oxford Street with your wife."

Danvers choked on his brandy spewing a spray of the amber liquid across the room.

Simon slapped him on the back. "Are you all right, old man?"

The baron waved Simon off, nodding as he took a handkerchief from his coat and wiped his mouth. "Good Lord, that's all Cornelia needs to inspire her cause for the American prisoners—a French girl whose father is privateering for the rebels."

"You are bold, Powell," remarked Eden. "Donet will have your head for this. With all your trips into Paris on the Crown's sensitive business, do you really think it was wise to put the tiger on your tail?"

"I thought it would be easier to sneak into a convent than it would be to venture into the pirate's den in Lorient. And I needed something to bargain with."

"A convent you say?" Eden's brows rose.

"That is where my intelligence told me I would find her. And the report was correct. She is a student at the Ursuline Convent in Saint-Denis. Or rather, she was."

Eden took a drink from his brandy. "A vulnerability the Frenchman had not considered, I would venture to say." The British statesman seemed to ponder this while staring at the glass he turned in his hand. "I wonder if we can use her to gain information we would not otherwise have, perhaps to gain even the pirate himself."

"No." The word came out more forcibly than Simon intended. He would not see Claire used by the government. It was bad enough he was using her for his own purposes. She was *his* captive and he'd not give her up to another.

"Very well. For the moment, you may keep your hostage. But know that her status could change at any time, depending on how things go in Paris. Donet has been a thorn in my side for far too long."

Simon set his teeth in firm resolve. Eden would not have his way in this.

"We received the messages you sent from Rye. Do you have more?" Danvers asked.

"Aye." Simon handed the missives to Eden. "When I was in Paris, there was much talk of peace and word of our representatives sent to bargain with the French. Perhaps these will prove useful in your negotiations."

Eden laid the three notes next to each other on his desk and to each he applied several drops of the chemical he kept in the small bottle retrieved from a shelf. Bringing the first message close to his face, he put on his spectacles and studied the page.

"Another shipment of Charleville muskets." His gaze locked on Simon. "If I did not need you in London for the next few days, I'd send you after those, but I suppose one of our cutters can do the job."

It would not be the first shipment of guns Simon had retrieved for the Crown, but at the moment he did not wish to be engaged in another battle while Claire was on board, and he would not leave her behind.

The second note brought a frown to Eden's face. "Damnation. That Frenchman Donet has taken over twenty of our ships in the last year. I had not thought him responsible for so many. I would dearly love to see the corsair dead. The man is indeed a nuisance."

"Aye, and slippery," added Simon. "No matter your efforts to bottle up the French fleet in port, Donet knows the Channel like the back of his hand and uses fog and bad weather to his advantage."

Eden handed the note to Danvers and then picked up the third. "Ah, this one is different. As you suggested, Simon, we have something here that may help in our negotiations. It suggests that Franklin is willing to talk terms in the absence of the French minister."

"That is good news," said the baron. "I was beginning to think Franklin and Vergennes were joined at the hip."

Eden suddenly stopped reading and looked up, smiling. "Why, this is a treasure map! The Scribe has done well." At their raised brows, he continued, "It's America's wish list of terms: In addition to independence, which we will concede, they want fishing rights off Newfoundland, acceptable boundaries for America, compensation for damages, all of Canada and an acknowledgement of Britain's war guilt."

"*All* of Canada?" sputtered Danvers.

Without responding, Eden handed the baron the note. "We must ask Lord Shelburne to insist America remain independent of France. He can add that to his goal to secure compensation for Loyalists."

Simon muffled a cough. He thought it unlikely the Americans would grant Britain the latter, but he was also aware that Shelburne, now the Crown's chief minister, would want to appease the Loyalists for his political survival.

"As soon as your work in London is done, Powell," said Eden. "I'll need you to return to Paris with messages for the Scribe. You will have them post haste."

❦

The maid brushed Claire's blue gown free of dust, placed it in the gilded armoire in the bedchamber that had been assigned to her, and then retreated from the room. Claire cast a glance about the room. "This is a lovely bedchamber," she said to her new friend. The pale peach curtains and counterpane on the four-poster bed were echoed in the flowers in the rug on the floor. She thought it might be French.

"You can see I like this color," said Cornelia. "'Tis shameless, I suppose, to use so much of a color that complements my own auburn hair, but there you have it."

Claire laughed. "I think it's lovely."

Cornelia looked about the room. "Do you have no chest?" At Claire's shake of her head, the baroness added, "Is that all you have by way of clothing?"

"That and what I am wearing." At Cornelia's look of surprise, Claire said, "In Saint-Denis, I have a chest full of gowns, but when one is taken from one's bed in the middle of the night, gagged and trussed up like a goose, there is little time to pack."

"He did not!" exclaimed Cornelia.

"He did. And it was quite frightening, I can assure you." Before she had known her captor was the golden one, she had been terrified. "I could see nothing."

"That scoundrel. If I did not like Simon Powell as much as I do, I'd be truly annoyed. But seeing as you are unharmed and noting the way he looked at you as we drank our tea—as if you were a delicate pastry he might consume—I think he must be treating you well, no?"

"Oh, yes," Claire admitted. "He's been most attentive to my needs." She did not mention his kisses, the guard who continuously followed her or the captain's many amusements at her expense. *Delicate pastry* indeed.

"Despite his obvious interest, I do believe he will act the gentleman," said the baroness. "But returning you to your father will have to be carefully done so your reputation in Paris is preserved."

"The nuns will say nothing." Of that she was certain. But, knowing the truth, would they allow her to return to the convent? Would the Reverend Mother want her back? After all, it had been she who had tried to persuade Claire against taking vows. And then there was her shameless response to the captain's kisses. Ursuline nuns took a vow of chastity. While she was still pure in one sense, her thoughts of the captain were not so chaste. It had been weeks since she'd made her last confession, though she had admitted her sinful thoughts to God while confiding to Him her concern for her future.

"Perhaps because he took you from the convent, the usual rumors will not abound."

"That was my hope," she said.

"But then you've been on his ship… "

Claire looked out the window and said nothing. She well knew the implications if the truth became known in Paris. She'd be ruined.

"Did you know that your father had seized Simon's ship?"

Claire averted her gaze. "I knew nothing of my papa's involvement in the war. I thought him only a man of business, a man of letters."

"Men are rarely of only one mind, Claire, especially in times of war. Even Danvers dabbles in the dreadful business in addition to his affairs in the Lords."

When Claire sighed, the baroness took her hand and smiled. "Tomorrow we will venture out for a bit of shopping. Oxford Street can be quite diverting. We shall have great fun ordering you some new gowns and other things you will need to go with them. Simon has been quite generous."

A sudden pang of conscience made Claire pause. "Do you think it wrong of me to accept his… his provision of clothing?" Claire had never taken money from any man save her papa and she felt badly doing so now, knowing it wasn't proper. "I have the gowns he has already given me. Those I accepted for I had no others. But surely I need no more for the short time I will be here. Papa would not approve."

"Certainly you will accept what Simon has offered. It was he who put you in this untenable position and he can well afford to see you are not embarrassed by a lack of proper clothing for a woman befitting your station. In England, Claire, you are considered the granddaughter of an earl."

Claire had never thought of herself in such terms, perhaps because her papa never mentioned his own father or the family title. She knew his strained relationship with the comte was caused by her parents' marriage. When, as a small girl, she had asked her mother about her grandpapa, she was told that her papa's love would make up for the grandfather she would never know. Thinking of it now, she recalled her mother had been sad that day.

"Besides, Claire, I want to have a soirée for you and a worthy gown is needed."

Claire suddenly felt anxious. *A soirée?*

Cornelia must have read her thoughts. "The English admire much about the French, Claire—their food, their dances, their fashion. Deep down they know they are poorly garbed compared to the people of Paris. That is why they ape your fashion. Why, they even teach French to their children! The war has changed none of that. Do not fret. Our friends will be delighted to meet you."

The butler entered carrying the package the captain had given him earlier. "My lady, Captain Powell has gone to Whitehall to meet with his lordship. He left this for you."

The baroness accepted the package wrapped in brown paper, nearly two feet long, her eyes glistening as she perused it. "I wonder," she said. "It's just about the right size." Retreating to the bed, she carefully laid the package on the silk counterpane and removed the wrapping. Her smile beamed her pleasure. "It is! It's one of those fashion dolls I asked Simon to bring me from Paris. My modiste will be thrilled."

The doll that held Cornelia in rapt attention was quite amazing. Its head, which appeared to be plaster with glass eyes and painted features, was exquisitely fashioned. The hair, which was auburn like Cornelia's, could have been real. The costume was elaborate, a miniature version of the gowns Claire had seen on the ladies who'd attended the masquerade two years ago in Saint-Denis. A gold silk skirt peeked out of a red velvet pelisse trimmed in what looked like Russian sable.

Cornelia squealed in delight, "Is it not wonderful?"

"It is one of the nicest I have ever seen," Claire responded. She had seen several in one of her shopping trips with her papa, but never one as well made as this one.

When Cornelia removed the pelisse, the gown was revealed in all its glory. Every detail was perfect, every stitch neatly done. Delicate lace circled the doll's neck and hung in two layers from the gold sleeves that stopped at the doll's elbow.

"I had heard that, despite the war, English dressmakers sent their employees to Paris to receive training in the latest fashions," said Claire, "but I did not realize the English used the dolls as well."

Still stroking the doll's gown, Cornelia said, "The dolls help our modistes see what the finished gowns should look like. Wisely, the government has exempted them from embargo. No matter we are at war, we women must have our fashion!"

Chapter 11

Claire awoke the next morning, tired from a night spent tossing and turning. No longer did she have the soft voices of the nuns singing at Compline to help her fall asleep. And the nightmares still plagued her.

As she slipped from the bed to her knees to say her morning prayers, she wondered if the Reverend Mother and Sister Angélique missed her as she missed them. She had often found convent life confining, yet the sisters and the other students had been her family for a very long time.

Determined not to let her fatigue spoil her day with the baroness, she rose, confident a loving God would forgive her failure to attend Mass, for the lack of it was not of her doing.

Once dressed in her new gown, helped by Cornelia's maid, she joined her new friend for breakfast. "Such a fine array of fruit!" she exclaimed, seeing the large platter of artfully arranged peaches, pears and figs topped with delectable black grapes. "Wherever do they come from?"

"The Kentish orchards grow many fruits for the London markets but we also have friends whose extensive kitchen gardens at their country houses keep us well supplied, and the quality of that is the best."

"We had very large gardens at the convent," Claire said wistfully.

"Do you miss the convent?" the baroness asked, her concern evident in her russet eyes.

"Sometimes, I do. But 'tis more like a childhood memory. Though my abduction was not one of them, I've had many wonderful experiences since leaving." Knowing Simon Powell was their friend, Claire declined to elaborate on the manner in which she had come to be in England.

"Well, you shall have other memories from your time here, good memories that will hopefully make you want to stay."

Stay? Did she want to stay? At the moment, Claire was torn. She had a vow to fulfill but her attraction for the English captain was pulling her farther from France.

Claire smiled at her hostess and selected some fruit and a warm roll. Not quite the brioche she had eaten on the ship but still very enjoyable in Cornelia's company. And the coffee was much needed if she were to remain alert.

"I've still to tell you about our friends invited to the soirée," remarked Cornelia.

Cornelia must have been busy if she'd already been preparing a list of guests. Claire furrowed her brow as she set down her coffee. Despite Cornelia's kind words, she was worried the English would not embrace a French woman among them when their countries were hardly friends.

Cornelia must have observed her reticence. "Do not fret, Claire. They will adore you. And I haven't even mentioned the men who I expect will be gawking at you and the lovely gown you shall wear. Mrs. Duval's shop awaits!"

Claire was cheered by her new friend's assurance the English would accept her and for Cornelia's enthusiasm for the day ahead. She'd never had a woman friend with whom she could shop for ladies' frippery. On her night adventures, Élise had been more like a younger sister, someone Claire had to watch over. A day of shopping with Cornelia would suit her just fine.

Late that morning, they departed for Oxford Street in a yellow and black landau carriage. Being a pleasant day,

Cornelia instructed the driver to leave the top down. With the driver in front and two footmen standing on the shelf behind them, they moved along smartly. To Claire, it seemed the grandest way to travel.

They arrived to find Oxford Street already bustling with people and carriages. Following her hostess, Claire stepped onto the stone walk in front of the shops. She had never been able to stroll along a street and take her time peering into shop windows, except in Saint-Denis, and that was only a village. When she'd been with her papa in Paris, he was always in a hurry, in and out of a shop in a minute with no time to peruse the goods on display. But today, she and Cornelia took their time, strolling along at a leisurely pace, sharing their delight at all they saw. Claire thought the shops even more splendid than those in Paris.

She stopped to admire the golden watches in the watchmaker's window. "So many," she remarked. "Why, there are even ones for women to wear as pendants."

"I gave Danvers one like that," Cornelia said, pointing to a handsome men's pocket watch, "when he won his last bill in the Lords. It is something he treasures, probably as a reminder of his brilliance," she said laughing.

Claire thought of the captain and wondered if he had such a watch. Perhaps she might give him one. But no. One did not give a gift to one's abductor.

They moved on to the jeweler's window where the gold bracelets displayed hinted at the richer jewels inside. She had only her moonstone ring and that she had left behind when she was taken.

When they came to the fan store, Claire paused. "The fans are so beautiful!" The display of painted silk fans was rich in variety, several were in red and blue with gold etching. And some in pink and peach with delicate flowers.

"We shall stop to buy a few," said Cornelia. "They come in most handy when batting away a rake." She winked at Claire.

"You are beyond hope, Cornelia! Besides, what rake would dare approach you with that handsome baron by your side?"

"You'd be surprised, Claire. Some men in the *ton* have no scruples at all."

They entered the shop and Cornelia talked her into acquiring several. Of course, Cornelia added to what she described as her collection of peach-colored fans. When they left, they handed their parcels to the footmen and walked to the milliner's where large, elegant, feathered hats graced the window.

Claire stood and stared. "I can't imagine wearing such creations on my head," said Claire. "They are huge!"

"Then you have never seen Georgiana, the Duchess of Devonshire. She wears the most outrageous hats of anyone I know, though I sometimes wonder if it isn't to garner the attention her dour husband denies her. Never did like that man. But I do like her."

Claire felt sorry for the duchess. A husband who adored you was worth so much more than titles, wealth and hats. "Do you know her well?"

"Not very well; we are acquaintances. I have greeted her on several occasions. I admire her ventures into the political fray. Danvers praises her efforts to help the Whigs stay in office, all the while she goes about wearing her eye-catching hats. Why the last time I saw her, she wore a black creation piled high with feathers and a huge, blue bow. It was most striking."

Claire thought she might like to meet the duchess but she had no desire to wear her hats. "I think I'll just stay with the smaller hats. Can you see wearing a large hat on a ship? The wind would carry it away in a heartbeat. The captain's crew would have me a laughing stock, I am sure."

"Yes, you're right," Cornelia laughed. "They most certainly would. The hats the duchess wears are not for windy days at sea."

When they reached the shop with the sign that read James Smith & Sons, Purveyors of Parasols, Cornelia paused to gaze at the umbrellas fashioned for a woman's fancy. "In this summer heat and with your fair skin, you simply must have a few parasols," she counseled from underneath the broad brim of her straw hat. "Later, after we've ordered your gowns, we'll return to select some."

"I had parasols for my outings with Papa, but I could not use them at the convent and I've not had one since the captain saw fit to take me aboard his ship. At least I have a hat," she said reaching up to touch the one she wore that went with her gown.

"That's a nice way of saying Simon has acted the knave, yet I cannot forget the way he looked at you over his teacup. I think he's quite taken with you, Claire. And why shouldn't he be? While he is not of your rank, you are a beautiful woman. And from what I know of Simon, he is not indifferent to beauty."

Claire could feel the blush rise in her cheeks. She remembered the way he'd responded to the trousered hussar, who as she thought about it now, had been beautiful. *Definitely not indifferent.*

Though Claire cared little for rank and knew her papa had planned to wed her to a lawyer, she couldn't fathom the idea Captain Powell had feelings for her. Attraction, yes, even desire. She'd detected both in his eyes. But not tender feelings. Surely not love.

"I hardly think he feels that way about me," she said as they walked on gazing into the windows of the other shops.

"Perhaps," conceded Cornelia. Then she shook her head. "No, I'm quite sure I saw that look men get when they are taken with a woman, when their eyes linger overlong. Danvers had that same look before he asked me to marry him."

The idea that the captain might care for her brought Claire a secret joy. But she must keep it a secret. Instead, she would ask about Cornelia's relationship with the baron. "Was it hard for you being in England as an American then?"

Cornelia stopped to admire a setting of china in a shop. "I came to London just before the Colonies declared their independence. At first I was accepted as a Loyalist, and then I married a member of the nobility." Looking away for a moment, she said, "But sometimes I do not feel quite one of them. And Danvers has lost friends in the war, which makes it more difficult."

"I'm sorry," said Claire seeing the sadness in the baroness' eyes.

"It's quite complicated," Cornelia went on. "My brother, Sean, is a patriot, you see. He fights for the new country he loves. Because he's in Baltimore, I don't often have word of him." Her face brightened. "But there's an American captain, one of the prisoners here in London, who knows him. He has told me Sean helps equip the American privateers."

"Oh, you must be torn."

"It is true that I have divided sympathies. I am as much an American as I am a citizen of London and loyal to my English husband whom I love." She let out a sigh. "I just want the war to be over."

In her own way, Claire had divided loyalties, too. She was French and happy her country was helping the Americans, yet she harbored tender feelings for an English privateer, and had since she was sixteen. "I want that as well."

"Oh fie," Cornelia said, "men and their politics—and their wars! If we women led the governments we would soon have peace."

"I am not so certain," said Claire. "As I recall from my history, the reign of England's Queen Elizabeth was fraught with war and conflict."

Cornelia let out an exasperated sigh. "Yes, there was the Spanish Armada. I suppose it is in mankind's nature to ever be at war."

As they turned from the shop, Claire thought she saw a man who'd been standing in the shadow of a building move to follow. A frisson of fear snaked through her spine. "Cornelia, I think we're being followed. No, don't turn just yet. But when you can, look without drawing attention and see if you agree."

Appearing to point to an item of interest in the window of another shop, Cornelia looked over Claire's shoulder. "Yes, there is a man some distance behind us who stopped when we did. I was going to suggest we walk to my modiste's shop as Mrs. Duval's is not far. But now I think we will ride. It's a short jaunt to Bond Street. I can alert my footman to the one who may be pursuing us."

They had just taken a seat in the carriage, the horses' hooves beginning a steady rhythm on the street, when Cornelia leaned in to say, "I wonder who would follow us. It makes me feel quite uneasy. Doesn't it you?"

"I don't like it, but the thought occurs it could be someone sent by Captain Powell," suggested Claire. "Since we've been in port, first in Rye and then in London, he's had one of his crew follow me about the ship. He fears I will try and escape."

"And would you?" asked her new friend.

Should she confide in Cornelia? Would the woman help her? "I might like to. And if I were successful, I would persuade Papa to free Captain Powell's men."

"Oh, Claire, you mustn't. London is dangerous enough for those of us used to living here. For a young woman alone, as pretty as you are, it would be horribly dangerous."

Claire had to confess that Cornelia was probably right. "I suppose to flee by myself with no idea of where to go would not be wise."

"No, and you must not think of it again. You can trust Simon to return you to your father. For all his privateering, he is honorable."

"It would seem so," Claire agreed. In her heart she knew he would keep his word. All he wanted was his men and his ship.

"Danvers has been telling Simon when the war is over, he

should marry, that he is old enough to be siring children." She sat back against the gray velvet of the padded seat. "I'm certain my husband would like to have little ones running about even if they are not his own. We've been married nearly seven years and I fear we are destined to be childless."

"Oh, Cornelia, I am sorry." Claire reached out and patted Cornelia's gloved hand. "But if it is any comfort, I shall never have children of my own either, as I intend to take vows to become one of the Ursuline sisters."

Cornelia gave her a long, studying look. "I cannot imagine someone with your zest for life seeking the cloistered life. Are you so certain that is what you want?"

Claire was not successful in fighting the heat that crept into her cheeks. Since she'd been aboard Simon Powell's ship, she was not at all certain she wanted that. She reminded herself she had made a vow. "I must."

"It sounds as if it is not your choice."

"It was not my first thought for my life."

The baroness gave her a penetrating look. "Well, we can hope it is not your last. Besides, I would miss you if you were not here."

Claire didn't want to remind her new friend that she was to be exchanged for Simon's men. "Papa wants me to wed. I was told he has arranged a marriage to a lawyer in Paris, but I did not have time to speak with him about my own desires before I was abducted."

"Then your future remains in doubt."

Claire reluctantly nodded.

The carriage pulled up in front of a shop with a sign of a spool of thread speared with a needle. The name in the shop window read *Mrs. Duval's*.

"We are here!" declared Cornelia. "I cannot wait to show my modiste my gift for her. She will be very excited for she can copy anything."

They entered the modiste's and one of Cornelia's footmen, carrying the fashion doll, followed them inside.

Cornelia introduced Claire and then held out the doll to Mrs. Duval. "For me?" she exclaimed.

"Indeed, yes!" said Cornelia. "To use to fashion my friend a gown such as she might have purchased in Paris."

Claire studied the older woman's face. She was elegantly attired in a soft gray silk with lace trim, her dark hair confined to a knot at her nape. The name Duval was French but the woman had an English accent. "Are you by any chance French?" she asked.

"My husband's family is French. They came to France early in the century. But I am very English, except when it comes to fashion. Then I am French."

All three women broke into laughter.

"Come," said Mrs. Duval. "I have some new silks to show you, and one that might just be perfect for this gown I'm to make."

The modiste put several bolts of shimmering silk on the table before them. Claire and Cornelia ran their fingers over the fine fabric. It was the gold one that drew Claire's attention. "I do like this one."

"Then you shall have it," said Cornelia and nodded to Mrs. Duval.

For Claire, shopping with a woman friend was great fun. Before an hour had elapsed, with the help of Cornelia and Mrs. Duval, Claire ordered three gowns. One was to be fashioned from the glistening gold silk moiré that Cornelia thought a perfect choice for the soirée to be held in Claire's honor.

Claire was quick to agree. She had never had such a glorious gown and wondered what Captain Powell would think when he saw her in it. It was for him she wanted to appear the lady.

Once they concluded their business with Mrs. Duval, Cornelia directed the coachman to the shops for shoes, reticules, shifts, corsets and other items she assured Claire were necessary. They returned to the parasol shop to find several that would match her gowns and keep the sun from her face, though Claire had to laugh at the thought of trying to hold one on a moving ship.

The baroness had asked the footmen to keep a watchful eye on anyone following them and Claire observed them studying the faces of the men on the street. But if the same man dogged their steps, Claire had not noticed.

When their errands were completed, with a gleam in her eye, Cornelia said, "I think before we return home, we shall stop in Mr. Negri's Pineapple shop in Berkeley Square." At Claire's puzzled look, Cornelia said, "… for some sweetmeats and ices. Many of his confections are from French recipes, you know."

"That sounds wonderful." A taste of home, and if she were honest, she had a sweet tooth which her papa had indulged with treats he brought her from Paris.

Once the driver had their new destination, from inside the carriage, Claire watched the shops they passed and spoke her thought aloud. "I feel guilty even thinking of a fête and such beautiful gowns while my papa is in France worrying about me, knowing I am the prisoner of his enemy, an English privateer." Claire remembered her papa as she'd last seen him, shouting orders from the deck of his ship in the midst of the Channel. He had been nothing like the papa she thought she knew.

"Not just any privateer, Claire," said Lady Danvers. "Simon is the natural son of an English earl, albeit he was never recognized."

"Do you mean—"

"Simon's father never married his mother, and then failed to acknowledge Simon before he died."

"Oh." Claire could not help but wonder how such a beginning contributed to the man he was today. "How awful for him."

"It's become all too common an occurrence in the aristocracy in the last several years, I'm afraid. He was the earl's firstborn son and should have been the heir but his father's failure to marry his mother made that impossible."

"Was his mother not acceptable?"

"Not to the earl. She was educated and beautiful, but a commoner," Cornelia remarked in a tone of resignation.

"Ah."

"When his mother died, he ran away to sea. Ships and sailing men are the only other family he's ever known."

"How long ago was that?"

"Well, let's see… He's five and twenty now, so at least ten years ago. He loved her, I know, and all Simon has told me of her suggests she loved her son."

"I lost my mother when I was younger than that," Claire sadly reflected. "But I had the sisters."

"They must love you," said Cornelia, her kind eyes conveying sympathy.

"I'm certain they are worried, but perhaps my papa has explained I am to be returned." She hoped he did not explain all that had transpired.

"I doubt they would find the truth reassuring. Snatched from your bed by an English privateer? No, certainly not."

Claire sighed. "You are right, of course." There was really no good way to explain that night. She decided to ask a question that had been bothering her since the baroness had spoken of Simon's mother. "Did his mother's family have money? Else, how did the captain come to own two ships?"

"He was poor as a church mouse until his father, on his deathbed, managed to make Simon a wealthy man. His mother had died by then. He has used the funds to great effect. In the last few years, he's become a successful ship's captain and, for his work in the war, respected by many at Whitehall."

Even if she were to forsake her vow to Élise, Claire knew her papa would never consider an Englishman, much less one who was illegitimate, for her husband. Had Providence brought Simon Powell back into her life only to send him away? It seemed so. Perhaps it was best to forget her longings and convince her papa to allow her to return to the convent.

Else she would have to marry the man her papa had chosen for her, a man she did not even know. The thought cast a cloud of anxiety over the otherwise delightful day. She shook it off, determined to enjoy Cornelia's company for whatever remained of her time in England.

☞ ♋ ☜

Leaving the baron to his port, Simon bid his friend goodnight and trudged up the stairs to his bedchamber, weary from a long day. The ladies had retired shortly after supper, tired from their day of shopping, leaving him and Danvers to linger over their port, discussing their meeting with Eden.

With an American wife, Danvers was hoping for a quick resolution to the war. Simon had his own reasons for wanting hostilities with the French to end.

Watching Claire across the table during supper had been a trial. She was lovely and tempting, her blue eyes lighting with mirth, her French accent beguiling, as she engaged in witty conversation with their hosts. A forbidden prize he very much wanted to claim but never could. The port wine and conversation with Danvers had helped to dull his desire, but only slightly.

Accustomed as he was to the rocking of a ship, sleeping in a bed on land always left him restless. He had just managed to drift off when a cry awoke him with a start. Rising on one elbow, he listened. There it was again, faint but real. Throwing off the cover, he slid from the bed, donned his breeches and padded across the room. When he opened the door, the cry grew louder. It was coming from Claire's room.

Dare he enter her bedchamber? Another cry pierced the night, vanquishing his doubts. He charged across the corridor into her room. She was tossing about in the bed, fighting the cover and shouting in muffled whispers, "*Non, non!* You mustn't follow. You will die!"

Simon strode to the bed and sat on the edge, reaching out

to grasp her flailing arms and lay them at her side. "Mademoiselle."

She did not respond, but tossed her head back and forth on the pillow, gasping the words, *"Non! Non!"*

Perhaps she would respond to her Christian name. With one hand, he gently shook her shoulder. "Wake up, Claire."

She uttered a sound deep in her throat that sounded like pain mixed with terror.

He gathered her into his arms and held her close. She was shaking. "Claire, sweetheart, 'tis all right. Was just a bad dream." Her warm body was pliant in his arms. She felt right snuggled close to his chest. He wanted to keep her there.

She woke then. "Captain? ... is it you?"

In the faint light from the window she would only know him by his voice. "Yes, Claire, 'tis Simon. You're all right now."

She clung to him as if he were the only raft in a storm-tossed sea. It tugged at his soul. At times, she was a wild child, at others stubborn, but at this moment she was vulnerable and he wanted to protect her, even from her dreams. He could never have explained the deep feelings that rose to the fore then. They were not feelings he'd had for any other woman.

He didn't want to leave her, but he knew he must.

The bedcover had fallen to her waist, leaving only the thin nightgown she wore separating them. Beneath it, the warmth of her skin and her soft breasts pressed against his bare chest tempting him beyond endurance. He wanted to crawl into the bed with her. He wanted to make love to her. "I must return to my chamber."

"No!" she cried. "Don't go. Not yet. Please... stay till the dream passes from my mind."

"All right." What else could he do? She was frightened and shaking, but why? "What has you so frightened?"

"Élise. Her ghost follows me. The dream is always the same."

He slid his palm up and down her back trying to soothe her. The heat of her skin beneath the thin cloth tempted him unmercifully but his intent was to comfort, not ravish.

After a minute she stopped shaking.

"Tell me, who is this Élise?"

"A girl who died because of my foolishness."

"What foolishness?" How could a young woman's silliness lead to another's death?

She looked up at him in the dim light, placing her hand on his chest, her cool fingers on his warm skin stirring his manhood. Their heads were so close he could smell her sweet breath.

"Two years ago, I sneaked out of the convent to see a masquerade. It wasn't the first time I had escaped the confines of the convent walls, nor the first time Élise followed me. She was really too frail to have done so, especially on that night. On the way home it rained and we were drenched. Élise took ill with pneumonia." He felt the dread that came over Claire as she sobbed. "She suffered so." Burying her face in his chest, she shuddered. "It was horrible and all because of me."

He held her close, his brows drawing together as he puzzled over her words, remembering a night long ago when he'd attended a masquerade outside of Paris. There had been a girl then, one who'd fallen from a tree. A girl who had fascinated him with her pluck and her mesmerizing eyes. "The girl in the tree at the château… that was *you*?"

She raised her head. "*Oui, c'était moi.*" Her voice was faint and somber as if she carried an overwhelming burden of guilt.

"I remember now. You ran away with another girl. Was that her?"

"*Oui.* She died a sennight later."

Suddenly he understood. She had tortured herself with the other girl's death. "You blame yourself. That is what troubles your sleep?"

She nodded. "Élise haunts my dreams, but there is more. Before she died, I promised her I would become an Ursuline nun and teach the children. It was her dream, one she would never realize because of me."

He let out a sigh. "A noble vow, perhaps, but I do not think 'tis your destiny. And Élise did not ask it of you, did she?"

"No, but I promised… I made a vow to her."

In the darkness of the room, he could not see her well, but he thought he heard a pout in her voice. She was so close, her breasts pressing into his chest. He kissed her hair. It smelled of lavender and the touch of it on his lips was like silk. "God will not hold you to a promise made when you were young and filled with remorse."

She tipped her head back, "But… "

Unwilling to let the moment go without acknowledging his desire for her, he brushed his lips across hers. They were warm, soft and oh, so sweet. She did not protest when he kissed her more deeply. He had to steel himself from claiming all he wanted, to keep from joining her in the bed. But it wasn't just her father and the crew of the *Abundance* that held him at bay. It was her innocence. It was not his to claim.

"Even that night I wanted to kiss you, Claire."

She stiffened. "But you were doing things with that… that trousered hussar!"

He let out a laugh, embarrassed by what she had seen, and at a time when she was even more innocent than she was now. "Aye, well, would it please you to know that we did no more that night and I've not seen her since?"

She settled into his arms. "It might, though I have no right to ask. What I saw was very… shocking, and if I am truthful, absorbing."

He laughed again and laid her back on the pillow. "That wild-eyed girl who fell from the tree all tattered and torn has come to my mind many times over the last two years. I should have recognized you, shouldn't I?"

"I have changed."

"Aye, I can see that you have." Lying there, her head on the pillow, her ebony tresses fanned out around her, she appeared the young seductress, more beautiful, more alluring than when he'd first glimpsed her. He wanted to press his lips to hers, to stroke her tender skin, to lift the thin gown from the curves it hid and make her his. Instead, he took a deep breath, gathered his resolve, and reminded himself she was not his to take. "Now, to sleep with you."

He rose to leave.

She stared up at him. "That night was the first time I saw you, but I never forgot the golden eagle."

Even in the faint light he could see her eyes fixed on him, the same azure eyes that had captivated him that night in Saint-Denis.

"Sleep, and that's an order."

Chapter 12

The sunlight was just slipping into his bedchamber when Simon rose and left for the Thames. He had not slept well after leaving Claire's room, troubled by her intent to become a nun. As the night wore on, he had come to a decision. He did not want to return her to her father, much less to a convent. If he could recover his crew, perhaps he could persuade her to stay in England. She could write her father a letter and tell him she'd chosen a new life. His imaginings did not dwell on what that new life might consist of. But one thing he knew: A convent was no place for her.

Once onboard his ship, Simon spotted Amos Busby, the first mate from the *Abundance*, talking with Jordan. With a jerk of his head, he summoned both men to follow him to his cabin.

He closed the cabin door as they entered and invited them to join him at the table.

"You're back already?" asked Jordan.

"My business in London is not yet concluded, but I have a task for Amos and I want you to be aware of it."

Simon could see from Amos' eager expression he was anxious for something more to do. He'd been in charge of the men watching Claire but it was not enough for a man who'd been first mate. And, after a day or two in port, his men were always impatient to sail.

"I've an idea to rescue the crew of the *Abundance* from Donet's clutches before the exchange." The two men leaned forward, interested. "But for that I need to know where Donet is keeping them."

Smiles broke out on the faces of the two men.

"Aye, Captain, 'tis a worthy idea," said the burly Amos.

"My first thought," ventured Simon, "was that the Frenchman holds them in Lorient where he has resources, but he may have moved them to another location. If I were him, I might have moved them closer to where I expected the exchange to take place. We must know if they are still in Lorient where I imagine he first took them."

Jordan leaned back in his chair and ran one hand through his curly brown hair. "Aye, 'tis logical, but the Frenchman has often done what we least expect."

Simon nodded. Indeed Donet had done some daring things in taking his prizes and avoiding the Royal Navy's frigates and cutters plying the Channel. And Lorient was his domain. "Amos, how would you like to go hunting for our men?"

"'Twould please me, Captain."

"Good. Take some of the idle crew from the *Abundance* with you to Lorient—the most skilled at stealth, the ones who speak French and can keep their heads when matters become difficult. You'll need to move fast; you don't have much time."

"I have just the men in mind, Captain," said the burly Amos, rubbing his rough hand over his dark stubbled chin. "We can leave this morning."

"Elijah and Giles may have learned something in Paris," said Jordan. "Might be they already know the place Donet wants the exchange to take place."

"I'm hoping they do," admitted Simon, "but I would not wait for them to return when Amos can be on his way to Lorient. It would be good to know if the men are there. Amos, when you've learned what you can, return to Rye, not London. By the time you're back, Elijah and Giles will have returned.

I'll meet you there."

Amos grinned. "Yes, sir."

"And, Jordan, I'll be expecting you to arrange the guards for Mademoiselle Donet for the few days we remain in London. She's our insurance for the return of our crew."

"I'll see to it," his first mate said.

It was a crazy scheme, Simon knew. And its success required much to go right if he were to find his captured crew before he had to meet Donet. He could only hope his idea worked.

෮ ෨෮ ෨

"Claire," Cornelia asked as she finished the last bite of roll, "would you like to come with me today? I'm to visit the American prisoners."

Her mind still on the captain and his words the night before, Claire was not certain if she had heard correctly. "Did you say American *prisoners*? In London?"

"Yes, though most are kept in the ports, like Plymouth and Portsmouth, we have a small number here, most of them taken off privateers."

She picked up her coffee and sipped. These were the men her papa was fighting to free. "I'd love to go with you."

Cornelia raised her palm. "Before you consent, you should know it may be unpleasant."

Claire frowned, puzzled. "Whatever do you mean?"

Her new friend let out a sigh. "Well, it was much worse earlier in the war when they were half-starved and sick, their clothes hanging in tatters with no blankets to keep them warm. They are better now, but the conditions are not ideal."

"Why were they treated so badly?"

"The British considered them mere rebels rising against the king, pirates charged with high treason. They had no status to protect them from harsh treatment. Then, too, the British never anticipated having to deal with such large numbers of prisoners. And most of us knew nothing of it."

"How awful."

"It was. But that changed when correspondence between Mr. Franklin and Lord Stormont, then our ambassador to the French court, made its way to the *London Chronicle*. It revealed the plight of the prisoners in graphic detail. Some of us in London formed a committee of relief with Reverend Thomas Wren, a minister in Portsmouth. Thankfully, it was successful. We raised over three thousand pounds."

"What did you do with so much money?"

"We took the prisoners clothing, blankets and food. Medicine when it was needed. They are so much better off now. Parliament finally designated them prisoners of war, so they can be exchanged for British prisoners."

No wonder Papa had wanted Simon's crew. Claire was relieved the Americans were being better treated. That they had not been so at the beginning of the war made her wonder at the British who claimed to be so civilized.

"But what the Americans really love," Cornelia continued, "is news from the outside world, the war and a kind word. I still bring them blankets, clothes and food. New prisoners arrive each week and have nothing save what we give them. Sometimes, I write letters for them. It gives them comfort to know their families have word."

"They let you send letters for the prisoners?"

"The letters are read by the military, of course, but they are generally allowed to go through. We send them to ministers in the main American ports who can read them to the families."

Claire's sympathy rose for the beleaguered prisoners. "I will gladly be by your side as you help them. I may not be able to write English as well as you, but I can distribute clothes and blankets and speak to them of the support France is giving them."

"They like to see an American face, but I know a French woman would be very welcome. They are well aware of

France's aid." Then looking at the gown Claire wore, she said, "You must wear your plainest gown. The blue one will do nicely. The place they are being held is not in the best part of town."

Not long afterward, Claire and her hostess left by carriage for what Cornelia had described as a warehouse in a rough area of London near the Thames. Two footmen accompanied them.

They arrived at the tall, wooden building, its paint peeling with age, to see British soldiers with their red coats and muskets standing guard outside the entrance. More waited inside the door as Claire followed Cornelia into the darkened space.

"Lady Danvers," a senior soldier greeted Cornelia, who was obviously known to him.

"Good morning, sir," Cornelia returned. When the guard's gaze shifted to Claire, Cornelia said, "I have brought a friend to assist me."

The guard tipped his head and allowed them to pass.

Claire trailed Cornelia into a cavernous room, her eyes adjusting to the dim light. Small windows at the top of the rough wooden walls and lanterns posted around the edges provided the only light. Some of the American prisoners lounged on pallets scattered around the dirt floor while others sat at a large, central table, appearing to be playing games. She counted about forty men.

The footmen who had followed them inside opened the baskets and bundles to allow the guards to see what they had brought. Once the search was complete, the footmen stood waiting for their mistress to direct them.

One of the Americans approached Cornelia, a broad smile on his face. The guard behind them moved closer, hands on his musket. "Lady Danvers," said the handsome American in an accent much like Cornelia's. "A welcome sight you are!" His left arm was in a white linen sling, but the injury did not appear to dampen his spirits.

"Mademoiselle Donet," said the baroness, "may I present Captain Thomas Field."

Claire was surprised at the youth of the American captain. "I am pleased to meet you."

"Captain Field is a privateer for America, Claire, taken captive a month ago. He's the one I told you about who knows my brother, Sean."

The face of the American, who appeared younger than Captain Powell, took on a serious expression. "My sloop was outgunned by the British. Lost half my men in that battle. 'Twas a sad affair."

"I'm so sorry, sir," Claire said respectfully. "I hope I can bring some cheer to you and your men. I am here to assist Lady Danvers."

"Your mere presence cheers me, mademoiselle. Have you traveled from France to be with us?" His gray eyes hinted of interest and mirth. In the candlelight, his clothes appeared fine but a bit threadbare, the coat and breeches the color of nutmeg, his shirt a faded ivory. His hair, brown and streaked with the sun, was neatly tied back at his nape.

"*Oui*," she said. "You could say that. We French are on America's side, and also like you, I am a captive, held hostage for a British ship and her crew."

Captain Field directed his confused gaze to Cornelia.

"It's a long story, Captain Field. Suffice it to say, Mademoiselle Donet has traveled here from Paris and is currently our guest. She was eager to join my efforts to help the American prisoners."

Captain Field beamed at Claire. "No matter the circumstances, I am pleased to find one of our allies in London. You are most welcome among us." He gestured into the room as if inviting her into a grand home when it was no more than a dark and dingy warehouse. "Other than Lady Danvers, we rarely get to see so beautiful a woman confined as we are. Most days all we have to look at are the surly guards and these four walls."

He pulled a face at the scowling guard who stood within hearing distance and Claire had to laugh.

"Lady Danvers," said the captain, "with your permission, I will introduce Mademoiselle Donet to my fellow prisoners. Some of my men want to send letters home. Others are anxious for word of the war. Did you happen to bring a newspaper?"

"Alas, I forgot, Captain," said Cornelia, bringing her gloved hand to her breast, "but I can bring some tomorrow. Claire, why don't you go with Captain Field? I'll distribute these blankets. When you're done with introductions, we can set out the food."

"Gladly," she replied, happy to be escorted by the handsome American.

Claire followed Captain Field around the room as he introduced her to his crew captured with him and others from different American ships. None wore uniforms, he explained, since they were all crew from privateers.

In response to her inquiries about their homes, families and health, they were very polite. Many were injured, their white bandages beacons drawing her attention and her sympathy in the darkly lit room.

The warehouse was dusty, the floor hard-packed earth. The men's clothes appeared soiled, their faces smudged with dirt, some of them still bearing signs of battle. The smell of too many bodies crowded together for too long rose to her nostrils. There was a stench of unemptied chamber pots. She wondered how long it was since any had bathed.

The eyes of the American prisoners followed her as she walked alongside Captain Field, but their stares did not make her feel uncomfortable. Perhaps it was due to the presence of the guards or the baroness, but they were all polite.

"It's been a long time since these men have had proper clothes," he said, "though Lady Danvers and her friends come often. I owe what I am wearing to her good charity." He lifted the lapel of his coat. "I believe this once belonged to Lord Danvers."

"It looks well on you, sir," she said with a small smile.

For a moment his gaze held hers. "You'll have to excuse me for staring. Never have I seen eyes such a vivid blue. They're like the open sea… and very beautiful, even in this place."

Claire hoped he couldn't see her blush. "Thank you, Captain. It seems I am destined to be surrounded by sailors. You are not the first to tell me my eyes remind you of the ocean. My captor, my father—who I have only just learned has his own ship—and now you—all are privateers."

"Your father is a privateer for France?"

"His ship was flying the American flag when I saw it last."

"Hmm," said the captain under his breath. "Perhaps he has a letter of marque from Dr. Franklin. I'd heard he was issuing some to French ships. Your father's efforts on America's behalf are most welcome, mademoiselle."

In the minutes that followed, in between chatting with his men, they talked about the war. "I do not know much of the battles," she told him, "but I have heard from the baroness the war draws to a close and negotiations for peace have begun."

"Yes, according to what we've heard, that news is all over London." Looking wistfully into the distance, he said, "Perhaps next Christmas, if not this one, we will be home."

"I shall pray toward that end, Captain."

With the assistance of one of the footmen and Captain Field, Claire distributed the clothing they had brought for the men. Afterward, Claire and Cornelia set out the food the footmen had carried in from the carriage. Those who could walk gathered around the table. To the others, Claire carried cold, sliced beef, along with bread, fruit and cheese. They ate as if starved. To her way of thinking, they were all too thin.

"Do they get enough to eat?" she asked Cornelia.

"Now they do. I try and fatten them up before they are

sent to other prisons. 'Tis not so bad as it was a few years ago, before the relief committee got involved. Now they have bread, meat and some kind of vegetable, often cabbage or turnips. A few years ago, they only had oatmeal or broth. Not enough to keep a grown man filling out his clothes."

Claire's heart went out to the American seamen, some of them barely out of boyhood. "How fare your sick and injured?" she asked Captain Field.

"As well as can be expected in this place. Better now with blankets and decent food," said the American, giving a nod of acknowledgment to Cornelia.

"Might I see them?"

Captain Field seemed momentarily flustered at the insistent look in her eyes, but reluctantly bowed in the face of her calm demeanor. He swept a hand toward the back of the warehouse where the light barely penetrated and a clot of men occupied the dirt floor.

"Oh," said Claire softly as she approached. The wretched state of the men was quickly apparent.

"You see, mademoiselle, it's not pleasant."

Claire brushed past him, her face softening with concern at the bloodstained linen and soiled bandages. In a matter of minutes, she had secured clean bandaging from Cornelia and bent to help the wounded men, changing their bandages and doing what she could to cheer them. One in particular tugged at her heart.

"What's your name?" she asked the young seaman.

"Alexander Monroe," he said rather shyly. Perhaps he did not often encounter women. "But everyone on Cap'n Field's ship called me 'Sandy'."

"What did you do on the captain's ship, Sandy?"

"I'm his cabin boy," the lad proudly replied.

She couldn't resist smiling at his cherubic face. Like her, he had blue eyes but his hair was a light brown. Her gaze drifted to the linen wrapped around his arm. It was dirty. "Can I change your bandage?"

"All right," he said, holding out his arm rather tentatively.

She thought she saw him wince in anticipation of being touched. "It still pains you?"

"Aye, a little."

As Claire unwrapped the soiled linen from his upper arm, she had to bite her tongue to avoid gasping at the deep irregular wound that was revealed. It would have hurt more than a little when it happened and likely still did. "I'll be careful, Sandy. It seems to be healing." She said the latter to encourage him. In truth, it would take a long time to heal.

"I don't mind when you touch it, miss. But the man who first tended it was not so gentle." Sandy was such a sweet boy, she had to fight the urge to take him into her arms and hold him as his mother might have done were she here, but she knew he would not welcome such attention in front of his fellow sailors.

She cleaned the wound, dabbed on the ointment one of the footmen brought her and wound a strip of clean linen around his arm. "There. Now it's clean again and the ointment will speed the healing. You'll be good as new before long."

"That's what the cap'n says." He beamed. The boy obviously admired his young captain. She wondered if Captain Field wasn't like a father to the lad.

"Do you have a family back in America?"

"Aye, miss, my mother and a younger sister, Katie."

She gave him a quick kiss on his cheek and squeezed his small hand in hers. "The war will be over soon, Sandy, and you'll be going home to them." Claire hoped it was the truth. She had to force herself not to cry, for the lad had stirred her heart.

There were a few others whose bandages she changed but none affected her more than the cabin boy. Though his accent was different, he reminded her of Nate. She would feel the same remorse had Simon Powell's cabin boy been wounded.

Hours passed as she listened to the men's stories of home

and the families they sorely missed. She understood, missing her papa as she did. She felt a pang of regret for what had happened to these men. Even though she was a captive, she was so much better off than they were. Still, they were alive and many were not.

੮ ୬୧ ੭

"You should have seen her," Cornelia told Simon as she handed him a brandy while they waited for Danvers in the baron's study later that day.

His gaze drifted toward the open door and the direction of the staircase. Upstairs, his captive changed for supper. He had not talked to her since the night before when he had come to her bedchamber to calm her fears.

"By the time we left the warehouse, the Yankee sailors were calling her 'the French angel'. Now that I think of it, Captain Field seemed quite smitten with her. She was just the thing to lift the prisoners' lagging spirits."

"Really, Cornelia. Do you think that was wise?" Simon was not pleased. "A young innocent like Claire Donet in a room full of American sailors—*prisoners*?"

"Why, Simon, you sound like Danvers." There was a gleam in her eyes. "You also sound jealous. Has she captured your heart as well?"

"Not at all," he protested, but he thought of the night before when he'd comforted her after her nightmare. The wild Claire Donet had turned into an angel in his arms. "I am merely concerned about the security of my hostage. The life of my men depends on her remaining safe and in my hands."

"She was never in any danger, Simon. Besides, Claire seemed to enjoy being useful."

"Who is this Captain Field anyway, and what was she doing with him? You were gone nearly all day."

143

"Captain Field is a privateer like you, except he's an American, from Baltimore, as am I," the baroness reminded him. "Claire was assisting me, changing bandages, listening to the men's stories of their families and handing out food, clothes and blankets."

He took another swallow of brandy, satisfied the burn in his throat had quenched his anger for the moment. "Ah yes, that charity work you do."

"Quite. And before you ask, Danvers approves. He was appalled at how badly the Americans were treated. I daresay it continues in some places, but at least in London we no longer treat them like dogs. Claire did the prisoners a good turn today, Simon."

"Do you intend to do this again soon? We will be gone in less than a week."

"Tomorrow morning, yes. I promised to bring them paper for letters and a few newspapers."

"Surely a footman can take them?"

"He could," the baroness agreed, "but some need their letters written for them—and we make sure the letters arrive in America. Besides, you know the American sailors would not derive the same joy from seeing one of my footmen as they would from seeing Claire and me."

Simon scowled at the baroness' impish grin. He had no meetings in the morning. Perhaps he would accompany them to see this Captain Field for himself if for no other reason than to prove there was no cause for this annoying flash of jealousy he suddenly felt picturing Claire tending the man's wounded crew. Perhaps the American captain was short, fat and ugly.

"If you're to leave in so short a time, Simon, I will have to arrange the soirée immediately."

"Ah yes, the soirée. However did I forget?" he asked in feigned innocence. An evening with members of the aristocracy was something to be endured, not something he looked forward to.

Cornelia slapped his hand. "You rogue. You'll be as charming as ever despite yourself, and Claire will be the envy of every woman there. Just wait till you see her new gown! By the by, I do not intend to mention how she came to be here, only that she is our guest, so I expect you to say nothing of it."

Chapter 13

Paris

François de Dordogne turned away from his friends who were enjoying a sumptuous dinner of salad, roast chicken and artichokes in the private dining room of the popular *taverne Ramponneau* in Paris.

Lifting his new snuffbox from the pocket of his ruby silk coat, he briefly ran his beringed finger over its top, admiring the sparkling diamonds inlaid in the polished black enamel. Raising the lid, he smiled just as he had when Jacques had presented the gift to him the night before in celebration of their year-old relationship. Painted inside were the words *gage d'amitié*, a token of friendship. It was a token of much more than that, but only his closest, likeminded friends were aware of the intimate relationship he shared with Jacques Régis.

"Is that the new trinket, François? Let us see," said Pierre, reaching out with his open hand.

"If I must." He set the box on his friend's palm, the diamonds reflecting the candlelight and sending glimmers of light dancing around the room. "But do take care."

Pierre turned the box in his hand, capturing the light. "Oh, it is lovely. He does treat you well, François." Pierre showed the box to his partner with a hopeful look that seemed to convey a desire to receive such a gift. Apparently not finding the assurance he sought, Pierre sighed and handed the

147

snuffbox down the table to Étienne who studied it for a moment before returning it to François.

"What has Jacques to say of your betrothal to Donet's daughter?" asked Étienne as he leaned against his latest lover, a man named Louis, some fifteen years his senior.

"He is pleased I shall have a convincing cover for our friendship. How could anyone question my manhood with a wife like Mam'selle Donet, who is rumored to be a great beauty?"

"Though we all know you're more interested in her gowns and jewels than in her face," said Pierre.

"If it were me," counseled Étienne, "I'd be cautious. Should Donet discover your ruse, the man will have your head on a pike. He may be the son of a comte, but that one has a dark side. What I see behind his black eyes gives me chills. I'd not want to cross him."

"Perhaps I can manage to get a child on her," said François, speaking his thought aloud. "That would be convincing, *oui*?" It might be necessary, too, he thought, though being with a woman in that way did not appeal to him and Jacques would not like it.

"Her dowry would be worth the effort," Pierre encouraged. "I hear Donet's as rich as Croesus."

"I have heard the same," agreed François. In fact, it was one reason he had quickly agreed to the match.

An hour later he and his friends glided out of the back room and into the busy tavern crowded with artisans, shopkeepers, lawyers and libertines. Few knew the private dining room they had left was often reserved by a particular group of men who preferred their own company to that of women. Men whose fashion would label them macaronies for the flamboyant way they dressed. Those of a harsher mind, aware of their proclivities, would say they were guilty of *débauche contre nature, sodomie* or worse. Paris was home to so many, unless there was another crime involved, the police rarely did more than issue a warning when one of them was discovered.

Donet would be a different matter, however. Were Donet to learn of his affair with Jacques, François' career in law—and perhaps his life—would soon be over.

෬ ൠ ෭

Elijah set down his wine and picked up his pipe, his mouth dropping open at the fops strolling from the back room of the tavern. "Will ye look at 'em Frenchies paradin' our way?"

Giles casually looked over his shoulder at the dandies slowly making their way through the long, crowded room. "Aye, frog-eaters every one. Enough lace to open a shop."

Elijah puffed on his pipe, then pulled it from his mouth. "Good thing the rest o' the crew ain't with us. They'd be laughin' their heads off. 'Twould draw too much attention."

"Paris is crawling with English just now," offered Giles, whose back was to the dandies. "The locals would not consider our presence strange even if the crew were here laughing above the din." The sailmaker brushed his reddish-brown hair off his forehead. "Trust me, the only thing that stirs the French these days is joy in criticizing their king."

"Speakin' of strange," said Elijah, shifting his attention from the fops back to Giles, "I thought the meetin' with the Frenchie's men went fine, but that quartermaster of his made me blood run cold. The man looked like the devil hisself, all dark scowl and frown, like a storm breakin'."

"I doubt he believed my assurances that Donet's daughter has been treated well. I had the impression Émile Bequel was of a mind to kill anyone who so much as touched her."

Elijah sent a puff of smoke into the air, took his pipe from his mouth and folded his arms over his chest as a picture arose in his mind. "Not unlike our cap'n. Ye know Powell harbors a fondness fer the demoiselle."

"Aye. 'Tis obvious as a red sky at morning," said Giles downing the last of his claret.

"She's a match fer 'im, 'tis certain I am." Elijah remembered well her tempest in the cap'n's cabin and the cap'n's reaction. "Fired his blood all right."

"Aye, but 'tis an unlikely match. Powell would never risk his men for a bit of French pastry, no matter how enticing."

Elijah considered the sailmaker's words. Gesturing with his pipe stem, he opined, "Mebbe, mebbe not. But mark me words, this one's different."

The effeminate fops paused to speak to some men drinking nearby. Elijah took in their clothing, all satins and silks with fussy, embroidered waistcoats and frothy, white lace. Their hair was left hanging in curls, or done in tortuous, puffed up styles even more exaggerated than the French aristocrats.

"'Tisn't proper," Elijah murmured under his breath.

Giles said nothing but he turned to glance at the fops, his eyes following them as they resumed their stroll toward the front of the tavern.

They passed Elijah and he got a whiff of their strong perfume. It made his eyes smart as the vapors engulfed their table. Even his tobacco smoke did not hide the strong odor.

Just as the dandies reached the entrance, the rotund proprietor wiped his hands on his apron and called out, "François!"

One of the fops turned to look back, a young one of slight frame with long, dark hair hanging loosely to his shoulders.

"*Oui*, Dordogne, I mean you. You have a message here." The hefty man picked up an envelope and shoved it forward on the bar.

The dandy ambled his way to the bar, picked up the envelope, waved to the proprietor and with a "*Merci*," left with his companions.

Elijah shook his head. "Damn me but those dandies turn me gizzard sour. Can't wait to be back in England." Then returning his gaze to Giles, he said, "I wonder if the cap'n's still in London. He'll be wantin' to know the exchange is set for Calais. 'Tis not far off either."

"We can be in Rye in three days if the weather holds. That'll be where he expects to find us."

Suddenly feeling a need for haste, Elijah rose, settled his knit cap on his head and dropped some coins on the table. "Aye, 'tis best we be on our way."

༄ ༜༝ ༅

London

Nervous with anticipation for the evening ahead, Claire held her hand to her midriff, studying her reflection in the mirror while Cornelia's maid pulled the golden gown's laces tight. This would be her first soirée. And likely her last. Since her vow to Élise, she had never thought to attend one, but Cornelia had insisted.

It might be her only chance to mingle with London's *beau monde*. Another adventure before she returned to the convent. *If* she returned to the convent. Her papa might not allow her that choice. A choice she was no longer certain she wanted herself.

She straightened the four bows made of gold silk that formed a column down the front of her bodice to meet the full skirt of the same silk fabric. The gown was one of those from Mrs. Duval's, this one copied from the dress worn by the fashion doll the captain had carried back from Paris. The sleeves hugged her arms till they flared at her elbows in golden flounces, each one with several dangling, golden beads. Beneath each flounce was a generous amount of ivory lace. Never had she worn a gown so fine. At her throat was a double strand of pearls Cornelia had lent her for the evening.

"I just need to fix your hair and then you will be ready, mistress," said the maid. "'Twould be nice to have some of your lovely black curls dangling on your shoulders. Perhaps I might take up just the sides and some of the back?"

Claire nodded and sat before the dressing table as the maid went to work.

Several minutes later, the door opened and Cornelia stepped inside, dressed in a pale blue satin gown that was lovely with her auburn hair, and smiled her appreciation at the job done by her maid who had just pinned the last curl in place.

"Claire, you look like a princess."

"All this is due to your good taste and the efforts of your maid," Claire returned with a smile. "But despite my appearance, my stomach is all aflutter."

"Come," Cornelia said, taking her hand. "The men are waiting for us. A glass of sherry in the library before the hurricane arrives, when the whole house will be full from top to bottom, is just what you need to calm your nerves."

Claire raised her palm to her breast to still her racing heart. "Yes, I think you are right."

Slowly she descended the stairs, her head held high, as she'd been taught. Knowing that Simon Powell waited for her made her skin tingle with anticipation. She wanted him to think her pretty, to see his eyes sparkle with delight at the gown he had given her.

He had come to the warehouse where they kept the American prisoners when she and Cornelia returned with the newspapers. Captain Field had bowed low over her hand and smiled up at her. In response, Captain Powell had quickly recovered her hand and tucked it into his elbow. She hadn't known whether to be flattered or annoyed at the possessive gesture. It wasn't as if he had a claim on her.

He had stayed by her side the whole morning. *Surely he must care.* Yet perhaps he only cared to protect his security for the return of his men. He had said it often enough.

It was more for her. She could not sleep nights for thinking of him. Since he'd held her and soothed her fears, the bad dreams had not returned. Perhaps the memory of his arms wrapped around her had driven away Élise's ghost.

She followed Cornelia into the library where he and Baron Danvers stood in front of the fireplace sipping what looked like brandy. Simon turned his gaze on her and, for a moment, there was no one else in the room. Only him and his brilliant amber eyes.

She took a step back, heated by his devouring gaze. Lifting her chin, she asked, "Do you like the gown?"

"That and more, I'd wager," said the baron, dipping his head to her.

"Indeed," said Simon.

"Darling," said Cornelia to her husband, "might you pour us a glass of sherry?"

"Of course, my dear." Ignoring the footman standing by the door, the baron proceeded to where the decanters of liquor were lined up on a sideboard. Cornelia followed him. "And aren't you a vision tonight in blue, my dear? I quite like that gown on you."

"Which is why I chose to wear it this evening, my lord."

Claire was vaguely aware Cornelia and her husband had stepped to the edge of the room, and though she could hear their conversation, she had eyes only for Simon. He had donned a chocolate silk coat and breeches with a waistcoat of gold brocade over his crisp, white linen shirt and cravat. His golden hair was neatly gathered at his nape with a black velvet ribbon. He looked every bit the young lord his parentage would have made him had his father not abandoned his mother.

No matter his beginnings, Claire was proud of what he'd become. He had accomplished much with no help save his own efforts and the guilt money from his father. He had gained the respect of his men and, likely, his country for his role in the war. Somewhere underneath it all she sensed the pain he harbored from his past, a pain that kept him distant from others. She did not want him to remain distant from her.

It was love she was feeling she realized sadly. A love that could never be.

"You are very beautiful tonight, mademoiselle," he said, setting his brandy on the mantel. Closing the distance between them, he took her gloved hand and brushed his lips over her knuckles, sending ripples of pleasure coursing through her.

"Thank you, Captain. And you are very dashing tonight. 'Twould seem London has been good for you."

"I can wear the costume when I must." He winked at her and she knew he was thinking of the night they had met in Saint-Denis, the night she'd fallen from a tree.

She decided not to allow his amusement at her girlish behavior to rouse her anger. "It suits you," she said.

Lord Danvers carried a glass of sherry to her and she happily accepted it, taking a swallow of the dry, nutty-tasting wine. She needed courage for the evening.

❦

Simon stood at the edge of the room watching the guests cluster around the beautiful French girl who, to all appearances, was practiced at her charms, handily trading quips with London's elite. Simon had anticipated that she would be the object of much male attention among those invited to the soirée, but he did not have to like it.

Underneath her carefree manner, he suspected she was still the innocent, convent-raised girl he'd met two years ago. Not as reckless and perhaps a bit wiser, but still innocent. She was blossoming into womanhood and the realization he would never see her as a mother of her own children or the grand hostess she would one day become hit him with a wave of remorse. If she had her way and returned to the convent, none of it would ever be. That he might want her to have children and they be his own was something he'd not fully admitted, even to himself.

The parlor was crowded with members of London's aristocracy, guests of Lord and Lady Danvers. Clearly, the young British lord and his American wife were well liked by members of the *ton*. That they had a friend who was a known privateer, rumored to be the bastard of an English nobleman, was just another interesting tidbit for conversation. He suspected some of the women who openly flirted with him believed him a rogue.

Lady Willowby, a young widow, who'd been looking at him over her fan all evening, sidled up to him then.

"Captain Powell," the pretty brunette said, touching her fan to his arm, "you are a welcome sight."

"Good evening, Lady Willowby."

At his use of her title, she gave a disappointed pout. "Are we not good enough friends for you to call me Amanda?"

"I should hardly think that proper," he returned, wanting to use the formality to keep her at a distance.

She moved closer until her rounded softness touched his arm. He could feel the heat of her breast through his coat sleeve. "But we don't have to be proper, you and I," she whispered behind her fan. "My carriage awaits outside."

That she would think he would jump at the chance to get beneath her skirts rankled. A year ago, perhaps, but not now. "I have a guest to look after," he said stiffly.

"Ah yes, the young French woman." She looked to where Claire was talking with several young men. "But she appears to be occupied with her many admirers."

Simon inwardly cringed at the reminder. "Just the reason I must keep watch."

"Like an older brother?" Lady Willowby batted her eyelashes in feigned interest.

He chuckled. "Just so." Let the woman think what she would. But he was no older brother and he kept watch over Claire as much for his own sake as for hers.

"Well, then," said Lady Willowby, turning to leave, "another time, perhaps."

He tipped his head and smiled as she joined the crush. He had long ago stopped caring what such women thought of him or what the members of the *ton* whispered.

Because she was American, Lady Danvers had once been a subject of gossip, or so she had told him. But that had changed in recent years with her husband's port-drinking Whigs who were sympathetic to America's desire for independence. And since they expected to soon be at peace with France, none held Claire's nationality against her. Like French food, fashions and brandy, she was another novelty to be examined and enjoyed. Why such a young woman was in London at this particular time was a matter of some speculation among the guests, but Cornelia came up with a convincing story of a distant relation that everyone seemed to accept.

He lifted a glass of champagne from the tray offered by the passing footman but refused the puffed pastry with beef and mushrooms. Sipping the golden liquid, he kept his eyes on Claire.

"You could ask her to dance," said Cornelia, joining him. "And perhaps you should. See the man just approaching her? He is the young Duke of Albany, just come into his title on the death of his father. He'll be looking for a wife soon. I understand he has ties to Scotland, and through them, to the French. You might want to be careful about leaving her alone with him too long."

"Matchmaking, Cornelia? A bastard and a future nun seem hardly a pair." Even as he said it, the hard truth grated. He could never compete with a duke, or any member of the nobility.

"Now there you'd be wrong," she said, rapping her fan on his arm. "Claire would care not a whit for your beginnings, Simon. She does not judge men that way. Of course, her father presents a problem."

"And do not forget it is my crew he holds captive. She is

my guarantee they will be safely returned."

"I have not forgotten," said the baroness, "and neither has Claire. Still, I'd like to see her remain in London. Can you not arrange that? I've quite gotten used to her company, you know."

"I do not think that possible." Simon said nothing more. What was there to say? Cornelia had accurately summed up the whole affair. Claire's father, his men, their ridiculous situation.

"Well," Cornelia whispered conspiratorially, "when the music starts, I suggest you be the first to offer Claire your arm. Or be content to have some young rake claim her."

At his frown, Cornelia sallied forth to join her guests. The baroness knew just how to stir his discontent.

A moment later, William Eden, attired in his customary shades of brown, replaced Cornelia at Simon's side.

"Finally alone. Good. I was hoping for a word."

Simon raised his brow as he lifted his champagne to his lips.

"When do you leave?"

"I sail for Rye as soon as my ship is loaded, tomorrow or the next day."

Eden directed his gaze to the object of Simon's attention. "And you take the mademoiselle with you?"

"I do." *What scheme was forming in Eden's mind now?* "I would not leave her behind when I need her for the exchange."

"Ah yes," said Eden, tugging his waistcoat down. "The exchange. I'd like to have word of the arrangements when they are made. 'Twould be a perfect time to capture the French pirate."

Simon nearly choked on his champagne. "It hardly seems the done thing, to coin a phrase of the *ton*. You would allow me to set up a prisoner exchange as a means to betray the trust implied? He may be our enemy, Eden, but I'll not do it. Besides, something is bound to go wrong and my men, unarmed and weakened by wounds, might be killed. Not to mention the girl. No, I like it not. And I'm surprised that you would risk provoking an incident on the heels of negotiations just commencing with the Americans."

"I will think on it more, but the idea appeals."

"I gave my word."

"To a pirate, one who serves the enemy, I might add." Eden smirked.

Simon's mouth twisted in a scowl. He did not intend to give Eden the chance to involve him in that kind of duplicity. Claire's father would only think worse of him than he already did.

"No longer a pirate, he is a privateer as am I." In the distance, Simon heard the music begin. "Excuse me," he said to Eden, "I must see to my guest." With that, he left the statesman and strode to Claire just as some young buck was about to ask her to dance.

"Mademoiselle," he said, offering her his arm, "This is our dance, I believe."

Chapter 14

Claire was startled for only a moment and then she allowed her pleasure to show, no matter his lie. "Of course, Captain Powell, how could I forget?" Making her apologies to the young man with whom she'd been speaking, whose expression made clear his displeasure at being cut out, Claire took the captain's arm and followed him to where the others had just begun dancing.

It was the same minuet she had watched him dance at the masquerade. Only now it was her hand he held as he adroitly stepped through the paces. And it was her he was smiling at. Joy rose in her heart. However fleeting it might be, she would not regret this moment. It was a memory no one could take from her.

"It seems you are forever sweeping me away to a place I'd not intended to go," she teased. "But this time, you have allowed me to realize a fantasy I've had since the night of the masquerade." At his questioning look, she added, "To dance with the charming golden eagle."

He chuckled. "I have not worn that costume since. It's somewhere with my things in Rye." At her puzzled look, he said, "I've a house there when I want to be off the ship."

"You did not think to leave me there when you sailed for London?"

"No, I never considered leaving you behind, mademoiselle." The longing she thought she saw in his eyes told her there might be more to his keeping her with him than her role in recovering his men.

Perhaps he cares a little, after all.

Claire felt the eyes of the other guests upon them as they danced together. She was a curiosity, as was the captain, he the bastard of an English nobleman, she a Catholic descended from French nobility. But she never saw herself as nobility, though Cornelia had told her the English would see her that way. In so many ways, she still felt like the convent student she had been for most of her life, ignorant of the schemes and flirtations that swirled around her. Compared to these worldly London aristocrats, she must seem like a girl playing at acting the lady. In the arms of Simon Powell, she felt protected. She was grateful for his daring, to ask her to dance before the whole glittering, London crowd. Well, she could be daring, too. They would be notorious together—the French convent girl and the bastard.

The sisters in Saint-Denis had taught her to think of others as equally loved by God. Honor and kindness would always mean more to her than position and power. And she was certain Captain Powell was a man of honor.

The room seemed to disappear in a blur as he smoothly led her through the steps of the dance. He was so handsome and tonight, he looked only at her. She had seen the women's eyes following him even as they gossiped behind their fans. She felt oddly protective of him, not wishing him to be hurt by their wagging tongues. What did it matter with so brave and daring a man how he had begun? Was it not how a man ended that mattered?

She raised her chin a bit higher, determined to show them all how fine a man it was with whom she danced, glad he would be her first partner for the evening.

Hours later, Claire had danced many dances, more than one of them with Simon Powell. When the guests finally began to leave, Claire was fighting a yawn. Only nibbling on the sweetmeats, candied fruits and sugared nuts set out for the guests on the sideboard had kept her awake.

When the last guest had bid Cornelia and her husband goodnight, Claire and the captain were left standing beside their hosts, with only a footman attending the door.

"You were quite the rage, Claire," said an excited Cornelia. "We enjoyed introducing you to our friends, didn't we, my lord?"

"Indeed we did, darling," said the handsome, young baron. "And they enjoyed meeting you, mademoiselle," he said to Claire. "The Countess of Huntingdon—who I was surprised to see accepted our invitation now that she's reached the great age of seventy—remarked to me that she was most impressed with your devotion to God."

"I enjoyed meeting the countess. Such an amazing woman and she has done much good with all the chapels she has caused to be built."

"Yes," said the baron, "her building projects are prolific."

"Had we not told our friends you were leaving London," said Cornelia, "you would have many calling cards stacked up on our silver tray come the next few days."

The captain frowned. "Just as well we sail shortly." He took her elbow and directed her to the wide staircase in the entry. "I will see you to your door."

She paused, turning to look back at Cornelia and her husband. "*Bonne nuit*, and thank you for the lovely evening."

The captain was at her side as she ascended the stairs, his tall figure a comfort.

"You danced every dance," he said. "The men of London Society were lined up for a chance to meet you."

She couldn't tell if he was complimenting or chiding her. "It will probably be the last time I dance. I did not want to miss any," she said by way of explanation. *I want memories to take with me.*

"Ah yes, the convent," he said. "I'd nearly forgotten."

Claire could not tell for certain but thought he was teasing her. He knew well her story and her plans. What he didn't know was that her heart was no longer in them.

At the top of the stairs he guided her toward the wing that held their bedchambers. "Some sleep will do you good," he said, pausing in front of her door, "though dawn is not far off."

It was true, she was exhausted, but she did not feel like sleeping. She wanted to watch the dawn with him, to have another memory of this special night before she returned to her papa.

He opened her door and gestured her inside. She took his hand and pulled him in with her. "I don't want to say *bonne nuit* to you just yet."

"This is dangerous, mademoiselle."

When she said nothing, he hesitated, but then closed the door. The maid must have lit the candle when she'd turned down the cover of the bed. The candle's soft light behind her lighted his face.

"Perhaps, but I would ask for a kiss before you wish me a goodnight." *A last kiss before I take my vows.*

He smiled. "Then you shall have one."

She went into his arms eagerly, memories of his last kiss rising in her mind. But this was not like the last kiss, or the one before it. He was not angry this time. He was tender and gentle.

His warm lips passed over hers, touching, tasting. Then he kissed her more deeply as she opened to him, returning his kiss and entwining her hands in his golden hair, setting loose the strands from the velvet ribbon.

Drawing her into the hard planes of his chest, his tongue invaded the soft recesses of her mouth, gently seducing her. His movements were slow, sensual as he slid his tongue over hers, taking more of her mouth. She was lost in the wonder of his kiss, in the feel of his body pressing against her. They melded together as one. Her breasts became sensitive with the quivers of pleasure that echoed through her body.

"Simon," she gasped as his lips slid to her throat where he

nibbled at the tender flesh. "Oh, Simon. I do not want to leave you." She had finally told him what was in her heart. She wanted to stay with him, even if it could not be.

He rained kisses on her neck sending shivers rippling through her body. Her breathing grew ragged and her heart raced in her chest.

With a deep breath, he pulled his head back. "I fear this is not a good idea, Claire. I want you but I cannot have you. We only tempt fate."

She dropped her forehead to his chest, resigned. "I know." Then she looked up again, unable to resist another look at his face. "But it might be the last time."

He held her away from him. "You are such an innocent and more tempting than any woman I've ever known. But I cannot forget you are the daughter of the man who holds my men. And you have made clear your intention to become a nun. In such circumstances, our feelings matter not a whit."

He was right, of course. But that did not stop the wanting that had nearly overwhelmed her. Nor the ache in her heart at the thought of never seeing him again.

☾ ⁀ ☽

Simon closed the door and took the few steps across the corridor to his bedchamber, knowing he might take to his bed but he would not sleep. He could still see the shock on her face from his words. He forced his body to calm even as his mind was filled with plans. Could he rescue his men before the exchange took place?

Claire.

Even her name made the blood surge in his veins. Rescuing his men was his only hope of keeping her. All he needed was the name of the location where they were being held. She had said she didn't want to go. If he had his men, she could stay.

A few hours later, the sun's first rays filtered in through

his window. He rose, quickly dressed and went downstairs.

At the foot of the stairs, Higgins greeted him. "Good morning, Captain Powell. His lordship and Lady Danvers have yet to rise. Would you have breakfast?"

"Thank you, just coffee."

In the morning room, he accepted the coffee a footman placed in front of him when another appeared at the arched doorway.

"Captain Powell?"

"Yes?"

"A young man has arrived from your ship. He identified himself as your cabin boy and says he comes on a matter of some urgency. I've put him in the baron's study thinking you might want to be private."

"Thank you, that was most kind." Setting aside his coffee, he hastily rose and strode through the door. *What could the matter be now?*

He entered the study and the familiar smell of old books rose in his nostrils. Nate stood in front of the large, carved desk worrying his tricorne in his hands. "Cap'n!"

"What is it, Nate?" The lad was obviously beside himself, his cheeks ruddy with exertion and sweat beading on his forehead. "Have you been running?"

"Aye, Cap'n. Mr. Landor sent me. There're men watchin' the ship. I slipped away while the crew caused a racket on deck, but just to be sure they didn't follow me, I took a windin' path down the alleys to get here."

He sat on the edge of the desk. "You did the right thing, Nate. Now, tell me, does Mr. Landor know who is watching the ship?"

"Zeb was the first to notice, sir. 'Twas yesterday. He told Mr. Landor that a man lurkin' about the cargo waitin' to be loaded looked like one of the crew from the ship that attacked the *Abundance*."

"Well, if it's Donet, he can want only one thing."

"The mistress?" the boy asked anxiously.

"Aye." Simon ran a hand through his hair as his thoughts raced. Donet had taken the same step he was planning, not waiting for the exchange. He could hardly blame the Frenchman for having a like strategy.

"Ye won't let them have her, will ye, Cap'n?" Nate's brown eyes pleaded.

Simon reached out to tousle his cabin boy's hair. "No, Nate. They'll not get her." *At least not yet.* "But if Donet's crew is watching the ship, it raises questions. Do you know if they have a ship in port or if the man Zeb saw is just a scout like the ones I sent to Lorient?"

"Mr. Landor did not say." The boy looked down at the rug he was standing on. "I think he does not know."

"Is the *Fairwinds* loaded and ready to sail?"

He looked up. "Aye, Cap'n. Mr. Landor asked me to tell ye that."

"Good. Now, listen carefully. I'll not risk a written message should you be discovered on your return. I need to talk to Mr. Landor. But I don't want him to come here. Tell him to meet me at the Bell Tavern on Fleet Street at noon." At the boy's questioning look, he said, "The first mate knows the place well. The crowds will be thick on the streets then. Tell him to depart the ship with two others, each going in a different direction to confuse whoever would follow."

"Aye, sir, I will." Nate headed for the door.

"And be careful," he cautioned the boy.

"Like always, cap'n." Nate grinned and was gone.

໒ ໑

Claire had awakened early to dress and pace in her room. She must do something! It had finally come to her sometime in the few hours remaining in the night that the Reverend Mother had been right. She could not live Élise's dream. Might she send a letter to her papa persuading him to free the English seamen he held? Ask him to allow her to stay in London? Cornelia had begged her to do so.

She had stolen down the stairs not wishing to wake any who still slept, then froze when she'd heard a knock on the front door. A footman had answered and Nate entered.

"I must see Cap'n Powell. I'm his cabin boy. 'Tis urgent."

"Follow me," had come the reply.

What could Nate have wanted that would be urgent? Carefully she had descended the stairs to hide in the recess next to the breakfast room as the footman had talked to the captain. He must have risen even earlier than she. Curious to know what was so urgent, she had sneaked to the study after the footman had passed her.

She had waited in the shadows as the captain walked to the study. The door was ajar and she listened as he spoke to Nate. What she had heard made her pulse speed.

Papa is in London? I must find him!

◌ ◌◌ ◌

Tobacco smoke assaulted his nostrils as Simon stepped through the door of the tavern. Shafts of sunlight filtering in through the paned glass windows illuminated the haze that hung in the air. The large room, crowded with unbathed men, smelled of sweat and sour ale. He had never liked such places overmuch, but this day the tavern served his purpose. He had chosen the Bell Tavern because it was a good place to hide in the open. And a meeting here wouldn't lead Donet's men back to Claire.

Ambling his way through the crowded wooden tables, avoiding outstretched legs and serving wenches carrying heavy trays, he slid into a chair at the back of the room where he could remain in the shadows. As more men entered the tavern, the noise of their midday conversations rose to a clamor.

Moving his chair to face the front door, he accepted a tankard of ale from the smiling barmaid while watching for

Jordan and any who might follow him, pondering his next move.

Now that his business in London was completed, his priority was returning to Rye. He had no intention of giving Eden more time to find a reason to involve Claire in his schemes. The British government could damn well negotiate peace without her as a pawn. Besides, he was anxious to know if Elijah and Giles had returned from Paris. Even more, he wanted to know what Amos Busby had learned in Lorient.

A movement at the front door caught his eye as Jordan Landor slipped in and doffed his tricorne, revealing a familiar head of curly dark hair. The first mate quickly scanned the room and then made straight for Simon.

His green eyes twinkling in amusement, Jordan pulled out a chair and sat. "Thought I'd find you tucked away back here."

"So you did." Simon waited till the barmaid brought another tankard and then, making himself heard over the din, got to the point. "How many are watching the *Fairwinds*?"

"Zeb thought he recognized two. But there might be more. Donet is nothing if not thorough."

"Any idea whether his ship is near? I'd like to avoid another encounter with the Frenchman. The mademoiselle would not take it kindly if I blew her father out of the water."

"There are so many ships in port just now, the Thames is like a kettle of stew on the boil. No way to tell if Donet is anywhere close. But if he is, he's not sailing his brig-sloop."

Simon thought of the possibilities. "Most likely he sails another of the ships he has seized, an English merchantman, perhaps. After all, he began as a pirate. Slipping over the side with knives between their teeth must be familiar to his crew. I've often thought his many disguises account for his successfully eluding our frigates."

"Aye, you're right. We cannot be certain of the ship he's sailing."

Simon had been toying with an idea, one that would be certain to keep Claire close to him and away from her father, at least for a time. And it might spare his men a fight in port. "Can you capture Donet's men watching the *Fairwinds*?"

"Aye, at least the ones we can see. We've plenty of extra crew from the *Abundance* to set a trap."

"Good. 'Twill slow down the Frenchman. Send word with Nate early tomorrow when you have Donet's spies in hand. Tell the lad to bring what he needs for the next few days."

"What are you thinking, Captain?"

"Donet will expect me to return to the ship with his daughter in tow unless he believes she is already there. But he might think her absent if his spies have not observed her on deck, or me either for that matter. He won't be expecting what I have in mind."

Jordan's brows drew together as he listened intently. "And that would be?"

"I want you to sail the *Fairwinds* to Rye while I take the lady over land."

A look of amazement appeared on Jordan's face. "He'd never expect you to travel by coach."

"My thought exactly, except that I plan to use a private carriage. It will take us two days to get to Rye. You can sail there in the same time if the wind and tide are with you."

"I've done it before," Jordan assured him. "Aye, I can do it."

"The mademoiselle won't like it, but then she wasn't too pleased when I carried her away from Saint-Denis."

Jordan chuckled. "Or when you forced her to sail from Dieppe. What are your orders should the *Fairwinds* be followed out of port by another ship?"

"Try to elude him on the Thames. Once in the Channel, use the schooner's greater speed to outrun her. Do not engage unless Donet forces your hand. Not even *he* would follow you into the maze of Rye Harbor."

Chapter 15

"We leave tomorrow," announced Simon at dinner. He regretted springing this on the baron and his lady but it could not be avoided.

For a moment Danvers and his wife said nothing. Next to him, Claire inhaled sharply.

"So soon?" asked Cornelia, struggling to find her voice.

"Aye, something's arisen. Mademoiselle Donet and I will travel by carriage. The arrangements are made. I cannot risk sailing the *Fairwinds* myself."

Simon watched the reactions of his friends. Cornelia shot a glance at Claire. Danvers' brow twisted in puzzlement. Neither he nor his wife asked Simon the why of his plans. By now they were familiar with his strange comings and goings and would not press him beyond what he offered by way of explanation.

"Where are you taking me?" asked Claire, turning to look at him, her azure eyes inquiring, her voice insistent.

"Back to Rye."

Her eyes flashed as if she might defy him, but before she could open her mouth, Cornelia interjected, "I will help you pack, Claire."

"Only what you'll need for one night," he counseled.

"This is all so mysterious, Simon," Danvers protested. "Have you told Eden?"

"No. And I do not intend to do so."

Danvers' forehead creased in a frown. "He will not be happy. Said he wanted to talk to you about the exchange before you sailed."

"My ship is under observation. So would I be if I went to Whitehall just now. The Frenchman would expect such a move. No, I cannot risk it. And I travel in haste."

"Ah, I see." Danvers nodded as if he understood, though the baron could only guess at all that was in Simon's mind.

Cornelia opened her mouth. "But—"

"Nay, darling. Do not ask him more," Danvers gently chided as he took his wife's hand. "Simon has no doubt considered carefully what must be done." The baron faced Simon. "We wish you and Mademoiselle Donet a safe journey."

❦

Claire sat back in the hackney she had hailed, relief flowing through her. Once she and Cornelia had seen to the packing of the portmanteau the baroness had loaned her, Claire had asked to be alone for a while. It had been her excuse to slip away.

Perhaps it was a foolhardy venture but she had to try and find her papa. If she were successful, and he knew of her wishes, if all he wanted was her safe return, wouldn't he allow the captain's men to go free? Might he even allow her to stay in London?

Leaving the mansion unobserved had not been easy, but she'd managed it, except for one young footman who intercepted her just as she was about leave. She stilled her racing heart long enough to give him the excuse of an afternoon walk in Mayfair. He had not been pleased but he could hardly hold her prisoner when Cornelia treated her as a guest.

There was no guard following her either, perhaps because she'd been with Simon. He had given her money the day she and Cornelia had gone shopping, and she still had it. The coins were safely stored in her reticule lying on the seat beside her.

Glancing out the window at the sun on the buildings, her spirits lifted knowing she'd have hours of light in which to accomplish her purpose.

Directing the hired coachman to the Pool of London had been easy enough but trying to recall where on the river the *Fairwinds* was anchored had been more difficult. She remembered the Thames was crowded with hundreds of ships the day they'd arrived. Into her mind came the picture of the huge mooring post nearly three times the height of a man to which ships had tied up. When she'd described it to the coachman, he had nodded as if remembering such a marker. He must have taken pity on her, a foreigner and a lady alone, for he agreed to see if he could find it.

If she found the *Fairwinds*, would she recognize her papa's men who were watching it? Other than M'sieur Bequel, she could only recall one or two who had come to the convent with her papa in all the years she was there, but their faces might be familiar. She hoped so. It might not be a very good plan but it was the only one she had.

A few minutes later, the hackney rolled to a stop. She took a deep breath, gathering her courage. The coachman climbed down and opened the door. Holding open his palm for the fare, he said, "Yer here, miss. The post ye described is just there." Her gaze followed the direction of his outstretched arm and she saw the mooring post, the ships tied up at the wharf—and the *Fairwinds*! Now all she had to do was find her father's men.

"Thank you, sir." She dropped the coins in his hand.

When the hackney had driven away, Claire walked to one of the buildings that faced the river where she stood in the shadows, observing what was before her. The smell she had inhaled that first day they'd moored in the Pool of London was there again, the stench of garbage and the smell of sour ale from the taverns. There were men everywhere, some carrying cargo to and from anchored ships, but some standing idly by, appearing to do nothing more than share bits of conversation with other men. Avoiding their curious gazes, she ventured forth as if she had come a purpose to seek passage on a ship.

She was not the only woman on the quay. A few leaned against the front of a tavern, wearing dresses revealing much of their bosoms, tossing seductive smiles to any man who walked by. There were others, more properly attired, who appeared to be passengers waiting for the small boats to ferry them out to ships. But unlike those waiting for ships, she was alone.

She studied the faces of the men whose gazes were fixed on the *Fairwinds*, hoping to recognize even just one. *There.* Was that man sitting on a cask in front of the tavern one of her papa's men? He looked familiar, a seaman by his dress. Could he be one of her papa's crew? If he were, he would have a French accent. Perhaps she might ask him a question.

She approached as if to walk by him and then stopped. "Sir, do you happen to know where a ship named the *Abundance* is anchored?" Why she had used that ship's name she wasn't certain. But any of her papa's men would recognize the name since her papa had seized that ship. And they would recognize her French accent.

"Aye, I do," said the man in a distinctive English accent. "Likely 'tis in Lorient."

Oh, no. A sudden dread took hold of her. She looked closely at the man and recognized him as the bos'n's mate from the *Fairwinds*. The one who had scrambled over the deck to secure the anchor the day they'd sailed for London. Only now he was cleaned up and had shaved off his beard. She couldn't even recall his name.

Rising, he fixed his steely eyes on her. "And what might the captain's passenger be doin' struttin' down the London quay and askin' questions about it?"

"Excuse me," she said, turning to go.

"Not so fast, mistress." He stuck out his hand to restrain her and her heart stopped. "The cap'n will be wantin' to know what yer about. Spyin' on the ship fer yer father, are ye?"

"No…" she stammered. He clenched her arm in a vise-like grip. "No I was just—"

"Come this way," he directed, as he pulled her behind him.

"No! Let go of me!" He did not let go, nor did he lead her to the ship. Instead, he yanked her around the building toward the rear of the tavern.

As he neared the back door, a man stepped into his path. He was garbed as an ordinary seaman but with a difference that spoke of France. The scarf about his neck, the color of his open waistcoat and something about his short dark beard told her he might be one of her papa's crew.

"I'll be seeing the mademoiselle to her papa," he said in a decidedly French accent as he reached for her.

He is French—and knows Papa!

The Frenchman latched on to her arm and tugged, but the bos'n's mate did not let go. Instead, he gripped her arm more tightly. "Nay, the woman is comin' with me."

Caught between the two men, she was being torn asunder. "Stop! You are hurting me."

The man from her papa's crew let go of her arm and swung his fist into the jaw of the English sailor. Claire lurched back, avoiding the two men now engaged in an all-out brawl in the alley. She thought of running away but the back door of the tavern swung open and men from the *Fairwinds'* crew rushed out.

One of them pulled the Frenchman off the bos'n's mate. It took two of them to hold the French crewmember, so violently did he struggle.

"He's one of them Frenchies," said the bos'n's mate wiping the blood off his mouth. Gesturing to her, he said with a swagger, "See what I caught in the net."

"The captain's lady," said a man she recognized as Mr. Anderson, the one who had guarded her door on the *Fairwinds*.

"Saved us the trouble of tracking down yet another French spy," said one of the others.

The Frenchman looked at her with regret in his eyes. "*Pardonnez-moi*, mademoiselle. I have failed. The *capitaine* will be most displeased."

Her heart sank. "I have failed, too, m'sieur, for I thought to find my papa, but as you see, we are both now captives."

The men from the *Fairwinds* led them into the small back room of the tavern, a storage room piled high with casks of ale. They forced the Frenchman onto a stool and tied his hands behind him.

Mr. Anderson turned to her. "What might ye be doin' here, mistress?"

"You'd never understand if I tried to explain," she said with a frustrated sigh.

"Find Mr. Landor," he said to one of the men. "The first mate will know what to do. Don't think he'd be wantin' us to take her aboard."

They escorted her to one side of the room where she gratefully slipped into a chair.

A few moments later, Mr. Landor appeared, frowning his disapproval.

"Mademoiselle Donet…"

She rose. "*Oui.*"

"What are you doing here?"

"It's a long story, Mr. Landor. You may not believe me, but I was trying to help."

"I doubt very much the captain would want you involved," he replied. "In fact, I'm quite certain he will be furious when he learns you are here. The wharf is not a place for a lady by herself. And he does not want you seen at the moment."

Mr. Anderson spoke up. "We've another one of Donet's crew, Mr. Landor." An explanation followed. In response, Mr. Landor whispered more orders and the French crewmember was escorted out of the room.

Mr. Landor faced the bos'n's mate, standing guard next to Claire. "Get me a hackney. I'll take her back myself."

The ride back to the Danvers' mansion was a long one

since Mr. Landor had directed the coachman to take a circuitous route. Claire sat stony-faced, angry with herself at botching her one chance to gain the captain his missing crew without having to let her go.

A gloomy silence hung in the air.

As the hackney jounced over the cobbles, the first mate studied her thoughtfully from the opposite seat, his green eyes boring into her. Finally, he spoke. "Seeking your father's men, were you, mademoiselle?"

"I was," she confessed. "When I learned my papa might be in London, I thought to persuade him to free the captain's men."

"Even if you had found him, it would have been a useless effort. Your father would not release our men unless we had you to exchange."

"But why? I would have been free."

"Because there is more to this than just your freedom, mademoiselle. Your father wants English prisoners to bargain for Americans. He wants both you *and* the crew from the *Abundance*. 'Tis why he attacked the *Fairwinds* on the Channel."

She sank back against the padded seat, a feeling of defeat washing over her. "I see. Then there really was no hope for what I did."

"No hope at all, and putting yourself in danger will not please the captain."

He was right, as Claire learned when they returned to the Danvers' home. Mr. Landor left her in the entry hall and the butler escorted her into the baron's study. Having apparently received word of her impetuous action, Simon was there, arms crossed as he leaned against the desk, a scowl on his face as he waited to hear her explanation.

"Well?" he demanded, his anger palpable. "What were you thinking by doing something so foolish? Did you plan to escape?"

She took a deep breath. "I only wanted to help. When I heard Nate say my papa's ship might be in London, I thought

175

if I could find him, I could persuade him to set your men free." *And to let me stay with you.*

"Naïve, mademoiselle. Very naïve."

Instantly her temper rose at his criticism. "Perhaps, Captain, but I had to try."

"You might have been harmed." There was concern in his eyes. She hoped it was because he cared for her. But perhaps he only wanted to retain his hostage.

"Or even abducted?" She could not hide the sarcasm in her voice. "As you know, I have journeyed that road before."

Ignoring her comment, he said, "In addition to that, some of my men now think you are a French spy."

"A spy? But why?"

"I should think that was obvious. You were on the wharf asking about the *Abundance*, my ship your father holds. And you have observed my comings and goings these past weeks. For all I know you may have learned things. Things I'd rather not have your father know."

"Do *you* think I'm a spy?"

"No, I think you too innocent to be a spy, but my men do not."

"May I have a brandy?" she asked, spotting the decanter at the edge of the room.

He gave her a curious look but did as she'd asked and poured her a small glass of the amber liquid that was nearly the color of his eyes.

She took a large swallow, forcing the grimace from her face, grateful for the distraction provided by the burn in her throat. "It's been a difficult day."

His harsh glare softened. "You may rest tonight." Then his jaw clenched. "We leave at first light."

With one look at his face, a face that was now precious to her, she set down the glass and turned to leave. "I'll be ready."

☙ ❦ ❧

The next morning Simon was waiting when Nate arrived, a small bundle over one shoulder and a note in his hand. Still disturbed by Claire's antics the day before, and the fear he'd felt when he'd learned she'd left the house, Simon accepted the note and lifted the seal.

Three Frenchmen in hold. Not talking. We sail with the tide. –J.

He looked into the lad's anxious eyes. "Thank you, Nate. Wait here." He headed toward the stairs. "I will return shortly."

Just as he raised his hand to knock on Claire's door, it opened and Cornelia came bursting out, her silk skirts rustling and her cheeks tear-stained.

"I will sorely miss her," said the baroness, dabbing at her eyes with a handkerchief, "as will our friends who, even in the short time she has been here, have come to love her."

He held Cornelia's gaze for a moment, then passing her, entered the bedchamber. He well understood what it would be to miss the French girl. He dreaded the moment when he must let her go. Though he knew it was inevitable, the prospect hung over him like a black cloud.

Claire stood in front of the bed, a portmanteau at her feet. "Lady Danvers loaned me her case."

She was wearing the simple blue traveling gown he had given her in Dieppe, the one she had worn for her jaunt to the wharf the day before. It only made her eyes, now filled with tears, a brighter blue. He steeled himself against the emotion he ached to allow himself. He had been concerned when he'd learned she had gone for a walk in Mayfair and angry she'd somehow slipped through his net, but to discover she'd been at the wharf! An innocent like her, alone on the quay, surrounded by purse-cuts, thieves, hard-faced doxies and the scum of the world's oceans. The mischief that might have happened to her gave him a chill of fear but her role in it made him angry.

He reached into his pocket and thrust a box at her. "Here," he said roughly. "Put it on."

She took the velvet box and opened it. Inside was the ring

he'd had a footman procure for him, a wide gold band of excellent workmanship.

She looked at the ring and then up at him. "A wedding ring?"

"Aye. You will pose as my wife. It will spare us questions and delay." He dropped his eyes, muttering, "...and it might keep you safe."

She slipped the ring on her finger. "How long will the journey take?"

"Two long days of travel with an overnight at a coaching inn." She looked up in question. "Trust me, by tonight you will be glad for a rest from the constant jarring on the uneven roads. It's not like the gentle roll of a ship."

"I've traveled by carriage before, sir. I know what to expect."

Her stubborn insistence made him smile. She was still angry—they both were. "I can see that you do."

She asked no further questions. By now she had to know something of his privateering and was well aware of the threat from her father's men so close in London.

He picked up the case and gestured her to the door. "We must go."

She gathered her cloak and stepped into the corridor, her shoulders back and her face set in determined fashion. Among the things he admired most about Claire Donet was that she did not engage in unnecessary prattle. She would walk bravely to her fate. Or perhaps she knew him too well to argue.

A short while later, they were seated across from each other in the carriage headed south to Sussex. Nate had asked if he could ride on top next to the coachman. When Simon saw how fascinated his cabin boy was with the heavy, old blunderbuss the coachman had stashed beneath the seat, he agreed. Simon himself carried a pistol in his coat and a knife in his boot, mindful that lurking highwaymen still presented a danger on the well-traveled roads.

He gazed across the carriage at the woman who had

vexed him the first night he'd encountered her in Saint-Denis. As a girl of sixteen, she'd been bewitching. At eighteen she was a dazzling beauty and more sensual than she knew. What would she be in her twenties when she came fully into womanhood? Even as an older woman, he was certain she would carry herself with grace and dignity.

"You would stare, sir?" she said, raising her chin defiantly.

"I would look my fill," he said in a low voice, holding her gaze. In truth, he could not look away.

The blush that spread across her face rendered her fair skin a warm pink, making him smile. Aye, he would like to look at that face and hear her sharp tongue for the rest of his life.

～ ❧ ～

Looking off the stern, Elijah stuffed his pipe into his coat pocket and shielded his eyes from the glare of the sun shooting through the clouds as the Fairwinds glided out of the Pool of London, heading toward the mouth of the Thames. He was relieved to be leaving London and its busy port. Rye Harbor was more his kind of place. There, he could lift a tankard with his mates at the Mermaid Inn and swap stories of their days at sea.

He lifted the spyglass to his eye to survey the ships on the river to see if any followed in their wake. He expected the Frenchie was there somewhere, lurking. Peering into the distance, he ignored the smaller ships. Suddenly a sloop flying a British merchant flag sallied forth as nice as you please.

Crossing the short distance to the helm, he handed the glass to the first mate. "'Tis a sloop followin', sir. Ye might take a look. I'd bet good coin 'tis the Frenchman."

Jordan took up the spyglass and leveled his gaze on the approaching sloop. When he lowered the spyglass, handing it back to Elijah, there was a deep scowl on his face. "You might be right. I'll do a few maneuvers to see just how closely she sticks with us." He turned and took the wheel from the helmsman.

The Thames was crowded with ships as it always was, but Elijah admired the first mate's nimble handling of the wheel as he tacked, testing the invisible tether that seemed to be tied between the two ships. The sloop fought to keep her sails billowing out as she tacked around the ships in her path to keep up with the *Fairwinds*.

No doubt remained in Elijah's mind. They were being followed. "Aye, 'tis the pirate hisself."

"He knows what he's about, that Frenchman," conceded the first mate, his hands steady on the wheel.

His gaze fixed on the sloop, Elijah silently agreed. No ship would take such risks unless her captain was determined to overtake the *Fairwinds*. And few were as good as Donet in navigating the ship-clogged river.

"A new set of clothes," said Jordan, "but still the same French privateer intent on rescuing his daughter. Appears the captain had the right of it in when he took his captive over land to Rye."

Elijah watched the sloop cutting smoothly through the waters like a dolphin and wondered how long they could stay ahead of it. The waters of the Thames were rough this day. The tide was running hard and there was a stiff counter breeze.

The sloop drew closer. Elijah lifted the spyglass to his eye. "She carries as many guns as we do, sir."

"I noticed that myself. I've no intention to become Donet's target in the Channel." With that, the first mate called "Ready about!" and turned the wheel hard to port.

The sloop made its own course change bearing down hard upon them. She was closing fast.

Elijah raised the glass and saw Donet striding the deck, his black hair blowing in the wind. "That's one persistent Frenchie," said Elijah, raising his voice to be heard above the wind.

"She may overtake us," said Jordan. "Or she may just dog

our heels until we are in the Channel and then use her guns. Either way, I'll not allow the crew to join those from the *Abundance*. We'll fight if we have to. Have men stand by the guns."

"Sir, ye might want to reconsider," Elijah cautioned, lowering the glass. "The Thames is no place for a game o' touch-and-go."

The first mate glanced over his shoulder at the sloop dogging them. "All right then. How about a game of hide and seek?"

Elijah grinned. He approved of Jordan's intended action. "Might jus' work, sir."

Jordan spun the wheel and the *Fairwinds* slanted away, cutting across the river to intersect a lumbering collier working its way upriver. The nimble schooner crossed in front of the slower ship and ducked behind her bulk. A smart move that, thought Elijah.

The first mate spun the wheel again, dodging between another collier and an anchored hulk. He spared another glance behind and grinned. "We got lucky."

To avoid a collision, the Frenchman was forced to tack away. Then, when he'd tried to tack back, his ship became mired in the snarl of the oncoming ships, falling hopelessly behind.

When it was clear Donet's sloop had been cut off by the collier, Elijah shared a smile with the first mate.

Elijah glanced aloft at the sails as the first mate spun the wheel again, threading their way through the armada of colliers to the clear flow of the river and out to the Channel beyond.

"That there was some fancy sailin'," he said to the first mate.

"'Twas more luck than skill—and it was close."

Chapter 16

"Oh!" Claire braced herself against the window as the carriage hit a rock nearly sending her flying off the seat.

Simon reached his arm out to steady her. "Are you all right?"

"Yes, I am now." The carriage was nothing like the ones she'd ridden in around Paris. For one thing, it lacked the springs she was used to. And the roads there were not so rutted. Still, despite the bouncing and the rough going, she could not tear her eyes from the handsome captain whose penetrating gaze was making her feel as if she were disrobed.

How was she to spend two days and a night with him?

She twisted the ring on her finger. His eyes darted to her hand. On his face was the beginning of a scowl. *He thinks I resent it and would take it off.* He was wrong. She wished the ring were not a ruse, but real. To share his life of adventure was only a dream, but one she cherished.

He turned his face to the window and the verdant countryside beyond. Looking at him now she wondered, what did *he* want? Surely it wasn't only the return of his men. But he'd made clear their feelings did not matter. But not speaking of them did not make them any less real. While she had not asked to love him, she could not deny the truth of it. She wanted nothing more than to remain by his side.

She had thought her vow to Élise right, even noble. But since she'd fallen in love with the captain, she now doubted her intended course. If she were honest with herself, guilt and good intentions did not amount to a calling to the habit, nor did it follow that her chosen course was God's choice for her. The Reverend Mother had been right. Claire sighed with the realization. She was trying to live another's life. When she allowed herself to dream of her own future, her thoughts were of an English privateer, not the cloistered life.

Turning to gaze out the window at the green countryside, she watched rolling hills covering the landscape dotted with small farms and copses of trees. It was not unlike the countryside of Northern France, which she had always thought romantically bucolic.

He had braced himself with his boot pressed into the base of her seat, his strong thigh muscles flexing beneath his tight breeches. She held on to keep from being jostled about, though she was not entirely successful. The constant bouncing was jarring.

They stopped more than once to change horses and to allow themselves a chance to take the air on solid ground and find some refreshment. Though the stops were only brief respites, the coachman had managed at each stop to accept a mug from one of the tavern girls.

In no time, they were back on the road. A sigh escaped her as she sank into the padded seat. The long silence between them had grown uncomfortable. She found that she could not make herself stay angry with him, not when it was obvious his main concern had been for her safety. So she decided to make use of the hours stretching before them by asking the captain about his youth.

"What made you choose a life at sea?"

His amber eyes turned from the window to focus on her. He hesitated as if deciding what he would say. "'Tis what any lad growing up in Dartmouth would think of. Merchant ships with their tall masts and bulging cargoes captured my interest from the time I was a boy. When the opportunity came to join the crew of a merchantman sailing to the Caribbean, I took it."

"And you liked it."

"I was good at figures, so learning navigation came easy. Before too many years, I was first mate. Aye, I liked it."

"And now you are a captain. You were good at more than figures." She thought he was better than good. From the words of his crew, he might be the best. When his hands took the wheel of his schooner, it was something to behold. "And you chose what you were to do."

"You did not choose the convent, I take it."

"No, my papa chose for me. But I am not sorry for it. I stayed longer than most of the students, of course. And because the Mother Superior took an interest, I learned much the other students did not. Unlike some girls of the aristocracy, I learned more than how to manage a home. I studied the world of literature and so much more. I am grateful for their instruction."

"Confined as you were, considering the result, I'd say they did you a good turn."

She couldn't resist a smile at his offhanded compliment. "They are very learned and very wise. It's a teaching Order, you see."

"Yes, I remember what you told me. And of your friend who died, the one who wanted to teach the children. Do you also want to teach children?"

The glint in his eyes hinted of amusement and more. Was his question aimed at her desire to teach the children at the convent, or interest in teaching children of her own? For some reason, she thought it might be the latter. "Why yes, Captain, I love children."

She looked out the window, thinking of the younger students at the convent. For a long time after Élise had died, the youngest of them had reminded her of the frail blonde girl, but no longer. The nightmares had stopped and she had begun to think of her young friend as being in Heaven. Did Élise teach children there? The idea brought a smile to Claire's face. If there were children in Heaven, and she was certain there were for death in infancy and disease had claimed many, then that is what Élise would be doing.

She returned her gaze to the captain, who was now watching the countryside go by. Her eyes lingered on his face, the high forehead, the strong nose, the determined jaw. A man whose very countenance told her he had faced his demons and overcome them. A man she respected. A man she loved.

Toward evening, the carriage slowed as they entered a village, finally stopping in front of a three-story, red brick inn. The sun still lingered in the sky reflecting off the gold lettering of the wooden sign that read The Rose & Crown. The coachman opened the door, pulled down the few stairs for them to alight and quietly informed the captain, "We have arrived in Tonbridge, sir."

The captain leaped out, turned and offered his hand. She took it, allowing him to help her down. An unexpected weariness washed over her when her feet touched the ground, making her glad for his strength. "You were correct, Captain. I will be most happy to have a night's rest in a bed that is not moving." He, on the other hand, did not even look tired, much less weary. "I envy your energy after so long in that bouncing conveyance."

He chuckled. "I don't mind the long carriage ride even if it is difficult to sleep or read for all the bumps. But it would have been slower had we taken the public coach. And just imagine the journey with the elbows of strangers in your ribs."

She cringed at the thought. "It was most kind of you to arrange for a private carriage." She knew it had to be costly.

"I would have preferred the ship."

Knowing the reason they did not take his ship to Rye, she said nothing. She had no desire to remind him that her papa had followed them to London and that she had tried to find him there.

"A ship is not so bumbling and rough, not so dusty," he continued.

"And not so many bruises," she said, feeling the effect of

the carriage's last encounter with a rock.

Nate climbed down from atop the carriage and caught her portmanteau as the coachman threw it to him. The captain gently cupped her elbow and guided her into the inn, his case in his other hand.

Her legs still wobbly, she was glad for the captain's support.

Nate followed them with his own small bundle and her portmanteau.

Inside, lighted only with lanterns and a small fire burning in the fireplace, the inn was dim until her eyes adjusted. She waited with Nate while the captain handled the business of securing them rooms. In the background, she heard the noise of many people and wondered if they were eating in the common room. She was hungry after their long day of travel.

"Nate," the captain announced above the noise of the inn upon his return, "I've secured a chamber for Mrs. Powell and a private sitting room for our meal; see about some food while I take my wife upstairs."

Claire was startled at the name and the status he'd bestowed upon her, but Nate didn't blink an eye. He merely nodded, handed her portmanteau to the captain and headed for the common room. The cabin boy must have been forewarned that she traveled as the captain's wife. How silly of her not to have anticipated the name when he'd given her the wedding ring. While the deception bothered her, the idea of being Mrs. Powell did not.

The captain took her arm and led her up the stairs. The room he opened with the key he took from his pocket was large though sparsely furnished with a four-poster bed, a round table and chairs. Since it was summer the green bed curtains were drawn back and tied at the posts. On a side table under the one window sat a flowered basin and pitcher of water. At least all appeared clean.

"I'll give you some time to freshen up. I'll send Nate up to escort you to dinner. I want to talk to the coachman before

I meet you in our private sitting room."

"Is your room next door?" She wanted to know if he was close should she need him—or his protection.

"Closer." He grinned. "I'll be sharing the room with you."

Shocked he would even consider such a thing, she spit out, "You will not!"

"Aye, but I will. The innkeeper would think it most unusual should a husband and wife have more than one room when many guests, even strangers, share beds."

"But I must protest."

"'Twill do you no good. I assure you it is necessary. You needn't worry for your virtue."

"But—"

He turned and left, leaving her staring at the closed door, wondering how she was to manage a whole night in the same room with him. He might have his reasons, but she was not pleased. He had just assumed it would be fine with her. It was not. She might have shared his cabin on the ship, but not while he was in it!

❦

Claire's look of incredulity when he'd told her they'd be sharing a bedchamber was nearly worth the agony he would experience spending the night in that same bedchamber unable to touch her. He must be one of her Catholic saints to even think it possible.

After a word to Nate, he left the inn to speak to the coachman. He found the man in the stable instructing the groom on the proper care of his horses. At his approach, the coachman waved off the groom.

"These are fine animals," Simon told the coachman as he ran his hand down the glistening, reddish coat of one gelding. In truth, he'd not seen finer horseflesh.

The coachman beamed his approval. "I've been on this route for several years and deal only with inns that keep good horses."

"I came to discuss tomorrow's travel. We start early, aye?"

"Dawn if you like, sir."

"Dawn it is. I'd like to be in Rye as soon as your fine horses can get us there."

He left the stable walking slowing back to the inn, reminding himself to ask the innkeeper to prepare some food for their early departure. The long day on the road suddenly caught up with him and he felt the protest of muscles that had not been used in a while. Keeping one's balance on a moving deck required very different muscles than a jarring carriage ride. But the thought of a good beef steak with potatoes, plum pudding and a hunk of Cheshire cheese revived his spirits and quickened his step. A dinner with Claire would be just what he needed.

He had just stepped into the entry when he heard a loud commotion coming from the common room off to one side. Striding towards the noise, a foreboding gripped him. *What trouble has arisen now?* He hoped Nate and Claire were tucked away in the private sitting room.

The sight that met his eyes in the busy common room had him reaching for the knife in his boot as he stalked toward the object of his ire. On the other side of the room Claire was pressed against the wall by a brigand, filthy from the road, who was running his grubby hand over her soft flesh.

Struggling against the man's greater strength for all she was worth, Claire shouted, "Let me go!"

Simon surged across the room, a primitive rage rising in his chest with each long stride. Reaching the brigand, he forced the edge of his blade against the man's neck. A trickle of blood ran into his collar. He froze.

In a too calm voice, Simon said, "Unhand my wife or you'll not see tomorrow."

Behind him, chairs screeched loudly as people rose from the tables and backed away. He could hear their intake of breath as they glimpsed his knife.

The brigand released Claire, raised his hands in the air, and slowly turned, sidling away. "Meant nothin' by it guv'ner. Just out for a bit o' fun. Thought she were a kitchen girl or one o' the wenches."

Claire rushed into Simon's arms. She was shaking and a sob escaped her throat.

"I'm sorry sweetheart," he said, drawing her close with one arm while holding his knife in the other and freezing the brigand with his harsh glare.

The serving wench, holding a tray of tankards, passed the brigand. "Told ye she were taken, ye dolt. Did ye not see her ring, her clothes or this fine gentleman who brung her in?"

The brigand slowly lowered his hands, his face pale beneath the dirt. "I see... now."

Simon was still deciding what to do with the man when, out of the corner of his eye, he caught movement across the room. There in the corner, Nate struggled in the arms of a rough looking character covered in dust from the road. Likely the partner of the one who'd assaulted Claire.

"Let go of the lad," Simon bellowed, "or I'll be sinking my knife in your gut."

The man's gaze shifted from Nate to the knife still in Simon's hand. He loosened his hold on the cabin boy just as Nate sank his teeth into the man's hand. With a curse, the man backhanded the boy, sending him flying across the room where he fell to the floor hitting his head on the edge of the hearth. Blood seeped from beneath his temple to the wooden floor.

Claire shrieked and ran to kneel by the lad, lifting his bleeding head into her lap.

Simon shoved his knife in his boot, stomped toward the man who'd hit Nate and sent his fist into the dirty face. The man lumbered away from the punch. His companion, who'd been standing their gaping, grabbed his companion by the jacket and, without a word, hauled him toward the door leading from the common room to the inn's entry.

Simon followed, his only thought to punish them for touching Claire and hurting Nate.

The innkeeper, apparently summoned to the room by the commotion, rushed to Simon's side, apologizing profusely. It did not slow Simon's advance on the two brigands who were hastening to the entrance to the inn.

The innkeeper kept pace with him, urging him to let the miscreants go.

Reaching the front door just before Simon, the two brigands took one look at Simon and fled.

The innkeeper shouted after them, "Yer business is no longer welcome! Stick to the highway where ye footpads belong." Then to Simon, "Sir, they won't bother ye again."

Concerned more with Claire and Nate than the two fleeing cowards, Simon turned from the door and hastened to where Claire knelt at Nate's side. He watched as she gently wiped the blood from the boy's temple with a cloth the serving wench handed her.

"How bad is it?" he asked.

"I think he's just knocked out," she said anxiously. "He's breathing and the cut is not too bad."

Simon knelt and brushed back the hair from Nate's face to examine the rising lump on his head. She was right; the cut was not deep though he'd have a bad headache from his head hitting the stone. "He's a good lad, and he's strong. He'll recover." He hoped it was true. The boy was like a younger brother to him.

"He should not be left on the cold floor," she said.

"Aye, you're right." Lifting Nate into his arms, Simon rose and carried him through the crowded common room toward the stairs.

Claire picked up the boy's hat from the floor and followed.

The innkeeper stepped into their path. "Sir, ye need not take him to yer room. I've a room in the back where ye can lay the lad. 'Tis warm and private. He'll be comfortable there."

The room the innkeeper led them to was just down the corridor from the common room. There, he found a small bed, some crates and sacks of flour. After opening the door for Simon, the innkeeper lit a candle and placed it on the small bedside table. "I'll see the leech is fetched. We've a good 'un in the village."

Claire looked up at Simon from where she had perched on the edge of the bed, holding Nate's hand. Her caring for the lad touched Simon.

An hour later the village healer had come and gone and Nate had awakened, his color returning to his cheeks.

Concern filled the boy's face as his eyes fixed on his mistress. "Are ye all right?"

Claire nodded and smiled. "I should be asking you that question, Nate. How do you feel?"

"There's a poundin' in my head, else I'm fine." Nate's hand rose to where he now had a large lump on his head and his gaze darted to Simon. "They were waitin' fer us when we came into the common room, Cap'n. 'Twas my fault. I shoulda seen 'em."

"It was no fault of yours, Nate. I should have stayed with you both. But I did not expect such a villainous act in The Rose and Crown."

The innkeeper, who'd been hovering outside, had apparently heard the comment. He hastened into the small room. "Yer right, sir. And 'twill not happen again. Why not let the lad rest and ye and yer lady have yer meal? Yer private dinin' room's close. Tonight ye'll eat at me own expense. And I'll see food is brought to the boy."

Simon studied Nate trying to judge for himself how the lad fared.

"I'll be fine, Cap'n."

"I don't think we should leave him alone," said Claire. "I can stay; I'm not very hungry." Simon was struck by what a good mother she would be, caring and sympathetic. But she needed to eat. His cabin boy would be well-tended while they were in the private room.

"Truly, mistress," urged Nate. "I'm all right. I'll just have me supper here. 'Tis not often I'm the one served."

"Are you sure?" Claire asked the boy. "I would be most happy to dine with you."

The cabin boy looked at Simon, then back to Claire. "Nay, you go."

"All right," she said with apparent reluctance.

Simon touched her shoulder and she rose.

"We won't be long," he assured Nate.

He put his arm around Claire's shoulder as they walked from the room, only to offer comfort, he told himself, happy she was safe.

They walked the short distance to the small, but well-appointed private room where he pulled out a chair for her and poured them both some of the red wine delivered by the innkeeper himself.

Soon after, a servant brought them their long delayed supper.

෬ ⁍ ෨

Staring into her plate, Claire shuddered at the memory of the horrible man pawing her. She could still feel his rough hands on her breasts and smell his foul breath. Thank God Simon had rescued her. It seemed she was ever running into the captain's arms—the one place she felt safe.

Adventure was all very well and good but it had its consequences.

From the time she was a young girl in Lorient, she had longed for adventure, inspired by stories her mother had read to her of an Englishman shipwrecked and imprisoned in a place called Lilliput, a land of tiny but aggressive people. She wondered now if she hadn't stumbled on to that very place.

Perhaps she'd had quite enough adventure. But upon reflection, she admitted to herself her adventures had brought her to Simon, her golden one, to her friends among his crew, and to Cornelia, the baron and Captain Field.

And her adventures had brought her love.

Looking into Simon's face as he ate his dinner, his golden hair more streaked by the sun than when she'd first met him, she knew she could ask no more of life than to remain by his side for as long as she could. The only adventures she wanted were with him.

She had learned one thing: People were just people. Everywhere there were good ones and bad ones, no matter they were poor or rich, common or noble. Whether they be French, American or English. While she hoped to meet no more bad ones, she knew life was not always a smooth road. More often it was bumpy like the road they'd taken from London.

"I'm sorry for what happened to you," he said, setting down his two-pronged fork. "I should not have left you and the lad alone."

She looked into his worried gaze. "It was... awful until you came. You were like a storm sweeping away the terror. But when the other man hit Nate, I was so worried the boy was hurt badly."

"I would have killed that stinking oaf had not the innkeeper intervened."

"It was good he did. I'd not want to see you hauled off to face a magistrate, or worse."

"The lad likes you, you know," he said, changing the subject, "more than a little."

"And I like him. He's like the younger brother I never had."

"He'd be most disappointed to hear you call him a brother," he murmured to his food. His eyes shifted to her still full plate. "Aren't you hungry?" he asked, stabbing another slice of his beef steak with his fork. He ate as if he hadn't eaten in days.

Claire glanced at the mushy vegetables and potatoes lying

on her plate alongside the too large portion of meat. "Not very."

"You'll need your strength for tomorrow," he urged. She could see he was worried. He wanted a sign she had recovered from the distress she had experienced at the hand of the pawing clod in the common room.

"Very well." She would not allow him to worry needlessly. She speared a small potato on her fork. It was highly seasoned with pepper but tasty. It reminded her of McGinnes' stews.

After a few more bites of potatoes, washed down with wine and accompanied by a small chunk of the yellow cheese, she felt full and was glad to see her efforts brought a smile to his face.

He reached out and squeezed her hand. "It will be all right, you'll see. After a good sleep, you and Nate will feel much better." His hand lingered over hers, sending warmth flowing through her. She would have been content for him to leave it there. Alas, he did not.

"Nate was very brave, you know," she said as he lifted his hand from hers. "He tried to protect me."

"The lad has a strong heart. And perhaps he is overly fond of you."

She smiled at him and the potatoes.

Once the captain had finished his pudding, he rose from the table. "We'd best check on Nate and then get some rest. Another long day awaits us tomorrow."

❧ 🙞 ❧

Nate seemed to be recovering well, stuffing his face with his dinner, when Simon looked in on him, Claire following on his heels. The innkeeper told them the room was Nate's for the night, which pleased Claire.

"How do you feel?" she asked him.

"'Cept fer my head, I feel good," Nate said with a mouth full of his supper.

195

Simon looked around the small room. It was warm and clean. "You're all right here, lad?"

"Aye, Cap'n."

Taking Claire's hand, Simon bid the boy goodnight and led her upstairs to the room they would share. He shut the door behind them as they entered. Doffing his coat and hat, he turned his back to her and removed his waistcoat and boots. "I'll not watch as you disrobe, though I'm tempted," he said with a chuckle.

"Don't you dare turn around, Simon Powell, till I tell you I'm ready."

He waited for some minutes, then smiled as he heard her climb into the bed. Not waiting for her assent, he turned to see the fetching innocent curled up on her side, staring at him.

"Somehow I knew you would do as you would," she said.

"I'll take the floor," he offered. He was certain with Claire so close, he would not sleep anyway.

"That is the least you can do considering how sinful it is for us to share a room. Here"—she handed him a pillow—"take this and the extra blanket."

"If you wish," he said accepting both the items and her criticism. Likely a convent-raised girl would consider the temptation presented to be the work of the devil. What did it matter if the hell he'd experience this night from being so close to her but unable to touch her was as hard as oak planks?

He blew out the candle and stretched out on the blanket he'd laid on the floor next to the bed, punching the pillow into an acceptable shape. Eventually, exhausted and with a full stomach, he drifted off to sleep.

When the small feminine cries of panic awoke him, he was not even surprised. But it was not the ghost of the French girl, Élise, who stalked Claire's dreams this night. From her muffled cries, he could tell it was the brigand who'd attacked her at the inn.

He rose and sat on the edge of her bed, soothing her as he brushed the sweat-dampened strands of her hair from her forehead. "'Tis all right, Claire. You're safe now. He'll never hurt you again."

After a while, she quieted and snuggled against his thigh resting on the bed. He was sleepy and began to sway in the dark room. Giving in to the temptation of the soft bed, he lay down beside her on top of the cover, breathing in the same lavender scent he had smelled earlier when she was in his arms. He knew, in that moment, temptation would forever smell like lavender.

Though she did not wake, she snuggled closer and, draping her arm across his chest, sighed. He reined in his desire for more, and placed his hand on her head, holding it to his chest, plagued with visions of making love to her.

And that is how he passed the night, she sleeping contentedly, tucked into his warmth, and he wide awake, hoping Amos was on his way back to Rye from Lorient with good news.

Chapter 17

Rye Harbor

The carriage arrived in Rye late the next afternoon. The three of them had ridden inside with Nate's head in Claire's lap for most of the day. Simon suspected the boy was taking full advantage of Claire's tender heart, but no matter. Though he would have preferred to be alone with her, the lad likely deserved her coddling after what he'd been through.

Simon stepped down from the carriage, thanked the coachman and handed him the agreed upon sum for their transport, and a bit more. He studied the sky, pleased that the heavy clouds were holding off their rain.

In the harbor, the *Fairwinds* sat at anchor bringing a smile to his face. His schooner was more home to him than any other place.

Once they were on board, he saw Claire to his cabin where he shed his hat and coat, ordered Nate to get them some food, and then sought out Jordan and Elijah. He was anxious to hear the news from France.

"Giles an' me jus' arrived when the *Fairwinds* sailed into the harbor, Cap'n," said Elijah, puffing on his pipe.

"I'd like to speak with Giles, as well," said Simon. Waving his hand in the air, he beckoned the sailmaker to where he stood with Elijah and Jordan on the quarterdeck.

When Giles reached them, Simon acknowledged him with a nod and turned to Jordan. "How went your departure from London?"

"We were not alone, if that's what you're asking. I wasn't sure at first it was Donet who followed us. He sailed another English sloop flying the flag of a British merchantman. But the sloop followed us closely and, at one point on the Thames, I got a glimpse of his black hair on the deck of the ship."

"But he did not overtake you?"

"He tried," said the first mate, "and nearly succeeded."

"Mr. Landor pulled some fancy sailin'," said Elijah.

"The truth is," Jordan clarified, "a lumbering collier helped us out. Sailed right across Donet's path so he could not tack, else the Frenchman would have had us."

"Well, however you did it, you brought the *Fairwinds* back," said Simon, "and I am grateful."

"My pleasure," said his first mate.

"How was your ride south, Cap'n?" asked Elijah.

"'Twas not without excitement." At their inquiring looks, he explained, "We had a bit of trouble in Tonbridge. Nate got a bump on the head for his efforts to protect the mademoiselle from a rough character taken with her beauty, but the lad's fine now. And so is she." Simon had no intention of revealing the horror he'd experienced at seeing the man's hands on Claire or the murderous intent it gave rise to. Reminding himself of the question burning in his mind, he asked, "Is Amos back yet?" He hadn't seen the *Abundance*'s burly first mate since he'd come aboard.

Jordan's brow furrowed. "No, but I've been expecting him."

Simon stared off the starboard toward France. "I hope I haven't sent him on some wild goose chase."

Returning his gaze to Elijah and Giles, he said, "I assume you have the arrangements for the exchange?"

"Ye won't like 'em, Cap'n," said the old salt. "'Tis Calais, four days hence. We lost some time returnin' from Paris with a broken axle on the coach and bad weather in the crossin'."

Calais. Four days more with Claire. It was not enough. He wanted more. Hell, he wanted a lifetime. "Four days doesn't leave us much time. Do you think the *Abundance*'s crew is there already?"

"Can't say," said Elijah, "but could be. 'Else he's bringin' 'em by ship just in time for the exchange."

Simon studied the faces of the two men he'd sent to Paris, wondering if they were holding back bad news. "Did Donet's man say anything about the condition of the crew? Did all survive their wounds?"

"I asked Donet's quartermaster, Cap'n," said Giles. "He's a gruff character by the name of Bequel. Seemed honest enough on that point, though. Said they have some physician in Lorient who works miracles. All have recovered or are on the mend."

Inwardly, Simon breathed a sigh of relief. Wingate and his men were well.

"And what of the ship? Has Donet agreed to return it?"

Giles and Elijah exchanged a look before the sailmaker gave voice to Simon's fear. "He won't return the ship, sir. Bequel said it was already committed to a purpose and when I asked, he declined most rudely to disclose what it was."

Damn. The *Abundance* had cost him thousands of pounds. He would not give her up so easily. "One way or another, once I have the crew, I'll go after my ship."

"The crew will be happy to join you," said Jordan, surprising Simon with the enthusiasm in his voice for what they both knew would be a dangerous task.

Elijah shoved some folded papers into Simon's hand. "From the Scribe, sir."

Simon tucked the papers into his waistband. "We'll wait two days for Amos to return. Then we weigh anchor for Calais."

Regan Walker

 ⟳ ⁕ ⟲

When she was alone, Claire surveyed the captain's cabin. It was just as it had been when she'd left. It smelled of the man who made it his home. Though she was well aware she was still a captive, she was oddly happy to be back on the *Fairwinds*. Not just because the constant swaying and bouncing of the carriage was at an end. She'd missed the crew. This time, when she'd climbed aboard the *Fairwinds*, some of them had waved her a greeting. Even the first mate, Mr. Landor, who must have forgiven her the escape attempt in London, looked pleased to see her. Perhaps he'd explained to the crew she was not a spy after all. The ship had begun to feel like home. More, it was his ship and she felt close to him when she was in his cabin, among his things.

Her fingers idly brushed over his chronometer sitting on his desk and she remembered with shame the time she'd tossed it onto a pile of debris on the deck. She valued such things now not just because she realized their worth, but because they were important to him.

How long would she remain on his ship? As the carriage had neared Rye, she had experienced anxious thoughts, knowing the inevitable exchange loomed on the horizon. Soon she would be returned to her papa. Soon Simon would have his kidnapped crew. And though she felt happiness at both events, they also portended ill, for soon she would see him no more.

Somewhere on the journey from London to Rye, she had decided not to return to Saint-Denis, except to say goodbye. Her time with the English captain had convinced her that whatever God intended for her life, it was not the life of a nun. If one day she taught children, they would be her own.

The cabin door opened and a beaming Nate stepped inside carrying a tray. "Hello, mistress. I've brought ye and the cap'n some food."

Before he had closed the cabin door with his foot, she

had noticed there was no guard posted even though they were in port. She supposed one was hardly necessary now. She had no desire to escape him and he must know it, too.

"Here, let me help," she said, taking the tray and setting it on the pedestal table. "How are you feeling?"

"Fine, mistress."

"Stay and keep me company."

"I suppose the cap'n won't mind if I stay a bit," he said, slipping into one of the chairs. "He's on deck talkin' to some of the men."

"Do you want some food?"

"I had a bowl of stew in the galley with McGinnes."

She removed the cover of one bowl and inhaled the rising steam. "It smells wonderful. Perhaps I'll have some before the captain returns." She was hungry and the stew was good, a hearty fare, tasting of the spices she had suggested to the Irish cook that went well with lamb. "McGinnes grows more expert at his craft."

"Aye. One of the crew told me they've been eatin' better."

"Did McGinnes say anything about trouble as they sailed from London?" She had to know if her papa had gone after the *Fairwinds*.

"Aye. McGinnes said a sloop followed them out of the Pool of London but with all the ships on the river, Mr. Landor was able to slip away. Once in the Channel, he set a fast course fer Rye."

The cabin boy rose with an apologetic look. "I'd best let the cap'n know the food's here. He'll be hungry."

When Nate left, Claire rested her chin in her upturned hand, her elbow on the table. So her papa had pursued Simon's ship. Was he hoping to rescue her so he didn't have to return the captain's men? She would never have allowed him to do that without arguing for their freedom. Would he have listened? The papa she had thought she knew would have listened, but the man he seemed now was so very different. She was not at all certain she really knew him.

Tired from their carriage ride and exhausted from the night before and her concern for what her papa had done, Claire looked longingly toward the bed. Perhaps she might have a small nap.

✺

Simon opened his cabin door. All was quiet within. His stomach rumbled when he smelled the lamb stew. Directly in front of him, the table was set with his meal, but beyond that, curled up on top of the blue cover on his bed, was the raven-haired beauty. A few strides took him to her. She was lying on her side, facing the cabin door. His hand caressed her warm cheek, her alabaster skin glowing even in sleep. Strands of black hair curled around her face. He brushed them aside.

Beautiful Claire.

Wild at heart, courageous and caring. A real lady. Too good for the likes of him. But he wanted her all the same. The urge to make love to her was so strong he had to turn from her or he would fail in his resolve to return her untouched. He must focus on his missing men.

Simon had never underestimated his enemies and he would not do so now. Donet would take vengeance on the *Abundance*'s crew if his daughter were not returned as she was when Simon had abducted her. Innocent.

But if the truth be told, neither he nor Claire was the same. Both had changed. He loved the wild girl he could tame with his kiss. And he wanted her for his own. He knew she had a certain fondness for him, had softened to her captor, else she would not seek comfort in his arms when she was frightened. In time, she might even come to love him. If he could find his men, he might convince her to stay. He'd hoped Amos had returned with news of the *Abundance*'s crew and was disappointed when he was not on the ship. Simon was nearly out of time.

Sinking into a chair, he pulled from his waistband the

papers Elijah had given him, glancing at them as he ate. More inane writings of Edward Edward that only Eden's chemicals could decipher. He would send one of his trusted men with them to London while he sailed to Calais.

༄ ༜ ༄

The next two days were given over to readying the *Fairwinds* to sail. As the duties assigned were completed, Simon kept one eye on Rye, the hill town rising behind the harbor and one eye on the Channel. There was only one question in his mind. *Where was Amos?*

Standing next to him on the quarterdeck, Jordan must have read his thoughts. "Elijah tells me there's been no word of our men sent to Lorient."

It was time to face the inevitable. "We sail tomorrow with the tide whether Amos makes an appearance tonight or not, else we'll be late to Calais."

"Aye, Cap'n. She's ready."

Simon knew his first mate referred to the ship, but he had to wonder. Was Claire ready to return to her father? He had steeled himself for what must be done, but he was none too happy. He'd long known that life sometimes required sacrifices, but this was one he was loath to make. Letting Claire Donet return to France was going to kill him.

Chapter 18

Lorient, France

Jean Donet set aside his copy of the Journal de Paris and picked up his café au lait to gaze out the large window overlooking the harbor in the room where he took his déjeuner when he was at home in Lorient. The article on the pending negotiations for peace that he'd found waiting for him upon his return had been most interesting. The people of France, increasingly unhappy with the king, were wondering what they might gain in the final treaty. Few knew just how much the American war had cost France, too much if the government's money woes were known. The war must end and soon.

His eyes focused on the harbor's cerulean waters where half a dozen ships and smaller boats were taking advantage of the strong onshore breezes. Though the sun was shining in a blue sky in the west, to the north dark clouds were dropping a curtain of rain. Was it raining where Claire was?

Impatience for her return made him anxious for action. He had waited long enough for this game to end. He must have his daughter back! He hoped she was still the Claire he remembered, the innocent daughter he loved. He had never stopped thinking of her in the time she'd been gone. Now he was desperate to know she was well.

Grudgingly, he acknowledged a growing respect for the English captain who held her as ransom for his men. Though Powell's spies sent to Lorient had quickly become known to Jean, and thus easily captured, he had to admire the Englishman's bold action in pursuing what he wanted. It had become like a game of chess, each stealing the other's pawns, a few knights captured and the queen threatened, the tension rising with every move. Still the game proceeded apace. What would be the English captain's next move?

He'd gained little from Powell's crewmembers and he would take no harsh measures to pry their story from them. He may have been a pirate but torture was not something he engaged in. He'd seen enough blood from battles at sea to be sickened by gratuitous pain. Besides, he knew why Powell had sent them. The English captain was searching for his men. Each held something the other wanted.

But was Claire safe in Powell's hands? Jean's men sent to Paris to negotiate the exchange had assured Émile she was unharmed and in good health, but the quartermaster had expressed his doubts, mirroring Jean's own thoughts. A girl as beautiful as Claire, alone with so many men, could hardly be out of danger. He would not turn over Powell's crew until he assured himself she was unharmed.

As for Powell's spies, what should he do with them? He could make a special gift of them to M'sieur Franklin, but perhaps it would be best to wait. After all, Powell had three of Jean's own crew. He was glad the Englishman had not captured all those Jean had sent to watch the *Fairwinds*. Those that remained had brought him word when the English captain made ready to sail. Losing Powell's ship in the congestion on the Thames had been a great disappointment. Had Claire been aboard? So close, yet still out of reach.

The repairs on *la Reine Noire*, made necessary by his tangle with Powell in the Channel, were nearly completed. He had been told that he would have his ship to sail to Calais. The sloop he had sailed to London was not the ship he wanted for the exchange. He wanted his own ship. He might need her sixteen guns to redeem his treasure.

There was still François de Dordogne to see to. Jean had managed to put off the young lawyer with the excuse of having Claire's wedding gown readied. It was not a lie. In truth, he had commissioned a gown of ivory satin embroidered with flowers from one of the finest modistes in Paris. But when Jean had made the excuse, Dordogne had not argued, saying Vergennes was keeping him busy drafting treaty provisions to be offered up to the British. Jean was glad Claire's betrothed remained unaware that she was being held prisoner by an English privateer. Her betrothed might reject her if he knew the truth.

All must believe she was with the good sisters in Saint-Denis.

Dordogne was young, ambitious and anxious to make a name for himself in serving Vergennes. That suited Jean. He wanted a man of good reputation for his daughter. But until he had Claire back, he could arrange no wedding.

Behind him his valet, Vernier, spoke. "M'sieur Bequel has arrived."

"By all means, show him in."

His quartermaster burst into the room with an uncharacteristic smile on his face. "Good news, *Capitaine*. The repairs on *la Reine Noire sont terminées*."

Jean rose, wiped his mouth on the napkin and set it aside "The guns?"

"All sixteen blackened and ready."

Jean slipped into his coat Vernier held open for him. "The new figurehead?"

"*Très bien*. She looks more like the Queen of France than before and she wears the costume of a shepherdess as you requested. All await your inspection."

"*Bien*, let us be at it." He cast one last glance through the window at the ships in the harbor whose sheets were filled with wind. "It's a good day to sail."

⌒ ๑ ⌒

Rye Harbor

It was the morning of the day they would set sail for Calais. Simon stood at the helm with his first mate, watching vessels moving in and out of the harbor while listening to his men attending their duty stations. The familiar sounds soothed him.

The anchor detail at the capstan winched in the cable, singing as they heaved against the bars. The sail handlers at their halyards were forming lines to be ready when the orders were given to haul away and set sail.

The deck had been swabbed, the guns blackened, the lines coiled and ready. And still there was no sign of Amos Busby or the men who had traveled with him to Lorient. Hard though it was, Simon had to face the unpleasant truth that even should they arrive before the *Fairwinds* sailed, it was too late to have any effect on what must now occur.

He was out of time.

With a heavy heart, he shouted, "Put the sails in their gear! Stand by to make sail!"

Jordan shouted the orders that would see the tasks done. In response, men scrambled aloft, halyard crews hauled their lines, and the *Fairwinds* slipped out of Rye Harbor heading into the Channel.

⌒ ๑ ⌒

Calais

Through the window of the captain's cabin, Claire glimpsed the golden rays of the setting sun reflected on the waters of the harbor as they arrived in Calais. Dozens of ships were tied up to the wharf, their bare masts testimony to the fact they were safely in port. Only one ship slowly sailed toward shore, its topsail unfurled and full of wind.

Nate had come to tell her of Simon's request that she wear the gown he had procured for her in London, the one she had yet to wear. She had managed to dress herself, as she had done many times. Anxiously, she smoothed the copper silk of the skirt, then lifted her hand to the pale blue-green satin brocade of the bodice, the same fabric that cascaded in a panel down the front of the copper silk skirt like a waterfall carrying with it small, black embroidered flowers. It was the most beautiful gown she had ever seen, much less ever possessed. And it fit her perfectly.

She took one last look around the cabin, her gaze pausing on the things she had come to treasure. His books, the ship's log, his spyglass, his favorite tankard. The things that would forever remind her of their time together. She slipped the wedding ring he had given her from her finger and placed it on his desk.

A knock sounded on the cabin door. She went to open it, thinking how ironic it was that just when she was leaving, she had finally gained her sea legs. The door opened before she reached it and Simon ducked his head to enter, coming to a sudden halt, his eyes roving over her. Was it regret she saw in his amber gaze?

"The gown is lovely," she said, suddenly caring that he liked her in it. "Thank you."

His eyes appeared to cloud with emotion. "I would not send you to your father in anything less than the finest silk, mademoiselle."

So, it was to be like that. He would put distance between them. A tear escaped her eye to carve a track down her cheek. She brushed it away, embarrassed to have allowed it, knowing the courage she must find to face what lay ahead.

Their situation was hopeless.

He had persuaded her that Mother Superior's words were true. She must live her own life; she could not live another's.

But in changing her life's course, he had opened her heart and called forth love. His kisses had awakened her to the passion between a man and a woman. The life she now wanted was with him and no other.

She must tell him before they parted, never to see each other again. "I do not want to go, surely you must know that."

He clenched his jaw, a reaction she had seen often enough to know his mind was set on a course he would stubbornly pursue no matter the cost. "I cannot sacrifice my men, and even if their faces were not always before me, your father no doubt has in mind a better life for you than one with a bastard sea captain. The convent might be preferable."

She stared at him, her love so bittersweet, the urge to run into his arms so strong, she dared not speak lest she lose control and beg him to let her stay. His circumstances of birth mattered naught to her. To share his life was her dream, a dream that could not be.

"Mr. Landor has made the final arrangements for the exchange. I wish you well, mademoiselle." He turned to leave. She watched his tall frame step through the cabin door and listened to the sound of his steps, taking with them her heart.

Alone, she broke down and sobbed.

Eventually, Nate came for her. "Mistress," he said with sad inflection, "Mr. Landor awaits ye on deck."

She wiped away the remaining tears and raised her head. "The captain?"

"He asks that ye fergive his absence."

She knew why he had given his first mate the task of accompanying her. Simon might not be able to do it himself and in that, she took heart. Though he had never said the words, she knew he loved her. She had seen it in his eyes when he'd left.

"I will miss you, Nate."

"I'm sorry to see ye go, mistress." He meant it, she knew. They had become good friends in the time they had spent together. And they shared their love for the captain.

She followed Nate to the companionway and took a deep breath, summoning her resolve for what lay ahead, before carefully ascending the ladder.

The minute she stepped on deck, her searching gaze found him. He stood at the starboard rail, looking into the sunset, away from his men assembled on deck and away from the wharf where a crowd had gathered. The orange and yellow light from the sun's rays cast a glow over his face rendering him the golden eagle he would ever be to her, now remote, and soon to be lost forever.

Her heart torn asunder, she ran to him and reached up to kiss him once more. It was a brief kiss, but in it was her whole heart. "I will never forget you."

His eyes were filled with unshed tears as he looked at her. Then he returned his gaze to the setting sun. "Go!"

She forced herself to leave him, to walk to where the first mate awaited her, his elbow offered in gentlemanly fashion, a kind look of sympathy in his green eyes peering at her from beneath the brim of his tricorne. She took his arm and they walked down the gangplank and across the wharf to where her papa, dressed in black coat, breeches and boots, a sword at his side, stood waiting with an anxious look. Behind him, a half-circle of men stood guard with their legs spread, their hands clasped behind them. Some of them looked familiar. Had they known her before? Had they just witnessed her display?

"Claire!" her papa exclaimed when she reached him. Taking her into his arms, he warmly embraced her. It was a small comfort and one much needed.

She smiled up at him. "Hello, Papa."

"You are well?" he asked.

"I am, Papa." He would note her red eyes and tear-stained cheeks but she would assure him she had been well treated. "They treated me as a guest." Turing to the *Fairwinds'* first mate, she offered her hand. "Thank you, Mr. Landor, for your many kindnesses." Her voice was stilted as she fought back tears.

He bowed over her hand. "It was my pleasure, mademoiselle."

"Mr. Landor," said her papa, "there will be a few more men returned to your captain than he might have expected." Then with a wry smile, he inclined his head. "Am I correct in thinking you sent some of yours ahead to Lorient?"

"Ah, yes," Mr. Landor said with apparent reluctance. "Are they here?"

"Indeed they are, with the others just there." He looked behind him to a group of assembled men. "And as I recall, you snatched a few of my crew in London."

Mr. Landor grinned. "We did. A full exchange, then?"

"My intent exactly," said her papa.

The first mate bowed over her hand before tipping his hat. "I'll see your men are released immediately, M'sieur Donet." He turned and joined the line of men now walking past them toward the *Fairwinds*. Some, she noted, were in a bedraggled state. From the happy words they exchanged in English, it had to be Simon's crew from the *Abundance*.

Shouts from the men lining the rail of the *Fairwinds* brought wide smiles to the faces of the English crew filing by, their eyes fixed ahead.

She looked beyond the men ascending the gangplank to the deck of the schooner, seeking the one who held her heart. But Simon was lost in the crowd of cheering men.

Turning back to her papa, she had to ask, "Why did you never tell me?"

"I wanted to protect you," came his reply. Claire could not fault him for that. She knew he loved her. She might have done the same in his place.

A man wearing a worn military uniform beneath which was a white linen shirt, open at the neck, strode toward them. She recognized Émile Bequel. She had met him years ago, never knowing he sailed on her papa's ship. Often, when her papa had visited the convent, M'sieur Bequel had been with him, often wearing the same attire. Looking at his harsh

214

features now with fresh eyes, she wondered: had this man, too, been a pirate? He could well have been.

M'sieur Bequel doffed his tricorne, his rough face breaking into a wide smile, softening his features. "Welcome home, little one."

"Thank you, M'sieur Bequel."

Her papa reached for her hand and slid a ring on her finger. The feel of the cool metal drew her eyes to her hand. It was her moonstone ring, his birthday gift to her more than a year ago.

"Sister Augustin gave it to me to return to you."

"Thank you, Papa." There was no reason not to wear it now. She would take no Ursuline vows. And since Simon Powell was lost to her, she would comply with her papa's wishes. What did it matter who she was to wed if it could not be the one she loved?

M'sieur Bequel and the men who had stood behind her papa walked away, leaving them alone for the moment. Her papa gave her an assessing look, his dark brows drawn together in a frown. "Are you all right? They assured me you were unharmed, and you assured me you are well, but I must ask again."

"I am fine, Papa. Truly." Tears welled in her eyes as she looked back over her shoulder to try and glimpse the captain for the last time. For a brief moment she thought she saw his golden head but then it was gone from her view.

When she returned her eyes to her papa, his face was lined with concern. "What is it Claire? Surely you are not sad to be leaving the English ship where you were held prisoner for so long?"

"And if I were? Would you let me return to Captain Powell?"

"I cannot believe you would entertain such a preposterous notion." He let out an exasperated sigh. "I saw your gesture bidding him farewell, the kiss you gave him." His dark eyes flashed. "Was it merely gratitude at their good treatment or do you have feelings for this man?"

She looked into the face she had loved all her life. He was a handsome man, her papa. And he had once been her age. Perhaps he, of all men, would understand. "Do we really have a choice in the person to whom we give our heart, Papa? I have thought much about it in recent days. Sometimes, when we least expect it, we catch a glimpse of someone, a face, perhaps only a smile, and our heart latches on and will not let go. It may not be love at first, but soon and for always." The tears welled in her eyes blurring his image. "Captain Powell is such a one to me, Papa."

"He is English, Claire! And no doubt a Protestant."

She gazed down at the worn planks beneath her feet, gathering her courage once more. Then she returned her gaze to his fathomless, dark eyes. "I have learned the heart cares nothing for such things. It can give itself away with no consideration for country, religion or wealth."

"I would never give your hand to such a man." His voice sounded like the steel in the sword at his side.

A small smile came to her lips. "I think he is not unlike you, Papa."

"You are young," he said dismissively. "You will forget him."

"Did you forget, Papa? When your own father, le comte, forbade you to marry Maman, did you forget?"

He pressed his lips tightly together and looked away, the wind blowing strands of his long, black hair from its queue to stream across his face.

She had her answer. But then she hadn't really needed to ask. He had defied his father, turning his back on his noble heritage, to marry the woman he loved. A woman his family had deemed unsuitable. Claire's sympathies reached out to him at that moment, as a greater understanding came to her. He had done what Simon's father had not done. And he had paid a price for it. No doubt, he'd become a pirate to feed his wife and child.

"Come," he said, wrapping his arm around her shoulder and drawing her close. "We will have supper and speak no more of this. Your future lies in Paris, Claire, not in England, nor at the convent in Saint-Denis."

He paused as if allowing her time to object.

Nodding her assent, she conceded the truth of his words. "You are right, Papa. My future is not in Saint-Denis, not anymore, nor, it seems, does it lie in England." Perhaps the will of God might be revealed in the will of her father. Or perhaps the marriage he had planned for her would be her penance, long delayed and now due.

They started to walk away when a shout was heard above the noise on the wharf and the sounds of the English ship making ready to sail.

"*Une frégate anglaise!*" An English frigate!

᠁ ᠁ ᠁

Jean's attention was drawn to the north, his gaze reaching beyond Powell's schooner to the ship bearing down upon the harbor. "He betrayed us!"

"No, Papa. Captain Powell would never do that!"

"We will see."

Émile rushed up to them from the edge of the wharf. "You must get away, *Capitaine*! A carriage awaits."

"*La Reine Noire?*"

"She is safe. After I unloaded the English prisoners, I hid her well. Once you and the little one are gone, I will take the men who are here and sail to Dieppe. By the time you reach Paris, I will be there."

"Very well." He looked at his daughter, sheltered beneath his arm. "Come, Claire. This may not be pleasant and I would spare you."

᠁ ᠁ ᠁

Simon lifted his spyglass to scrutinize the approaching frigate. "Eden!" *Damn the man.* This could only be his doing.

"What's going on, Simon?" asked Wingate.

"It's Eden, my contact in London. He must have sent the frigate hoping to capture Donet. I knew he was up to something, damn him." Simon anxiously looked toward the shore. "I must block the frigate's access to the harbor so Claire and her father can get away."

"You would aid Donet?"

"'Tis a matter of honor—my own. And there is more, but I have no time now to explain." Leaving Wingate with a perplexed look on his face, Simon strode to the helm, yelling as he moved aft, "All hands on deck! Stand by to make sail!"

"Right now, sir?" queried his first mate as he passed him.

"Yes, damn it—now!" Then to his crew, "Ready the mainsail halyard! Ready the foresail halyards! Stand by to cast off moorings!"

Confusion reigned for only a moment, then quick as lightning, his crew not already at their stations rushed to their places.

From amidships, Jordan shouted, "Mooring lines manned and ready! Halyards manned and ready."

Simon bellowed, "Cast off the bow line! Cast off the stern line! Haul away the halyards! Haul away smartly, men!" His heart pounding in his chest as the frigate moved closer, Simon shouted, "Fill those sheets with wind!"

As the sails went up, the mooring lines splashed into the water and the *Fairwinds* slanted off the wharf, heading straight for the incoming frigate.

Taking the wheel from the helmsman, Simon gripped the spokes, staring intently at the looming warship, alert to any change of course. The frigate drove on, straight toward the *Fairwinds.* Half a dozen startled faces popped up above the frigate's rails.

Simon grinned and held the wheel steady.

From the frigate came a shout. "Bear off! Bear off, you grass-combing lubber!"

"You bear off, you slab-sided scow!" Simon barked back.

"Damn you, sir. Damn you for a pig-headed… " The bellowing voice of the frigate captain broke off cursing and rose again in a volley of commands. "Hands to the sheets! Let fly the headsails! Let fly, I say!" The big triangular jibs sagged and spilled their wind. The frigate veered off the wind, slowing as it turned, like a lumbering wagon with a broken wheel.

As soon as he heard the shouted orders, Simon spun the wheel hard to port and held his breath. The nimble schooner turned on a shilling and shot past the frigate with mere feet to spare.

Above the rail of the frigate's tall quarterdeck, a red-faced captain wearing the familiar blue frock coat with a gold epaulette on each shoulder shook his fist in the air.

Simon laughed and gave him a wave as the *Fairwinds* caught the wind and flew away, gathering speed as she left the harbor behind.

As the euphoria wore off, Simon's heart sank at the grim realization of what he'd left behind in Calais: His heart and the azure-eyed, French girl who held it in the palm of her hand.

❧ ☙ ❧

From the top of the hill where the carriage waited, Claire gazed back at the two ships in the harbor. "Papa, look! The English ship is stalled."

Her papa set his cocked hat on his head and stared into the distance where the schooner glided away from the frigate and its flapping sails. "It would appear you are right, my dear."

"See, Papa. I told you Simon Powell would not betray us. His honor would not allow it." Pride welled in her chest as tears filled her eyes. He was daring, her golden one.

"In war, Claire, one man's honor is another man's shame. He may pay for that maneuver with his superiors in London.

But I must concede the English captain has done me a favor this day."

Claire's heart had been in her throat when the frigate nearly collided with the schooner. But when the *Fairwinds* sailed away, silhouetted against the muted colors of the fading sky, the sun having set below the horizon, she brought her fisted hand to her mouth and let the tears fall.

Farewell, my love.

Chapter 19

Paris

Claire was home, yet Paris didn't feel quite like home anymore. After hearing only English for so long, her native tongue sounded odd to her ears now that she was surrounded by people speaking only French. Despite the profusion of flowers and color she had always loved, she found herself missing the ship, and more, the face of its captain.

After the tumultuous events in Calais, she and her papa had spent that night at an inn, sharing a meal and the joy of being reunited. The next day, rain had followed them as they traveled south to Amiens. Inside the carriage, a cold, damp chill wrapped itself around her, matching her mood. After another long day on the road, the sky cleared as they neared Paris, leaving a few white clouds floating listlessly in a blue expanse.

Across the carriage, her papa smiled. "Since I saw you last, I have purchased a townhouse in Paris knowing you will most likely be here from now on. I want to be close enough to see you from time to time."

Claire felt her future rushing toward her, a future she didn't want. "Papa, there is no need for haste, is there? Surely we can have some time together before I must marry?" Claire would put it off forever if she could, but she knew her papa would not. He had already selected the man who would be her husband.

"It will be a few weeks before the wedding can be arranged, but I want you to meet your betrothed. He'll want that time to court you, I am certain. And you must be fitted for your wedding gown and trousseau. I would like you to have the wedding that was denied your mother."

Claire could muster no enthusiasm for a grand affair, particularly if Simon Powell was not her intended. But she knew it would make her papa happy, so she did not question his plans.

She glanced out the window as the carriage drove through the *porte cochère* of an elegant, stone townhouse to a landscaped, inner courtyard. Balconies on the second and third stories were railed with scrolling wrought iron. It was so different from her childhood home on the hillside in Lorient she had difficulty picturing her papa here. Of course, he had been raised among aristocrats so, at one time, he must have been used to such opulence.

A footman opened the carriage door and her papa stepped out, then helped her down. "I know the journey has been long, Claire, so I'd suggest you rest this evening. I've hired a maid who will see to your needs. Tomorrow you have an appointment with the modiste and in the evening, we will dine with certain men of influence and some of my friends. And your betrothed, of course."

A footman held open the door to the townhouse and they entered, her papa still speaking. "I've invited the American commissioner, M'sieur Franklin, our Foreign Minister, the comte de Vergennes and the provost of Paris, Antoine-Louis de Caumartin. Your betrothed, François de Dordogne, is anxious to meet you."

She had heard of the American Benjamin Franklin. All of Paris seemed to adore him. But she had not met Vergennes, Caumartin or her betrothed. It was the first time she had heard the name of the man she was to wed and it made her pause.

He was now a real person, someone to contend with, not just a vague concept. The prospect of the unwanted marriage settled in her stomach like a bad meal.

"I'd like to visit the convent—to say goodbye, Papa."

"*Oui*, the Mother Superior would like that. She was understandably upset by what happened to you. Seeing that you are well will give her great comfort."

After introductions were made to the butler and to her new maid, Claire retired to her bedchamber, barely noticing the elaborate furnishings. Instead, her thoughts strayed to the *Fairwinds*. Was McGinnes telling stories of Irish fairies in the galley with Nate listening enraptured? Was the ship in Rye, London or somewhere else? Was Simon striding the deck with his golden hair streaming out behind him?

Did he think of her?

༄ ༒ ༄

London

"The skipper's turned into a curmudgeon!" McGinnes huffed, dropping the wooden spoon into the kettle, splashing the dark brown broth from the stew onto his work table.

"Nay, he's a man in love," said Elijah sitting on a stool nursing a mug of coffee, his pipe lying across his thigh. "Worse than a wounded bear. Everyone's celebratin' the return of the *Abundance*'s crew 'cept the cap'n who made it happen. He sulks."

As if he hadn't heard Elijah's remark, the Irish cook droned on. "'Tis the second time today he's sent back his stew. Sure an' it might be a good thing he stays with his fancy English friends now that we've anchored in London."

"As I recollect, he intends to do jus' that," said Elijah.

"Sure an' he even barked at Nate. Poor lad came to see me this mornin', his face so long 'twere nearly draggin' on the deck."

"Aye, well that may be due to the lad's fondness for the demoiselle. He misses his mistress."

Ignoring Elijah, the cook persisted in his rant. "... mopin' around like the lad lost his best friend."

"The cap'n's like a dog deprived of his favorite bone, McGinnes. Snarlin' at everyone. Ye and Nate are bein' treated no different than the rest of us. Ye could show a bit more understandin'."

"Well, if'n that's the way of it, he should just go get her."

"'Tis not so easy, that. She's with her father, the Frenchie, now. Or mebbe the nuns, now that I think o' it."

☞ ༄ ☜

Climbing into Danvers' carriage with his friend, Simon left Whitehall in a foul mood, still smarting from Eden's stinging rebuke, one that Simon considered totally unjustified. He'd refused to apologize for interfering with Eden's unforgivable action in sending a warship into Calais. It could have spelled disaster had he not been there to intervene. An image of gunfire on the wharf and Claire falling to the wooden planks, wounded, filled him with dread.

"You need not fret. Eden will return to his good-natured self in time."

"Good-natured? Surely you jest. The man's insane," Simon returned.

"He's got a lot on his mind these days. The treaty negotiations have him worried. The prime minister rejoices in the rumor that the Americans will abandon their friends in France, but Eden's suspicious."

"As tight as America and France have been, according to the Scribe, I'd be suspicious, too," he grudgingly admitted. "Perhaps Lord Shelburne is too trusting."

The carriage pulled up in front of the Danvers' townhouse and Simon stepped down, waiting for his friend.

"Cornelia will want us to join her for afternoon tea. You'll not disappoint her?"

"I shall not," Simon said, though he knew it would commit him to at least an hour of chatter. Then, too, Cornelia might ask about Claire. What could he say?

Soon the three of them were seated in the parlor with a tray of small sandwiches and sugared cakes.

Cornelia, who sat across from him, set down her cup. "I wonder if Claire is yet wed."

"Wed?" Simon nearly spit out his tea, the porcelain cup clattering against the saucer. "I thought she was returning to the convent."

Cornelia gave him an incredulous look. "However did you get that idea? Oh, I know Claire thought at one time to become a nun, but it was clear to me her heart was not in it. And, it seemed her father had other plans. Why, he even had someone picked out for her." Her gaze assessing him, she added, "By the time she left, Claire realized she was not suited for the cloistered life."

Simon's eyes narrowed. "Who?"

Studying her nails, Cornelia said, "A lawyer, I think. Someone in Paris."

It was one thing to let her go to a convent because of a vow made to a dying girl. It was quite another to send her into the arms of a suitor. What kind of a man was he? One more worthy of her? "Do you have a name?"

Cornelia looked up, unfazed. "Alas, no." At her side, Danvers munched on a sandwich, seemingly indifferent to Simon's predicament.

"I see."

With a heavy heart, Simon returned to his ship that evening, and had Jordan call together his men who'd had been in contact with Donet. Wingate and Busby had been the Frenchman's prisoners and both Elijah and Giles had been in Paris to arrange the exchange. Once they were seated around his table, he asked them, "Did Donet or his man, Bequel, ever speak of a lawyer in Paris to whom Claire Donet was betrothed?"

The men exchanged glances, then shook their heads.

"The subject never came up, Cap'n," said Elijah. "Bequel asked after the girl, 'o course, and Giles told him she was bein' looked after, that no harm had come to her."

Giles nodded his agreement.

"None of us in Lorient were in a position to hear of such news," said Wingate.

"I want to know who this lawyer is," Simon coolly replied. "I'll not see her with a man who would not treat her well," he murmured.

"Our contacts in Paris can tell us," said Elijah chewing on the end of his unlit pipe.

Simon turned to Wingate. "I'd ask you to stay in London to find us a ship to replace the *Abundance*. Make sure your idle crew is paid as we'll soon need them."

Wingate nodded. "Aye, I'll see it done."

Simon rose and walked toward the small windows, looking south toward France. "We were going to Paris for Eden; now 'tis urgent I go for more. I won't be left in the dark about this man Donet has chosen for his daughter." His mind whirring with plans, he turned to face his men, his jaw set in firm determination. "And, John, I'll need a favor from Lord Danvers. It's just a contingency, but he'll understand when he gets the message. I'd ask you to deliver it."

Wingate nodded. "Of course."

Giles opened his mouth to speak and then paused as if he suddenly remembered something. "Cap'n, when Elijah and I were in Paris, we spent some time in a tavern that is a favorite spot for lawyers."

"Ye'd not believe the dandies that traipsed through there," said Elijah grimacing. "Enough fancy dress to make ye sick."

"Then we'll begin our search there," said Simon. "Load what supplies we need. We sail with the tide."

⟨ ❦ ⟩

Paris

Claire felt like she was sleepwalking, going through the motions of living while detached from everything around her. She'd been to Mass that morning and made her confession before going to the modiste's with her maid. Thus, her conscience was clear, but her thoughts were still a world away when the guests began arriving for dinner. Even the beautiful wedding gown her papa had ordered for her had not improved her outlook.

Her papa's salon, an ornately decorated room with red ceiling and gilded panel walls, soon filled with the chatter of men and women from very different walks of life: statesmen, business partners of her papa and their wives and some of her papa's men who were dressed as gentlemen for the evening, including Émile Bequel, who she had learned was her papa's quartermaster. The language spoken was French and the praise for her papa's new townhouse effusive.

She knew which man was François de Dordogne the moment he stepped into the room. He was the only one under thirty. In appearance, he was slender, almost feminine. The finely tailored, black coat he wore over an elaborately embroidered ivory satin waistcoat suggested a narrow frame beneath. There was much lace at his neck and wrists. He was not much taller than she, and his sable-colored hair hung to his shoulders framing features delicate enough for a woman. Still, for all that, he had a pleasant face, his skin pale and smooth with no hard lines suggesting cruelty or arrogance. She had to remind herself he was a lawyer. A sigh escaped her. He was so different from the men of the *Fairwinds* and their ruggedly handsome captain with his skin rendered golden by the sun.

François de Dordogne looked more like a poet, or a tutor of the violin. A man who worked inside all day with paper, quills and words, she reminded herself. She wondered if he'd ever been on a ship.

"Claire, allow me to present M'sieur Dordogne," her papa said.

The young man took her outstretched hand in his slim fingers, several of which bore rings with glittering jewels, and bowed gracefully. "*Enchanté*, mademoiselle. Given our pending nuptials, you may call me François."

He gave her a smile, but it was a cool one. There was a decided lack of warmth in his brown eyes. And no glimmer of interest either, or any hint of amusement. In fact, she detected no emotion at all. He seemed almost… bored, like he was meeting a total stranger on the street, rather than his betrothed. At least he was refined, she reflected. But even as she had the thought, it struck her that his demeanor was more like that of a dilettante, politesse for a mere show of manners, rather than from any sort of respect for her as a person or desire for her as a woman. Her heart sank. She tried to think of something comforting, something positive. *Perhaps he will not be unkind.*

He made a few pleasantries, saying he looked forward to some time with her. She nodded her agreement, all the while feeling guilty knowing she could never give François de Dordogne her heart. But perhaps he would not expect it. Arranged marriages were often merely alliances for land and wealth.

As Dordogne sauntered away, she exchanged a somber look with her papa, and saw the disappointment in his eyes at the lack of any spark in her first encounter with her betrothed.

The din of the conversation among the guests faded into the background as Claire found herself longing for a moving deck, the wind off the Channel and a schooner captain with golden hair shouting orders to his men. The sigh that escaped her lips was involuntary, but not unnoticed.

"Claire, are you all right?"

"Yes, Papa, just tired, I think." *And weary of the evening before it has begun.*

The dinner that followed passed in a flurry of conversation as M'sieur Franklin expressed his hope for the negotiations for peace, which had apparently broken off some weeks ago, and the comte de Vergennes spoke of his concern for the outcome of the recent assault on Gibraltar by the combined forces of France and Spain. The battle did not seem to be going well from what Claire could determine. To her relief, the only ships the men spoke of were warships, not those of privateers.

Her betrothed said little. She glanced about the dining room she had glimpsed for the first time only the day before, admiring the walls that were the rich color of burnt sienna, complementing the rug of scrolling design in similar hues. Her papa had certainly taken pains to provide a beautiful home in the city.

❦

The next day, the sky threatened rain as Claire took the short carriage ride to Saint-Denis to pay her respects and say her goodbyes.

"You can remain in the carriage if you like," she said to her maid when they arrived in front of the convent. "I won't be long."

The girl nodded, "*Oui*, mademoiselle."

Claire stepped down from the carriage and looked up at the gray-colored stone of the four-storied structure that had been her home for so long. Now it seemed strangely confined to the past, no longer a part of either her present or her future. Was it only months ago she had been here? So much had happened it seemed like years.

The Reverend Mother and Sister Angélique met her as she entered the office, their familiar black and white habits flowing around them, as their faces drew up in broad smiles.

"You are well?" Sister Angélique asked enthusiastically.

"I am much like I was when you last saw me."

"Only different, I think," said the Mother Superior examining Claire with her intense gaze, always seeing more than anyone else. "You have changed, Claire."

"Yes," she looked down for a moment fighting tears, and then met the Reverend Mother's clear gaze. "I have learned you were right, but then you had no doubts I was not meant for the Order, did you?"

"No, Claire, I had no doubts. I believe you have your own, very special path to tread. One that God will make clear in time."

"You know Papa means me to wed M'sieur Dordogne?"

"Yes," said the Mother Superior, watching Claire like a hawk, seeing too much as she always did.

Sister Angélique put her palms together and held them close to her starched wimple, the excitement in her expression almost more than Claire, in her sadness, could bear. "When is the wedding?"

"'Twill be in Paris a sennight from now," Claire informed them.

"You do not appear to be pleased with the upcoming nuptials," said the insightful Mother Superior. "There is another, perhaps?"

"Well, there was a man I met in England... " Claire's voice trailed off. How could she explain Simon Powell and her love for him to the sisters? Would they even understand?

"Ah," said the wise Mother Superior. "Then I will pray once again that God's will be done. Never doubt, Claire, He has you in the palm of His hand. All will be well."

Claire fought back tears as she considered the Reverend Mother's words. Her broken heart left little room for hope. But she would not ruin her time with the sisters or the students she had yet to see. "I thought to say goodbye to my friends and those students for whom I was *dizainière*."

"Of course," said the Reverend Mother, leading her into the convent, "they are anxiously waiting to see you."

It was a sad afternoon for Claire, realizing that this was yet another goodbye that she could not avoid. But she was glad she had come for it had reminded her that here, at least, she had done some good.

The days after her visit to the convent passed through Claire's fingers like so many beads on her new rosary, the practiced routine comfortable but requiring little of her active mind. Her appetite had waned though her papa had plied her with her favorite foods and sweets and taken her to a private showing of art in one of the salons of the day. Without the man she loved, even the joy of being with her papa often failed to bring a smile to her face.

Her betrothed, the young Dordogne was something of an enigma. One evening, he'd joined them for dinner and afterward he had read her poetry. She'd had the oddest feeling it wasn't her he was thinking of, but someone else as his eyes filled with a longing she'd never seen before. Of whom had he been thinking? She was still wondering as she bid him goodnight.

He would not be a difficult husband, of that she was certain, but would he be much of one at all? Having loved a bold man of the sea, could she settle for less? Could she bring herself to give Dordogne more than a sisterly peck on the cheek? Doubts settled around her like so many brooding vultures, ready to snatch away any chance for happiness.

೨ ༀ ೧

Simon leaned back in his chair to watch the large room crowded with men. A haze of smoke hung in the air of the *taverne Ramponneau* in Paris. Elijah and Giles, sitting on either side of him, nursed their glasses of claret as they surreptitiously looked about, searching for some familiar face. It had been nearly a week since they'd left Rye. A rough crossing and rain had delayed their arrival in Paris. He'd left Jordan with the ship in Dieppe while he, Elijah and Giles traveled to Paris.

Only that morning, he had learned the name of Claire's betrothed, a lawyer from a good family who apparently worked with the French foreign minister. From the description he'd obtained, it sounded like François de Dordogne might be an acceptable choice for the convent-raised daughter of a French comte's younger son. It grieved him to acknowledge that her father may have made a wise choice, someone more worthy of her than a bastard English sea captain.

But before he conceded defeat, he would know more.

Elijah crossed his arms over his chest, his pipe in one hand. "That name ye were given sounds familiar, Cap'n, like I heard it before. And this place, 'tis ticklin' me memory."

Giles stared at the bar. "…Dordogne… Dordogne. Ah! I have it!" he said, slapping the table. "Elijah, recall the last time we were here, the proprietor shouted to one of the dandies as he was leaving?"

"Aye," said Elijah, "I remember. The Frenchies strollin' out the back room wearin' all that lace."

"Dordogne," Giles repeated. "That was the name!" he exclaimed. "Captain, if 'tis the same man, he'd not be a fit man for the mademoiselle's husband. Nor any woman's husband, come to that."

"What?" Simon said with a start.

"He was with the group of fops Elijah spoke of, Cap'n," explained Giles, as if that told Simon much. It did not.

Elijah leaned in to whisper, "They're effeminate frog-eaters." When Simon frowned in puzzlement, the old salt clarified. "Mollies, sir. Sodomites."

Simon drew his head back. "*Damn.*"

"Just what I was thinking," said Giles.

"Why," Simon wondered aloud, "would such a man take a wife?"

"So as to keep his pretty head on his pretty shoulders, likely," said Elijah with a shrug. "He wouldn't be the first to put on a masquerade to fool the rest o' the world. Likely won't be the last neither. 'Tis a crime that could see 'im hanged in most places."

"Donet must have no inkling," said Simon, shaking his head.

"Half the aristocrats in Paris dress like that, Cap'n," offered Giles. "'Tis likely Donet sees nothing unusual in the man's appearance. But it was clear to us that his affectation and that of his companions was more than a tribute to fashion."

"And Donet ain't a man to judge another by the cut of his coat," said Elijah. "He's jus' lookin' at the fop's pedigree, not the... er... stud horse hisself."

"Gelding, more like," muttered Giles.

"Well, I'll be happy to enlighten him," said Simon, suddenly smiling at the turn of events and glad he'd asked Danvers for that favor. He would not see her go to such a man, no matter his pedigree. *If she'll have me, I will have her for myself!*

By the end of the day, Simon had gained the location of Donet's Paris home and the date of the wedding: the next day.

He made plans accordingly.

The afternoon of the wedding, Simon and his men took up positions around the townhouse. He'd hoped for a glimpse of Claire, but never saw her. As the afternoon waned, carriages began arriving and passengers alighted, dressed in finery fit for a celebration. With the guests creating a distraction, the time had come.

At his signal, Simon's men fanned out around the rear of the townhouse, finding hiding places among the trees and the boxwood hedges. Scanning the various approaches, Simon's gaze came to rest on the inner courtyard and what he could see of balconies. They would lead to the bedchambers.

"I'm going up," he advised Elijah. "You and the others wait below with the rope. I'll signal when I want it. You and Giles will be needed to lower Claire safely to the ground, assuming she will come with me."

"The demoiselle will come," said Elijah. "When the first mate led her to her father, I'd never seen a woman so miserable."

Simon hoped the wizened old bos'n was right. She'd be leaving her country and her beloved Papa to take up with a bastard English privateer. But he was encouraged when he remembered her words that she did not want to leave him. If she came he would spend his life making sure she never regretted her choice.

At Elijah's signal, Giles brought the rope, while Simon looked up to where curtains covered the windows and glass doors.

He ran to the tree nearest the tall structure and began to climb. One branch took him to another and to another until finally, he could jump to a balcony and climb over the railing. Flattening his body against the side of the townhouse, he peered cautiously through the glass into the bedchamber, detecting no light. He tried the handle of one of the tall, paned glass doors. It opened. Beyond the heavy curtains, the chamber was dark. He paid it no mind, but strode through it to the corridor and began cautiously opening doors. Behind each of the doors was a darkened room. As he made his way down the corridor, from below the stairs, he heard music and the sound of many voices in conversation.

Time was short, but only one door remained. He tried the handle, relieved when it gave way. With barely a sound, he stepped over the threshold and into a room bathed in candlelight. Carefully, he closed the door behind him.

In the middle of the room, in front of a four-poster bed, stood the woman who haunted his dreams. She was dressed in a gown of ivory satin, embroidered with red roses. It was lavish and hugged her small waist like a second skin. Even with her back to him, he could see it was trimmed in a good deal of fancy lace. *Her wedding gown.* He shuddered to think how close he'd come to losing her.

His heart pounding in his chest, he spoke the name that had been in his mind every waking moment since he'd left her in Calais, "Claire."

Chapter 20

Lost in her thoughts, at first Claire thought she was imagining his voice. But it sounded too real, too close. She whirled. "Simon!"

She ran into his welcoming arms, hugging him with fierce determination, inhaling his scent of salt and the sea. His warmth encircled her as she tipped her head back to welcome his urgent kiss, tears streaming from her eyes in glorious happiness.

Their hungry mouths seemed starved for each other. Too soon, he broke off the kiss.

"You're here," she said. "Why?"

"It seems I cannot live without you," he said, a faint tone of amusement in his voice. "And I could not allow your father to give you to so unworthy a man."

"Oh, Simon. It matters not to me if he is worthy; he is not *you*. I was just gathering my courage to tell Papa I could not go through with it, not even for him."

He held her away, his expression serious. "I want you by my side Claire, for always. But if you come with me, your home will never again be in France."

Tears filled her eyes as she spoke the truth that was in her heart. "My home is with you."

His smile was brilliant and his amber eyes glistening as

he asked, "Will you marry me?"

Her heart soared. Her most fervent prayer had been answered. "Yes. Oh, yes."

A knock at the door made her jump. He looked down at her wedding gown. "There is no time to change," he whispered. "We must go."

"*Une minute*," she shouted to the door, hoping to buy them time.

Taking her hand he pulled a letter from his waistcoat, laid it on the pillow of her bed and hurried her toward the balcony. At his wave, a coil of rope flew up from the courtyard below. He caught the end, looped it around her hips and swiftly tied some kind of seaman's knot, forming a loop for her to sit in. Leaning over the balcony, he tossed the other end over the stout branch of the nearby tree and waved to his men waiting below in the gathering darkness. They grabbed the rope and braced themselves while Simon gathered her into his arms and lifted her over the edge of the balcony.

She looked at him in rising panic.

"Don't look down," he whispered. "Hold on tight. I'll lower you. Elijah and Giles are just below."

She nodded but could not hide the fear in her eyes.

Gradually he let the rope take her weight as his men below lowered her down. By the time she shed the rope from around her hips, Simon had scrambled down the tree with easy agility and stood beside her.

Shouts from the balcony above followed them as Claire gathered up her long skirts and they ran from the courtyard. On the street, a carriage awaited. It was not unlike the night he'd taken her from Saint-Denis, except she was running beside him and wore no blindfold. Could she be that same girl?

෴

Jean looked down at the note he held in his hand, shaking with anger, and leaned toward the candle to read.

M'sieur Donet,

I love your daughter and I believe she loves me.

Having learned the man you have chosen to be her husband is not worthy of her, I have claimed Claire as my own. Know that she went with me most willingly this time or I would not have taken her.

I have sought a special license from the Archbishop for us to wed, but as she is not yet one and twenty, we must have your consent if we are to marry under England's laws. I will give you a week to come to Rye where my ship is anchored. If you do not come, we will sail for Scotland where I will assure we are legally wed.

Come with your blessing, sir. Attend the wedding. It is what Claire would want above all. If you do, I promise our firstborn son will bear your name.

Yours most sincerely,
S. Powell

So, the chess game had ended. The queen had been captured, this time with her willing consent. Jean let out a deep, resigned sigh.

The sound of footfalls made him turn. His quartermaster stood in the open doorway.

"*Capitaine?*"

Jean ran his fingers over his slight mustache, still trying to take in all that had happened. Looking into the deep-set eyes of the man who had been his friend for the last many years, unable to hide his pain from one who knew him so well, he said, "François de Dordogne hides a secret, Émile. Under threat of death, if necessary, learn the truth of it. And then send a message to the crew to change *la Reine Noire* into her British costume. We are bound for Rye Harbor."

"Aye, *Capitaine.*"

Jean looked down at the note in his hand, once more reading the words. "Émile?"

237

The quartermaster paused at the door. "*Oui?*"

"Have the messenger see me before he leaves. I have a thought about the name I would have the ship bear."

෴ ঔ৫ ෴

At last Claire was finally alone with the man she loved. Simon had asked his men to ride on top of the carriage that would take them from Paris to Dieppe. She hoped it was the last long carriage trip she would have to endure for some time. While they did not have to contend with rain, traveling on the road north was still rough as the driver urged the horses to a fast run. Curled next to Simon as she was, the bumps and jolts she experienced were soon forgotten for the joy of being with him again.

He pulled her into his arms, a fierce passion burning in his eyes. "You are mine now, Claire."

"Kiss me Simon."

His mouth descended on hers. It was a deep, searing kiss, more passionate than his others, and it left her heart racing and every part of her body sensitive to his touch. She kissed him back, mating her tongue with his in rampant pleasure. Leaving her mouth, his lips sought the tender skin where her neck met her shoulder as he pulled her tightly into the curve of his body.

"I love you, Claire."

She responded with moans she could not hold back as he kissed the pulse at her throat. "And I you. I feared never to see you again."

He ran his fingers through her hair, sending pins flying around the velvet seat, freeing heavy, black curls to fall around her shoulders. Her palms smoothed over his chest and his shoulder, unable to resist touching him. He was hers, this golden man she had dreamed of for so long.

His hand stroked her breast, his fingers lingering over her nipple, causing her to experience pleasure she had not known before. She pulled him closer, wanting more.

With a deep sigh, he pulled back and looked at her. "You're even more beautiful tousled in the moonlight. It requires all my will not to take you here in this carriage. But I'd rather our first joining not be in a bumping box on the road to Dieppe. I want to make slow love to you on my ship. In my bed. I want you to remember it all of your life. For this night I intend to possess you, Claire, body and soul. Unless you insist I wait, I'd prefer not leave your innocence unclaimed. There is still the possibility your father might yet try to rip you from me."

"I am yours now, no longer under my papa's control. I will not ask you to wait."

He kissed her again and, for a moment, she was lost in the feel of him. His masculine scent surrounded her. How she had missed him!

When he raised his lips from hers, she asked, "What did you say in the note you left my papa?"

"I invited him to our wedding and asked for his blessing, for without it, we must sail to Scotland to be wed."

"Oh my. I wonder if he will come. He will be very angry, I think."

"Perhaps, but I am hoping he will not want to miss the chance to see you wed. But then again, he may yet try and take you from me. Even if he agreed Dordogne is not right for you, he may want you to marry another Frenchman."

He kissed her forehead and pressed her head to his chest. "I could not allow that."

She nestled her head under his chin, content just to be with him. She could feel his heart pounding a fast rhythm beneath her palm where it rested on his chest.

"Sleep, sweetheart, for I will not give you the chance to do so once we reach the *Fairwinds*."

Excited for the future that lay ahead of her, she did not think she could sleep. But she must have drifted off, because the next thing she knew she was being carried in his arms, her head in the crook of his neck. She opened her eyes to a predawn light that outlined his chin. Ahead of her were the dark cliffs of Dieppe and the waters of the Channel lapping on the shore. She kissed the warm skin of his neck. "We're in Dieppe?"

"We are. And you had best stop kissing me if we are to make it to my cabin."

"Over here, Captain," shouted the sailmaker, Mr. Berube, gesturing to a skiff pulled up on the sand. Simon lowered her onto one of the wooden bench seats and leapt in behind her. Mr. Hawkins, Mr. Berube and two others, who must have been waiting with the skiff, took the remaining seats.

Soon, they were gliding over the water toward the schooner anchored off shore.

∽ ❧ ∽

Once onboard, Simon hurried Claire toward the aft hatch, shouting over his shoulder to Jordan, "Ship's yours." His crew, bearing huge grins, headed for their stations, preparing to sail.

Nate stood to one side of the hatch, on his face a satisfied smile. "I left a tray for you and the mistress, Cap'n."

Simon acknowledged the lad's thoughtfulness with a nod and drew Claire closer, about to descend the ladder. Nate's words made him pause.

"We're all glad ye're back, mistress," said his cabin boy.

"Thank you, Nate," said Claire. "I am very happy to be here."

Simon urged her through the hatch and down the companionway.

Once inside his cabin, he turned to face his prize. "Ah, sweetheart."

She was a vision, more seductive than she could possibly know. Her blue eyes glowed with happiness from a face that was sun-kissed from her time on his ship. Her long, raven hair, slightly tousled from their carriage ride, fell to her shoulders in wild abandon. The bodice of the ivory satin gown she wore drew his eyes to the tempting mounds of her breasts.

Like a man long starved for his lover, he reached for her, unable to leave any distance between them. She came into his arms, smiling. His kiss was frantic at first, his longing suddenly a reality. His tongue explored the depths of her sweet mouth, as his groin swelled at the press of her soft breasts against his chest, his body ready for the woman he had wanted for so long.

She returned his kiss, threading her fingers through his hair and holding his head to her.

Each vied for the other's mouth.

He felt the ship lurch and held her steady. "You are still certain you want this, and now, before we marry?"

She smiled and reached her fingers to touch his face. "I told you my home is with you, Simon. I have agreed to become your wife. I do not want to wait."

It was all the encouragement he needed. He glanced down at her clothes, tempted to rip them from her, but he remembered she wore her wedding gown. "If you think to wear that gown to our wedding, you'd best take it off. Besides, I want to see you, sweetheart—all of you."

Claire blushed and began to pull at her laces.

"Here, I'll help. I'm good at this part."

She rolled her eyes. "Of course you are."

He turned her and began stripping the laces. The frippery fell to the deck, her gown, petticoats, corset and shift forming a pile.

She kicked off her shoes and picked up the gown. Carefully making her way across the rolling deck, she laid it aside.

As she moved, his eyes feasted on her rounded breasts, her narrow waist and enticing hips and buttocks. Standing there in only her silk stockings, she was delectable. And embarrassed, he noted, when she turned and faced him, covering her breasts with her arms.

"Don't fret, sweetheart. I'll be as naked as you in a moment." He ripped off his cravat and waistcoat, having already shed his coat and boots. Pulling his shirt over his head, he was left in only his breeches as he reached to touch her arms. Slowly, he backed her toward the bed.

"I don't know what to do," she said, her innocence rising to the surface.

He smiled at her and reached his hand to cup her cheek. "Just respond to me, sweetheart. I've imagined you like this, you know, so many times." He drew her arms from her perfect breasts, their honeyed tips calling to him. "You are so beautiful, Claire."

She blushed. He should have expected it. She was neither a practiced courtesan, nor a bored lady of the *ton*, but a convent-raised, sheltered young woman. It was a miracle he had found her at all and another that she had given him her love, accepting him as he was. He couldn't help but wonder if he could ever be worthy of that love. Silently, he vowed to prove to her and the world that he loved her above any other treasure life could offer.

When he had backed her to the bed, he began undoing his breeches. His sex sprang free, bold and hard. Oh God, he wanted her so. She looked down and inhaled sharply.

"'Tis all right, sweetheart. I mean to go slow."

Stepping out of his breeches, he leaned into her and a bolt of lightning coursed through him as they fell onto the bed together.

☞ ✑ ☜

Claire gasped as Simon fell on her, his long, lean body pressing against her from her breasts to her thighs. The hard flesh of his man part pressed into her belly and a frisson of fear coursed through her. He was so large and she was new to a man's loving. But this was Simon, she reminded herself, her golden one, the man she loved and had agreed to wed.

He braced himself on his elbows and dipped his head to her kiss her.

She wrapped her arms around him and held him close. She would think only of his kisses and not what came after. The scrape of his unshaved face as he pulled his mouth from hers was tantalizing. His warm muscled body glided over her woman's softness as he moved his mouth to her breasts, setting every nerve on end when his rough, whiskered skin encountered her nipple.

When he covered one breast with his mouth and began to lick and gently suck, ripples of pleasure coursed through her and an ache arose between her thighs. He moved his mouth to her other breast at the same time he moved to one side, placing his palm over her woman's mound and moving his hand in slow circles.

She moaned with pleasure and held his head to her breast.

As if he knew what she needed, his finger was suddenly stroking her woman's flesh and then it was inside her, touching some sensitive spot that made her crave more, made her suddenly slick. His finger stroked her and she rocked her hips to meet his touch. It was alarming and wonderful as her body responded of its own accord to his touch.

He brought his mouth back to hers and kissed her deeply as he moved above her.

She spread her legs allowing his hips to rest between them, wanting his hardened flesh against her soft, hungry flesh. At her core she experienced a quiver when he pressed against her, rocking his hips so that his hardened member glided along her tender flesh that was now seeking, wanting more. Fear and excitement wrestled within her.

When she thought she could bear no more pleasure, she whispered, "Oh, Simon." It was a plea for more.

She felt a shudder run through him. "I had wanted to go slow, sweetheart, but it seems I... cannot."

The tip of his hardened flesh probed between her thighs. It frightened her for what she knew it was, what she feared was coming. But longing to be joined with him, wanting him to be inside her aching core, she raised her hips in invitation.

"I can't stop, Claire, can't…go slow." With one sure thrust, he buried himself deep within her.

She expected it to hurt and it did. But with their joining, she felt complete. They were one.

He pulled from her slightly only to enter again, his hard flesh filling her, stretching her.

I love you.

She lifted her legs to wrap around him and gripped his shoulders with her hands. His thrusts grew more rapid and the pain turned into something else, something more, as a rising pleasure drew all her attention to the center of their joining. They were moving together even as the ship moved beneath them.

She raised her hips to take him deeper with each thrust. A sudden tightening of her muscles grew more intense where they were joined. The tension was building, like a wave taking her higher and higher to some unreachable crest. Suddenly the tension burst and she felt suspended in air as spasms rippled through her.

Simon stiffened above her, then threw back his head, his eyes shut tightly. One harsh, guttural groan and he collapsed on top of her. She held him to her as the ship rolled in the waters of the Channel, loving the feel of him around her, inside of her.

༺ ❦ ༻

Simon awoke to a different sort of light filtering in through the windows of his cabin. Afternoon sunlight, he thought. The ship rocked gently, telling him they had anchored in Rye Harbor.

He felt Claire's warm body nestled against his, her arm draped over his chest and one of her legs slung over his thigh. His manhood stirred. He wanted her again. Reaching his hand to her long, dark hair where it spread out over his chest and her shoulders, he ran his fingers through the tendrils of black silk. Nudging his face against hers, he kissed her temple. *Lavender.* He had slept with her scent all around him. No wonder he was hard and ready.

Turning into her warmth, he kissed her forehead, her cheeks. She made small, kitten-like noises as she rose from the depths of sleep. Softly, he kissed her awake. "Sweetheart," he whispered.

"Hmm?"

Unable to wait for more words, he rolled her beneath him and kissed her again. She was so warm and soft. "I love you, my own."

She opened her eyes and smiled. "Simon, my love."

"Aye." He grinned. "So I am."

She reached for him, twisting her hands through his hair, freed from its queue long ago. Their love ignited a flame that swept them higher as their passion demanded fulfillment. This time, he took her more slowly, she, his willing partner in their leisurely lovemaking.

What a fortunate man he was to have tamed the wind and won such a woman as his bride.

❦

A few hours later, Simon was busy on deck, whistling, his mind filled with images of Claire sleeping curled against him, when Elijah, standing at the starboard rail, interrupted his thoughts.

"Well now, there's somethin' I ain't never thought to see in me lifetime!"

"What is it?" he asked coming up behind the old seaman who'd just blown a puff of smoke into the air.

Elijah squinted his eyes. "I only know'd 'er 'cause I seen 'er before." Pointing to entrance of the harbor, he said, "Look ye there, Cap'n. See that ship, jus' a-comin' in? She's all decked out like a lady in new petticoats an' flyin' His Majesty's silks, but damn me eyes if that ain't the painted doxie of a certain French pirate, lately a privateer."

Simon caught up the spyglass from the binnacle and aimed it toward the ship just entering Rye Harbor. A wide smile spread across his face when he saw the name on the hull.

Jordan joined them at the rail, raising a quizzical brow.

Still grinning, Simon slapped the spyglass into the hand of his first mate and pointed. "She's flying false colors with a new rig and he's covered some of the gun ports with painted canvas, but Elijah has the right of it. That's *la Reine Noire*. I'd know her anywhere."

Jordan extended the spyglass looking toward the incoming ship and frowned. "What the devil is he—"

"Look, sir! Look what's comin' up behind her!" shouted Nate, pointing and jumping up onto the rail in his excitement. "It's the *Abundance*! She's come back to us, sir!"

"So she has," said Simon, "so she has."

The *Fairwinds* crew left their chores and gathered around to watch as the brig-sloop, rigged as a schooner, sailed closer, followed by the ship they knew so well.

The two vessels under full sail crossed the harbor swiftly, skimming the water like white birds, heading straight for the *Fairwinds*. British colors fluttered from their mainsails. The Navy cutter making its customary rounds of the harbor ignored them completely.

Amos Busby joined Simon at the rail. "The *Abundance*!"

"Aye," said Simon. "She's with him."

When the larger ship was a mere biscuit-toss away, Simon heard a cry of orders from her deck. With a rattle and a bang, all her canvas came down at once, the wheel was turned hard to port and her anchor splashed into the harbor not twenty yards from their own taut cables. The French ship doused her sails and glided smoothly into place just off their starboard quarter—as neat a job of anchoring as Simon had ever seen.

"Go, quickly, Nate. Fetch your mistress," he ordered.

"Tell her nothing. I want to see her face when she learns her father has come."

Simon's gaze fixed on the deck of the French ship. His nemesis, Jean Donet, stood on the raised quarterdeck, a tall figure in black, his stance sure, his eyes focused ahead. A vision that Simon knew had struck fear in the hearts of many a British seaman.

"There stands a gen-u-ine pirate, lads," said Elijah to the crew of the *Fairwinds* gaping at Donet.

"No," said Simon. "There stands courage. He risked his life to sail to England to give me his daughter's hand. He does it for love of her." Turning to face his crew, he said, "Hear me well, men. While Donet is in England, he is my guest and under my protection."

❦

Claire had been talking with McGinnes in the galley, urging him to try some new spices, when Nate came rushing in, breathless.

"Mistress. Ye must come!" Exchanging a glance with the cook, she dried her hands on a cloth. "What is it, Nate?"

"I'm not to say, mistress. Cap'n wants it to be a surprise."

There had been so many surprises of late, she supposed one more was not unexpected. "All right," she said and followed the cabin boy to the companionway.

Once on deck, she headed toward Simon's beckoning hand where he stood with a cluster of his men watching two ships anchored nearby. His welcoming smile made her cheeks heat at the memory of their lovemaking that morning.

The crew parted for her to join him at the rail.

"Look, sweetheart," Simon enthused.

Her gaze followed his and when she took in all that was before her, she raised her hands to her cheeks. "Papa!" He was just climbing over the rail of his ship and down a rope ladder to a small boat.

"See the name on his ship?" Simon asked.

Shielding her eyes against the sun, she looked toward the ship's hull and read *Blessing*. "Oh Simon!"

"Aye, sweetheart, a clever way of letting me know I need not fear his guns. He comes for our wedding."

She waited excitedly as her papa and M'sieur Bequel were rowed across the small distance, then climbed up the man-rope of the *Fairwinds* and dropped onto the deck where she and Simon stood waiting.

"Oh Papa," she exclaimed rushing to him, "you came!" He embraced her tightly. She looked into his dark eyes. "Thank you for giving us your blessing."

He stared into her eyes for a moment. She hoped he saw her happiness there. Then looking over her head, he said. "As you might imagine, Powell, I am not pleased about the manner in which you chose to collect my daughter. But I concede, I owe you. I had not chosen well." Claire stepped out of his arms, and her papa glanced at her before saying, "I can see Claire is determined to have you. Given that, I'd be a fool to withhold my permission."

Simon chuckled. "You are no fool, sir."

Claire returned to Simon's side. He wrapped his arm possessively around her shoulder and drew her close. His warmth reassured her that she was where she was meant to be.

"I see you have returned the *Abundance*," Simon remarked.

"*Oui*, it was to be part of my daughter's dowry. Seeing how it was yours to begin with, I could hardly refuse."

"It is most welcome. Did I mention that I like your new name for *la Reine Noire*?"

"It is only temporary," said her papa, "and I have you to thank for the idea."

Simon held out his hand. "You have my thanks, sir, for your blessing and for the gift of Claire's hand in marriage."

Her papa shook Simon's hand. It was enough to show her the two men she loved had made peace. Given their prior relationship, she couldn't see her papa giving Simon the traditional French kiss on both cheeks.

"I trust you will take care of her, Powell. She'll not be forced to live on a ship?"

"I will love her all of my days," said Simon, "and she'll have a fine house in London."

Claire listened to the exchange, happy her father and the man she loved agreed on something involving her. Simon had told her the terms of the treaty ending the American war were not yet agreed to. Until they were, her papa and Simon were officially enemies.

Her papa narrowed his eyes on Simon. "And you will keep your promise?"

"Aye, sir, I will," Simon confidently replied.

"What promise?" she wanted to know.

"I think you will find it most acceptable, sweetheart, but I'll tell you when we are alone." He faced her papa. "Will you and your quartermaster join me in my cabin for some brandy?"

"French brandy?" her papa inquired with a wry smile.

"Aye, only the best."

"*Oui*, I accept." Her papa beckoned M'sieur Bequel closer. Simon welcomed him and, after the quartermaster greeted Claire and Mr. Landor, they walked to the aft hatch, she and Simon with her papa and Mr. Landor and M'sieur Bequel walking together behind them.

"By the way, sir," Simon said to her papa. "The wedding's in London as soon as we arrive. It was my hope you would give away the bride."

"If you allow my crew to sail the *Abundance*, I shall gladly go to London. I'm afraid were I to take my own ship, even disguised as she is, I would soon be discovered."

"I will agree if you allow the *Abundance*'s first mate, Mr. Busby to take command. The captain, Mr. Wingate, is in London just now but Mr. Busby is also a familiar sight on the London quay on that schooner and 'twould be best if he were on deck when she sails up the Thames."

"*Oui*, that is acceptable. But my daughter sails with me."

Chapter 21

London

Two days later, with the wind billowing her sails and Simon at the wheel, the Fairwinds sailed up the Thames, followed by the Abundance, captained by Amos Busby. Simon keenly felt Claire's absence for he'd been two long days and nights without her, his only glimpses of her lovely face the ones he'd had through his spyglass. He bided his time, knowing soon they would be together.

He'd not been surprised when Donet had insisted she sail with him on the *Abundance*, and though Simon would have preferred otherwise, he could hardly protest since propriety dictated she remain with her father until the wedding. He knew Claire would want time with her beloved papa before he returned to France.

Notwithstanding the pirate had given his blessing, Simon still had a lingering fear her father might try and dissuade her from her intended course. At dinner that first night in his crowded cabin, he had been encouraged to see the Frenchman's penetrating gaze had seemed to discern that Claire now belonged to Simon. Perhaps it had been the glances he and Claire shared throughout the meal, or the little touches they could not resist. He'd hoped the message he'd sent Donet was clear: *She's mine, she's happy and she's not going back to France.*

They sailed into the Pool of London, where the *Fairwinds* and the *Abundance* tied up at the wharf. Standing on the quay with Claire and her father, Simon explained that he and Claire would stay with Lord and Lady Danvers where the wedding would take place. Donet could hardly object with the baroness as chaperone. Anxious to speak to Cornelia about the plans for the wedding, Claire urged her father to agree, which he did.

Simon suggested Donet also might lodge at the Danvers' townhouse, but the invitation was declined. "That will not be necessary, m'sieur. I will make my own arrangements."

It was probably for the better that Simon did not know where Donet was staying. Eden was certain to ask. "Until this evening, then?"

"*C'est bien,*" came the reply as the Frenchman kissed his daughter's cheeks and walked briskly down the quay with his quartermaster and a few of his men. The thought occurred to Simon that Donet had been in London previously and knew the city well. It should not have surprised him, though he could not help wondering just how many times the pirate had crept into the city for his surreptitious dealings while the British military remained unaware. Probably too many for comfort.

Once Simon and Claire arrived at the Danvers' townhouse, he had a word with Cornelia and then left Claire and her friend to their plans while he left for Whitehall.

⟡ ᘛ⁐̣ᕤ ⟡

"How wonderful to have you back!" Cornelia said, embracing Claire. "But that rogue of yours might have given me more notice! A wedding with mere days to plan. I should have known when Captain Wingate brought that message asking Danvers to secure a special license Simon would be in a hurry. I shall be frenetic before 'tis over."

""I'm sorry, Cornelia. But then I had no idea either."

Cornelia gave Claire one of those looks that told Claire men rarely gave notice of their intentions. "Oh, well, I do love a challenge." Tapping her chin, the baroness began to speak her thoughts aloud. "We shall need the servants to go to market and shop for the wedding breakfast. We must have a house full of flowers. And champagne. Yes, there must be champagne."

Claire felt a twinge of guilt for all the work she and Simon were asking of Cornelia. "It is good of you and the baron to allow us to be married in your home."

"Oh, but you *must* have the wedding here. I would not hear of it taking place anywhere else. Besides, I adore parties!"

""Twill only be a small affair, certainly."

"Not too small," said Cornelia, gathering her paper and quill to take notes as they sat down to tea. "I'm so excited I can hardly think where to begin."

"I already have a gown," offered Claire. "That's one thing we need not bother with."

"Do you?"

"Papa had it designed when he thought I was to marry in Paris."

"And you would still want to wear it?"

"Oh, yes. Papa had it made especially for me and it's truly lovely, Cornelia. You will see when we go upstairs. It's in the chest the footman brought in." Claire thought of the gown and could not resist sharing the details with her friend. "It's made of ivory satin and embroidered with roses on delicate, green vines. The bodice is edged in Brussels lace with more at the elbows."

"It sounds beautiful. Your father must be an unusual man to have such elegant taste."

"He is," she said, feeling a sudden fondness for her papa. "I'm so glad he's agreed to the marriage and come for the wedding. Simon wasn't sure he would and that's why he—"

"Your father is here in London?"

253

"Oh, yes. He came on Simon's other ship, the one Papa has returned."

"I see. Well, I don't see precisely, but you can explain it all later." She brought her teacup to her lips and then, without taking a drink, returned it to the saucer. "I am most anxious to meet him. Just think, a real French pirate!"

"He isn't a pirate any longer," corrected Claire.

Patting her hand, Cornelia said, "Oh, I know. He is a privateer like Simon and Captain Field. Now there's an idea! Wouldn't it be grand if I could secure permission for the American privateer to attend the wedding and meet your father?"

"Could you?" Claire asked, hope rising at the possibility. "Papa would like to meet one of the Americans he has been working to free, though I don't imagine the English attending would be very pleased that one of their prisoners was invited. Or a French privateer for that matter."

"We will see. After all, the war is over for all practical purposes. They've resumed negotiations on the terms for peace. They only hold the Americans as insurance for the treaty. With Danvers' influence, we might just be able to see our American captain included as one of the guests. We women shall banish war forever, at least for the day of your wedding!"

Scribbling some notes on her paper, Cornelia ran the feather of her quill over her lips, thinking. "I shall have my maid dress your hair for the wedding. You will be ever so beautiful. Oh, Claire, how wonderful to think you will be married in our parlor!"

"Will the one marrying us be a member of the English clergy?"

"He must be if you are to be legally wed."

Claire brought her hand to her throat trying to still her raging pulse. She supposed it didn't matter really. "Papa would prefer a priest, but as long as the one performing the ceremony is a man of God, I will be satisfied. Frankly, I'm a bit overwhelmed at how hurried everything is, but Simon won't hear of any delay. He's quite insistent."

"I am not surprised," said Cornelia, smiling. Leaning toward Claire with a decided gleam in her eye, her friend whispered, "I knew he was in love. You must tell me all that has happened to bring you back to my door."

Claire felt the heat rise in her cheeks. She could never tell Cornelia all that had happened.

"You do look happy," said her friend. "Are you?"

Claire could not hide the truth of it. "Oh, yes, I am."

"I was right about Simon and how he feels about you, wasn't I?"

Claire looked down at her tea she had allowed to grow cold. "Yes," she said, furiously blushing at the memory of their lovemaking. She raised her head and looked into Cornelia's warm russet eyes. "You were right."

"However did Simon get you back? Do tell. I cannot believe your father agreed to the match. He was the one I was concerned about from the beginning."

"The story is a long one. Perhaps while I unpack, I can tell you."

Cornelia rose. "A good suggestion. And my maid can help. When we've finished in your chamber, we can be about our plans. Cook will need to be advised of the wedding breakfast and the food she must prepare. We will need sweetmeats from Mr. Negri's Pineapple shop, of course. And then we'll have to sit down and make a guest list. The invitations must be carried by messenger today."

They walked toward the wide staircase as Cornelia chatted on.

"Did Simon happen to mention a few extra guests for dinner?" Claire asked, embarrassed to be foisting all this off on her friend, but remembering Simon had requested her papa join them.

"He did. Not to worry, Claire. It is fine with Danvers and me."

⌒ ༺༻ ⌒

A black cloud followed Simon to Whitehall that afternoon. He dreaded having to advise Eden that Jean Donet was in London, but since Eden would be a guest at the wedding, he'd know soon enough. And Simon wanted Eden's word that Claire's father would be safe while he was here. Would Eden give him such assurance? And, if he did, could Simon trust him? Eden had already proven he was capable of deception to get at Donet.

When he arrived, Simon realized he needn't have worried. Eden was in very good spirits. "Come in, come in, Powell!" Eden cried. "Danvers is due here any minute. I've invited him 'round for a toast to Lord Shelburne."

"What's the prime minister done that has you raising a glass in his honor?"

Just then Danvers strode in. "Welcome! I see you made it to Paris and back."

"May I pour you both a brandy?" offered Eden, with an uncharacteristic smile.

Simon nodded and accepted the drink, as did the baron.

"I was just about to tell Powell here about Shelburne's latest coup in the negotiations."

"The old boy's done well," said Danvers, taking a sip of his drink.

At Simon's raised brow, Eden explained, "Seems the PM managed to enlist the French admiral de Grasse—who, you may recall, spent the summer in London as a prisoner on parole—to carry England's peace terms to Vergennes. In response, the French minister sent a close associate of his to London."

Reminded of the note he carried in his waistcoat, Simon handed Eden the missive from the Scribe. "Here," he said, "from my trip to Paris a week ago."

Eden set his glass on his desk and opened the letter,

laying it down and applying the chemicals as he had done countless times before. Reaching for his spectacles, he perused the paper. "Very interesting, this," he remarked. Taking off his spectacles, he raised his head. "Now we know precisely why Vergennes sent the representative he did to meet with Shelburne. It seems Grasse was not trusted."

"Who is the representative?" asked Simon.

"Gérard de Rayneval, the French Under Secretary of State. A trusted ally of Vergennes. He's been meeting secretly with Shelburne. Word has it that when Rayneval first met with Shelburne, the PM disavowed the message Grasse delivered to Vergennes. Things were a bit sticky after that, but Shelburne prevailed upon Rayneval to stay when he would have gone, and the two struck up a friendship. Now Rayneval will return to Paris convinced of Shelburne's sincerity and with a new set of terms we approve."

"A grand result," said Danvers. "We need Vergennes to help bring Spain to the table."

Simon sipped his brandy. "And the Americans?"

"More good news," said Danvers. "We have reached a separate agreement with them, though Franklin will likely have to apologize to the French for his breach of etiquette in doing so."

"A very good day," said Eden.

Realizing he would never have a more perfect moment, Simon said, "Since you are both in such good humor, I'd ask a favor." With their attention focused on him, Simon launched into his tale of personal success. "I've regained the *Abundance* and her crew—and much more. I've gained a French beauty who will soon become my bride."

His colleagues gaped at him.

"So the special license was for you and Claire Donet?" asked Danvers.

"Aye, just so. And thank you for procuring it." Simon couldn't resist a grin.

"You intend to marry Donet's daughter?" asked Eden,

disbelieving.

"Well she *is* the granddaughter of the comte de Saintonge," said Danvers. "He could do worse. And so could she. At least she'll have a man who is besotted with her." The baron slapped Simon on the back. "Well done, old thing, well done."

Eden harrumphed. "If you can talk that pirate into parting with his only daughter, Powell, it occurs to me we should have sent *you* to Paris to negotiate our terms for peace. What is this favor you want?"

"Donet has come to London for the wedding. I want your guarantee he will not be harmed nor any attempt made to capture him while he is here."

Eden stiffened and his face formed a frown. "You mean I'm to let him off scot-free?"

"Something like that," Simon muttered.

"Where is he?" Danvers asked.

"I have no idea where he is staying," said Simon, "but he intends to give away the bride at the wedding."

"And when is that?" Eden inquired.

"Two days hence. You're both invited, of course. Oh, and Danvers, I think you should know that your wife has graciously offered to hold the wedding in your home."

The baron choked on his drink.

Eden sputtered.

But in the end, Danvers recovered, the favor was granted and Eden grudgingly gave his word.

Simon was pleased.

Chapter 22

That evening in the Danvers' townhouse, Claire witnessed a miracle. Her papa and her new friends all toasted her upcoming marriage to an English privateer. She would never have believed it possible that persons of three nationalities and such different walks of life could gather in London to celebrate an English Protestant marrying a French Catholic and before the American war was officially at an end.

They began the evening in the baron's study, a footman circling with a tray of sherry and brandy. As she sipped her sherry, it occurred to Claire that her papa had never looked more like a French aristocrat than he did this night in his black silk coat and breeches set off by a claret brocade waistcoat and much lace at his chin. His black hair neatly queued at his nape and a gleam in his dark eyes, he appeared a well-born gentleman, not the pirate she knew he had been.

When the three men began speaking of the negotiations underway in Paris, Cornelia beckoned her aside. "Your father, Claire, is going to create quite a stir at your wedding."

Worried for her papa, she asked, "Why? Is there something wrong? Should I warn him?"

"Oh, no," her friend whispered. "You misunderstand." Shooting a glance at Claire's papa, Cornelia said, "I daresay there won't be a woman in the room who does not find her heart all aflutter. You never told me how handsome he is. How polished his manners. And there is something most mysterious about him, something almost… dangerous. I predict he will be quite the sensation."

Claire had always known her papa was a handsome man. Few men had his presence or his striking dark looks, but she'd never thought of him as an object of other women's admiration. "Oh my."

"Do not worry, Claire. I'm certain he knows how to handle such attention."

Simon came to her side then and slipped his hand into hers. "What are you two clever ladies discussing on your own over here? I am missing my bride." His amber eyes seemed full of mirth, happy in his teasing.

"We are discussing my papa if you must know," Claire said, teasing him.

Simon cast a glance at her father who, Claire thought, looked very much like the aristocrat he was raised to be. "He appears to be enjoying the baron's company," said Simon. "Perhaps we should join them before your father has the baron investing in one of his more questionable enterprises."

Cornelia gasped. Claire laughed. And Simon ushered them both back to the other men.

෧ ৩৫ ৯

The morning she was to be wed had arrived. Claire knelt beside the padded bench in her bedchamber and folded her hands in prayer. Though she would not be able to attend Mass in London and her wedding would be presided over by an Anglican clergyman, she could still make her confession before God and thank him for the man He had sent her.

When her papa had learned she would not be married by a priest, he had said nothing. Perhaps he had been resigned to that since he'd given his blessing to their marriage. Having allowed her to make her choice, he was apparently accepting what she could not change. She would hide her own discomfort. Simon might not be Catholic, but he was God-fearing, honorable and true. She would cast no cloud on their happiness.

Cornelia burst into the room shortly thereafter with a maid carrying a tray set with coffee and breakfast foods. The aroma of the dark brew and baked bread filled the room, reminding Claire of her hunger.

"The servants and Cook are all in a dither over the wedding," said her friend, "so I thought we'd have a bite together. After all, the wedding breakfast won't be for hours yet and we can't have you fainting. What say you?"

The maid set down the tray and asked if that would be all. At a nod from her mistress, she left the chamber.

"I have never fainted, Cornelia. But food sounds delightful. What about Simon?"

"Simon was all nerves this morning, so Danvers insisted they go for a ride in Hyde Park. 'Twill do them both good." Then with a wink, "And will keep them out of our way!"

"You and the baron are so good to us."

"Nonsense. I am having fun. And to see Simon happy after all these years brings us great pleasure. As for you, I look forward to having many adventures together. Just think, when your husband is off on one of his voyages, and Danvers is buried in his political scrabbles in the Lords, you and I can go to Bath or Brighton. And I've a few ideas for charities that will be needed following the war. So many families will have lost their men folk. It's a chance to do much good."

Claire's sprits rose thinking of the friend she now had. "Oh, Cornelia. I am so fortunate to have found you. I would love to help in your charities."

"I am counting on it. And I know Danvers is expecting to be an honorary uncle to your children."

The thought of children warmed Claire. Yes, she very much wanted to have Simon's children.

"Come now, Claire, wipe that smile off your face and help

me eat these pastries. I made sure they purchased some for us when the servants went for the sweetmeats for the wedding breakfast."

Claire bit into a fig pastry and a question rose in her mind. "I wonder where we shall live. Simon told me he has a house in Rye, but he said something to my papa about a house in London."

"You'll be pleased to know that last night he told Danvers and your father about one of the newer houses in the Adelphi Terrace he wants to purchase. 'Tis a good location for a sea captain as it's right on the Thames. I think after their ride this morning, they were planning to meet your father to view it."

Claire picked up her cup of coffee. "It will make Papa feel better about leaving me here if he knows Simon has plans for a home."

"It's a lovely area, Claire. And the best part is that you will not be far away."

When they'd finished their breakfast and had marveled over all that had happened to Claire since leaving the convent, Cornelia's maid came to supervise the lads carrying pails of hot water to her chamber for her bath. At Cornelia's request, the maid agreed to stay to assist Claire with her dressing.

Cornelia left Claire to her bath, but a few hours later returned with a box and a bouquet of flowers, which she set on the dressing table.

By that time, Claire was dressed.

"The men are back," Cornelia announced, "and have dressed for the wedding. You must hurry. The guests are beginning to arrive."

Butterflies began to flutter in her stomach, but Claire took a deep breath, resolving to stay calm.

Cornelia wore a gown of peach silk with lace at the snug-fitting bodice and sleeves. It was simple but elegant and went so well with her auburn hair and russet eyes.

"You look beautiful, Cornelia."

"Danvers likes me in this color, so I wear it often. For

your wedding, I wore my favorite."

Picking up the box she had set on the dressing table, Cornelia said, "Simon brought this for you. I'm dying to know what jewels he has bestowed on his bride."

Carefully, Claire opened the blue velvet box. "Oh my!" Sparkling inside was the most exquisite necklace of diamonds, rubies and gray pearls. Loops of diamond chains were draped over a thin collar of rubies. Hanging from the sparkling loops were pear-shaped pearls. "He must have remembered my wedding gown, Cornelia. Look how well this goes with the roses!"

"It would appear your sea captain has excellent taste. Those pearls are nearly silver. Here, allow me."

Claire held out the box and Cornelia took the necklace and fastened it around Claire's neck. In the box were also ear bobs of diamonds and the same pearls. When she put them on and stepped in front of the mirror, she was amazed at her transformation. No longer the young, convent student dressed in drab, dark blue, she was now a woman grown, adorned for her wedding. If only Maman could have lived to see this day. Would she approve? Somehow Claire thought the woman who had married a man who turned pirate for love of her would approve her daughter's choice.

"I like what my maid did with your hair," said Cornelia, fingering one long, dark curl. On the crown of Claire's head was a mound of curls save for one long curl draped over her shoulder. "And the gown is just as lovely on you as I pictured it, Claire. So unique. I've not seen one in London to compete with the workmanship of these embroidered flowers. Why they almost appear real."

"Papa was very proud of this gown. He selected both the fabric and the style. Your maid was kind to use the pressing iron to smooth the wrinkles. It was a bit crumpled as a result of our escape from Paris." She did not mention the carriage ride to Dieppe or the gown's brief sojourn on the deck of Simon's cabin afterward.

"You are all ready, save for this." Cornelia handed her the bouquet of orange blossoms that she'd brought with the jewel box. "It is tradition and represents the bride's purity."

Claire felt her cheeks flush. Simon had already claimed her virtue. Though the Reverend Mother would be horrified, Claire had no regrets. She had promised to marry him when he came for her in Paris. There would be no other for her. Only Simon.

He was waiting at the bottom of the stairs when she and Cornelia began their descent, his gaze fixed on her as a smile began to spread across his face. The sea captain had once again become the well-attired gentleman but with a vigor in his appearance that bespoke of his days spent in the sun, his hands steady on the wheel of his ship. His golden hair was confined to a neat queue, his broad shoulders encased in a cinnamon jacket with gold buttons. Beneath it was an ivory waistcoat trimmed in gold braid and dark brown breeches that hugged his thighs. Instead of his boots, he wore silk stockings and black shoes with gold buckles. Her golden one waiting to claim her as his bride.

"You take my breath away, sweetheart," he whispered in her ear as she reached him and he offered her his arm.

"And you mine," she whispered back.

The rising noise from the many voices in the parlor some distance away caused Claire to experience a sudden anxiety. *It must be a large crowd.* She had thought it would be a small affair. "You should have warned me."

"'Tis only the same friends of the Danvers who came to the soirée," he assured her. Then with a chuckle, "Well, and perhaps a few more."

Coming up behind them, Cornelia said, "They want to see the woman who has captured the gallant Simon Powell. And I am certain word of your father's coming has stirred quite a few to accept my invitation. Already the females attending are all a titter."

"Cornelia, you will make Claire nervous," Simon chided

the baroness. Then he smiled at Claire and all in her world
came right. "'Tis a grand day for a wedding, no?"

"Oh, yes. Yes, it is." It was a grand day to leave the past
behind and step into a future that was theirs. A future she very
much wanted.

He covered her hand with his palm. "You are the most
beautiful bride. But then your father has been telling me that
for hours. In the spirit of comity, I felt compelled to agree."

"You jest. But since it helps my nervous condition, I'm
grateful. Oh, and thank you for the necklace. It is the most
gorgeous thing I've ever owned."

"I'm pleased you like it. Of course, it's your own radiance
that makes the gems sparkle."

She returned his brilliant smile.

They entered the parlor and her gaze was drawn to the
many faces that turned toward them. Her papa, wearing a
black velvet jacket and his burgundy waistcoat, waited just
inside the door. "Claire." His dark eyes sparkled as he smiled
at her.

"Oh Papa!" So much emotion lay in their brief exchange.
He kissed her on the cheek and took her hand from Simon
and placed it on his own arm. Soon he would giving her back
to her golden one for always.

The Anglican clergyman was easily identified by his
appearance and where he stood on the far side of the room. A
white linen vestment covered his black robe and at his neck
were white Geneva bands. Though his gray hair gave him a
stern appearance, on his face was a smile, and for that, Claire
was grateful. Did he mind that Simon was marrying a Catholic?

"Don't worry, Claire," her papa reassured her, patting the
hand that rested on his arm. Then his eyes narrowed. "You
want this, *oui*? It is not too late to change your mind. I could
whisk you away to Paris where you'd have your choice of
many men."

"*Oui*, Papa, I want this. I love him."

"Then you need only repeat the vows the minister gives

you and you will belong to him. Baron Danvers does you an honor. The officiating clergyman is the Bishop of London."

When they reached the bishop, she let her hand fall to her side and joined Simon who was waiting for her, so that she was now standing between him and her papa.

The bishop made a few brief words of introduction explaining the solemnity of the occasion and then began the ceremony. Simon took her hand in his warm grasp. She was glad for his strength as she was trembling.

"Dearly beloved," the bishop began, "we are gathered together in the sight of God, to join together this man and this woman in holy matrimony… "

Claire stole a glance at Simon. His face was inscrutable. Did he have second thoughts?

The bishop continued, "… and therefore it is not to be taken in hand, unadvisedly, lightly, or wantonly, to satisfy men's carnal lusts and appetites, like brute beasts that have no understanding; but reverently, discreetly, advisedly, soberly, and in the fear of God…."

The bishop asked Claire if she would have Simon for her husband.

"I will," came her reply.

Then the bishop asked, "Who giveth this woman to be married to this man?"

Her papa said, "I do," and stepped back.

They exchanged vows and Simon placed a gold ring on her finger. She was certain it was the same ring he'd given her for their carriage trip to Rye. When she looked at him, questioning, he smiled. *It is the same ring.* Somehow that reassured her. Even then he had wanted her as his wife for he had purchased a ring too fine for a ruse. On her other hand she wore the blue moonstone ring her papa had given her, another symbol of love.

Holding her hand in his larger, stronger one, Simon said, "With this ring I thee wed, with my body I thee worship, and with all my worldly goods I thee endow: In the name of the

Father, and of the Son and of the Holy Ghost."

Sill holding her hand, they knelt and the bishop prayed. Simon squeezed her hand, assuring her of his presence, his love. She said a silent prayer, thanking God for leading her back to her golden one.

When it was done, they rose and Simon leaned down and kissed her. It was a tender kiss but in his eyes she saw the promise of more. "Mrs. Simon Powell," he said, "I like the sound of that."

"Me, as well."

Cheers went up from the guests as she and Simon turned to see their friends and well-wishers smiling at them. The bishop gestured them to a registry where they entered their names.

Her papa was the first to approach them. He shook Simon's hand and embraced her. "I expect you to visit Paris from time to time."

"I will Papa." She turned to Simon, seeking his agreement. He nodded.

"And I will come here," said her papa with a wink. "The war will be over soon and then I can travel more openly to England."

He bid them well and turned aside as other guests approached. She looked over the shoulder of one smiling guest to watch her papa walk into the crowd and noticed the eyes of many women following him. *So it is true what Cornelia said.*

Lord Danvers joined them then, Cornelia at his side. "Congratulations, old boy," he exclaimed to Simon. "You've done well."

"And so has Claire," Cornelia told her husband. "A fine match all around, one that happily keeps Claire in London. I couldn't be more delighted."

"Thank you for all you have done for us," said Claire.

Simon chuckled. "Aye, well, I suspect a large part of it is wanting me out of their townhouse."

"Too true," chimed Lord Danvers. "But then you bring

with you such interesting guests." The baron looked toward a group of men standing to one side. Claire's gaze followed.

"Simon, it's some of the crew! Why, there's Mr. Landor and Captain Wingate. Oh, and Mr. Busby and Mr. Hawkins. I almost didn't recognize them in their fine clothing. It's a far cry from the garb they wear on the ship."

Cornelia and her husband, pulled away by some of their guests, provided Simon and Claire a moment alone.

"I suspect that was Jordan's doing," said Simon. "He wouldn't let my men come in less than their best. And he could not have kept them away if he'd tried. They were determined to see us wed. Even young Nate is somewhere around here," he said, casting his gaze about the crowded room. "Or he was earlier."

Elijah Hawkins sidled up to them when he caught them looking his way. "Knew the cap'n was done fer the minute I saw ye," he said to Claire.

She felt herself blush. She had no idea the old seaman had considered them a match.

"'Tis clear you were meant for each other," said Mr. Landor, joining them, "and you make the captain very happy, madame."

"Thank you, Mr. Landor," she said, remembering his kindness in Calais. "I'm glad you and the others came to share this day with us."

She had met John Wingate since she'd returned to London, but did not know him as well as the others. When he, too, came to join them, she held out her hand. He bowed over it. "I hope you do not hold against me or my papa your imprisonment in Lorient," she said. *Surely he must.*

"It was war, Mrs. Powell, and 'twill soon be over. We are safely returned with none lost. For that I am most grateful. And I do not forget that you, too, were a prisoner. One, it seems, who has been captured for good."

Simon chuckled. "Aye, 'tis true."

She smiled, grateful for Mr. Wingate's understanding.

Simon's men waved as they walked away, promising to see them on the ship for Simon planned to sail to Rye the next morning.

Claire looked up to see M'sieur Bequel approaching her. He acknowledged Simon with a nod and then turned to her. "Little one, *vous êtes très jolie*, and the most beautiful bride I have ever seen. Alas, you marry an Englishman, but the *Capitaine* tells me you are happy, so I cannot object."

She kissed him on both cheeks as was their custom. At her side, Simon bristled. She turned to him, "I have known M'sieur Bequel a very long time, my love."

"It matters not," he said. "I'm just stingy when it comes to your kisses."

"Since her papa has given her to you with his blessing, *Capitaine* Powell, I wish you well." He bowed and left them.

Simon leaned in close and whispered. "Coming from your father's formidable quartermaster, that is a very large concession."

She nodded. "Oh, look, Simon, there's the American, Captain Field, over there with Cornelia. She told me she was going to try and obtain permission for him to attend. Isn't it splendid she was successful?" She waved to the handsome, young captain. "Do you mind if I go and greet him?"

Simon let out a sigh.

"Simon, I'm a married woman now. You can hardly object to me showing kindness to one of Cornelia's countrymen."

"I suppose not. But only a quick greeting and then you're mine. I'm hungry, and not just for food."

Claire felt her cheeks heat. "You are incorrigible."

"Aye, I am. But I've had only my men and Danvers for company. I long for yours."

Chapter 23

Simon watched his bride walk toward the American captain who had once before stirred his jealousy. Field must have been given new clothes with his invitation as he was much better attired than when Simon had last seen him in the warehouse.

The American captain kissed Claire's hand and Simon scowled just as Eden sidled up to him.

"Finally got to meet the infamous Jean Donet," Eden said. "Was rather surprised that he seemed so much the gentleman."

Simon wondered if Eden had forgotten his own spies could don a disguise if need be that rendered them quite different than their ordinary demeanor. "It's a wedding, Eden, and he's now my father-in-law. How would you expect him to act? And do not forget, he was raised a comte's son."

"Oh, trust me, Powell, I forget nothing. Might be able to use that connection at some point."

"You wouldn't dare."

"Oh, but I would," replied Eden. "Did you never wonder how it is he came to speak English so well?"

Simon shook his head. He had not given it much thought since Claire also spoke English.

"Seems he had quite a smuggling business into our southern ports at one time, Rye included. But then you were only a boy at the time. 'Twas before he became a pirate."

"He is a pirate no longer."

"Perhaps you are right."

Simon shrugged. Donet was well able to take care of himself. It would be unwise of Eden to tangle with him, pirate or no.

Higgins stepped into the room and announced, "Breakfast is served."

Simon reclaimed his bride and led her to the eating parlor, the ceiling of which he had long admired. Its corners featured casts of the four seasons: spring with garlanded flowers, summer with ears of corn, many fruited autumn and bearded winter.

The long table at which the guests were taking their seats was set with flowered china and crystal glassware. Simon thought the tall, silver candelabra marching up the center of the mahogany table surrounded by many hued flowers a bit much, but then it was a grand occasion. The grandest of his life. Cornelia had pulled out all the stops.

"It's all so splendid, Simon," Claire remarked as he escorted her to her chair.

"As long as it makes you happy, sweetheart."

Danvers took his place at the head of the table and remained standing to greet the guests as the footmen poured champagne. Cornelia was just taking her seat at the other end with the young Duke of Albany on one side of her and some peer Simon thought he'd met at the soirée on the other.

Simon helped Claire to her seat, next to his, in the middle of the table. Across from them was Claire's father. On Donet's right was a woman in a dark blue silk gown. Simon returned her smile but could not, for the life of him, remember her name. *Must be one of the baroness' friends.* She seemed rather taken with the French privateer who was smiling at something the woman had said.

Danvers claimed the guests' attention. "Lift your glasses as I toast the newly wedded couple. May mirth, love and children grace your home!"

Glasses were raised by all and the guests shouted, "Mirth, love and children!"

Claire blushed, but she recalled that Cornelia said Danvers had wanted children about even if they weren't his own.

Simon stood, glass in hand, and faced Claire. "To my bride and to our life together," he said, bringing another lovely blush to her cheeks. "I still can't believe, of all the men in the world, I should be so fortunate to have won your heart."

"To the bride!" echoed the guests.

Claire said, "And I am glad I have won yours, my love."

Simon smiled at the woman who held his heart in her hand and remained standing. Directing his next toast to Donet, he said, "To peace!"

Claire's father and the other guests seated around the elegant table raised their glasses as one. "To peace!"

Donet slowly rose from his chair, his face set in stone. Simon felt a wave of trepidation wash over him as he sat down. Whatever the pirate was about to say, he would say in dead earnest.

Simon had hoped they could avoid toasts to America's freedom or the British Crown. He did not wish to alienate his friends or cause a commotion at the wedding feast. He wanted the day to be a happy one for all.

Donet raised his glass and his dark eyes bored into Simon. "May you love my daughter as I loved her mother—more than my own life."

For a moment, silence prevailed as the other guests stared at the Frenchman.

Simon stood and, with his eyes fixed on Donet's dark countenance, lifted his glass. "More than my own life." Then he downed the rest of his champagne.

Again silence reigned. Then the women began to smile. The particular woman seated next to Donet stared at him with a look of longing. A tear streaked down Claire's cheek. At the far end of the table, Cornelia beamed at her husband at the other end. Then smiles broke out on the faces of the other guests until everyone at the table was smiling their approval.

Simon and Claire's father resumed their seats. Simon looked at his bride. Her eyes were filled with tears but there was a smile on her beautiful face. Their gazes met and the room seemed to disappear. His whole world was this woman whose love he had somehow managed to win.

Danvers cleared his throat.

Simon turned to consider his friend. "Aye, we should eat. After all, you and Lady Danvers have gone to much trouble for us."

Danvers glanced at his wife, his mouth twitching up in a grin, then he lifted his fork.

What followed was a sumptuous feast that resembled dinner rather than a breakfast, but since it was before noon, Simon recalled it bore the name of the earlier meal. Egg dishes and ham were accompanied by breads and pastries with butter and pots of honey and marmalade. As if that weren't enough, there were also plates of fresh fish in sauce and sliced cucumbers. Bowls of peaches, plums, figs and dark purple grapes were set between the candelabra. Simon plucked one pear from a bowl, supposing it was for eating as well as decoration.

After the guests had filled themselves, the footmen brought trays of sweetmeats and small cakes of various kinds. And more champagne, coffee, chocolate and tea.

When the wedding breakfast was nearly finished, Simon drew Claire from her seat. "I've a surprise for you." Her papa exchanged a glance with Simon and then rose and promptly left the table. Cornelia and her husband also rose, excused themselves from their guests, and exited the room.

"What is it, Simon?" Claire asked. "Where are we going?"

"You will see," he said wrapping his arm around her waist

and ushering her from the room. They crossed the entry hall to the baron's study. He opened the door and bid her enter.

In the middle of the study to one side of the desk, her papa and a Catholic priest stood talking together. Next to them stood Cornelia and her husband. Claire came to a sudden halt. "Oh, Simon!"

"I thought you might want a second ceremony. When I suggested it to your father, he wholeheartedly agreed."

Tears filled her eyes as she looked at Simon. He could not know how much it meant to her that he would honor her faith on their wedding day. It was a kindness she had not expected and a daring move. One she would never forget. "Thank you."

She walked toward the priest in his black robe and short, white vestment that indicated he was about to perform a ritual of the church. It was not unlike the one the bishop had worn, though perhaps simpler, less ornate.

The ceremony was short but very meaningful. And she could see her papa was pleased that her English husband had arranged it.

When it was done, Simon and her papa thanked the priest. Not everyone who had attended the wedding would have approved of the private ceremony. In truth, Claire knew many would not. Cornelia had told her that only a few years before there had been riots in London against the Catholics and now many worshipped only in house churches. But because he loved her, Simon had arranged for a Catholic wedding. How could she not love such a man?

❦

That evening, after many tearful goodbyes on the quay, Claire boarded the *Fairwinds* just behind Simon. Before they went below, he drew her to the stern rail to admire the sunset. Not far away, her papa stood on the deck of the *Abundance*.

They had shared a light repast with her papa before departing for their separate ships. Now that she was Simon's wife, she would sail with him to Rye and her papa and his men would sail back on the *Abundance*.

Claire looked into the clouds surrounding the setting sun. "It was the most wonderful wedding, Simon. I'm so glad the rain did not fall."

"It wouldn't dare," he said turning his back to the rail to look at her. His amber eyes glistened with desire.

"By the by, your father approved my choice for our new home."

"Did he?"

"It's one of the newer homes in the Adelphi Terrace. Just think, you will be able to watch me row from my ship to the front door."

"I would like that. But I would also like to sail with you." Seeing the frown that creased his brow, she added, "at least until the children come."

His eyes twinkled as he stepped closer and kissed her forehead. "Children. Aye, I want children. That reminds me. I never told you the promise I made to your father."

"Oh yes, what was the promise he was determined to see you keep?"

"I told him if he gave us his blessing our firstborn son would bear his name."

Claire couldn't resist a smile. "I would like that," she said. "Jean Powell."

"How does Jean Nicholas Powell sound?"

"It's a nice name, but why Nicholas?"

"Nicholas is the name of the captain I first sailed under, the one who taught me all I know about ships and the sea. He gave me a chance to rise in his crew. I owe him much."

"And so do I," she replied. "If you had never become a captain, I might never have become your captive. If God gives us a son, my love, then I agree Jean Nicholas is a fine name."

He led her aft, passing the smiling faces of his crew, who tipped their hats to their captain's new wife.

Once in his cabin, he lit a lantern and Claire suddenly felt shy. It wouldn't be the first time he'd made love to her, but it would be the consummation of their wedding vows. She was now a wife.

Looking back, she could see all that had happened that had led her to this day. Had she always loved him? She was certain the spark of love had kindled that night more than two years ago at the masquerade in Saint-Denis. Had God been guiding her all that time? *Perhaps.* She was more certain than ever the wise Reverend Mother would say so.

"Come, sweetheart, I can wait no longer for my bride."

She turned in his arms and allowed him to free her from her laces and stays. Soon they were both naked and standing before each other.

He took her face in his hands. "I intend to love you this night and all our nights for the rest of our lives." She opened her mouth to accept his kiss. "Now let's get started on making that son, shall we?"

❧

Rye

A few days later, after a dinner with Claire's father at the Mermaid Inn, Simon and Claire bid Donet goodbye on the wharf.

The Frenchman embraced his daughter. "When the peace treaty is signed, you will see me again." He held her away from him, smiling. "Perhaps I will come for the christening of that son who will bear my name."

Claire attempted a smile but, faltering, began to weep. "Oh, Papa, I will miss you so."

"I will take care of her, sir," Simon assured him.

Donet nodded, looking a bit careworn, Simon thought. Even a pirate could become emotional at having to say goodbye to his only daughter. Leaving her in a country that was not his own had to render the parting more difficult.

Bequel waited next to the skiff that would take Donet to *la Reine Noire*, anchored in the harbor just off shore, still bearing the name *Blessing*.

"I will write, Papa," she said through her tears.

Simon shook Donet's hand before drawing Claire close and kissing her temple.

"It will be all right, sweetheart."

Donet walked toward his quartermaster. Just before Donet stepped into the skiff, he turned and raised a hand in farewell.

Claire waved to him. "Papa… " she said in a forlorn tone. "What will happen to him?"

Simon turned her into his chest and with one finger under her chin, raised her face to his. Her eyes were troubled. He pressed a gentle kiss to her lips.

"You need not worry for your father, sweetheart. He will be fine." He kissed her forehead and then turned her so they could watch Donet settle into the skiff, looking toward his brig-sloop. "I have a feeling his story is just beginning."

And so it is.

Post Script

Not too long after Simon and Claire were married, on November 30, 1782, the United States and Great Britain signed the preliminary articles of peace to end America's War for Independence. By their terms, America received acceptable boundaries (greatly expanding the young country's territory), fishing rights and the right to navigation of the Mississippi River. The British acknowledged America's independence and promised to withdraw their troops. In exchange, Britain received little except America's agreement to honor its debts and a vague promise that Congress would recommend the states give fair treatment to the Loyalists.

On April 11, 1783, Congress officially declared an end to the first successful colonial war of independence against a European power. Though the preliminary articles did not become the formal Treaty of Paris until September 3, 1783, America had become a sovereign nation.

As for Claire and Simon, they were to have four strapping sons, the first of whom would be born in 1783. Each of their sons would have French and English given names. Their first-born son, Jean Nicholas Powell, named after his pirate grandfather, became a sea captain like his father. Nick is introduced in *Against the Wind* and his story is told in *Wind Raven*. Sir Martin Edward Powell, the second son, became a spy in Paris and England. He is introduced in *Racing with the Wind* and his story is told in *Against the Wind*. Lastly, Claire and

Simon had two twin boys, Robert Pierre ("Robbie") and Nash Etienne ("Nash") Powell, whose story will be told in *A Secret Scottish Christmas* where they vie for the love of a Scottish lass. You can get an idea of it from *The Holly & The Thistle*.

As the ending of *To Tame the Wind* indicates, the dark and dashing Jean Donet's story is just beginning. If all goes according to plan, *Echo in the Wind* should be released in 2016. It will be set in France in the years before the French Revolution. *To Tame the Wind* is thus both the prequel to the Agents of the Crown trilogy and book 1 of the Donet duology.

Author's Note

I hope you enjoyed my story of the American Revolution from a different perspective. To me, this time in the history of England, France and America is fascinating, but rather than set my story in America, I chose to set it in England, France and the English Channel.

In London, the War for Independence was known as "the American War". However, some members of Parliament argued it should be called "the French War" because of France's immense assistance to America. That France made possible America's victory cannot be doubted. It cost the French much to aid America, and the debt France incurred on America's behalf would set the stage for the French Revolution. But for the money and forces contributed by France, America might not have prevailed. According to Benjamin Franklin, our wily commissioner in Paris, France was having difficulty meeting its own expenses, "yet it has advanced six millions to save the credit of ours."

There were, of course, more players involved in the peace negotiations in Paris than my story would indicate. A few years earlier, John Adams had been charged with the mission of negotiating a treaty of peace with Britain. But the French did not approve of Adams' appointment and, on the insistence of the comte de Vergennes, Benjamin Franklin, Thomas Jefferson, John Jay (America's minister to Spain), and Henry Laurens were appointed to work with Adams, although

Jefferson did not go to Europe, Laurens was posted to the Dutch Republic, and much of the time, Adams was not in Paris. It was Benjamin Franklin who worked tirelessly to win the respect of Vergennes and the purse of France.

Franklin also worked to gain the freedom of American prisoners in England. As my story suggests, they were treated abysmally and died at an appalling rate. Hoping to gain British prisoners to exchange, Franklin issued letters of marque to three vessels that became American privateers: the *Black Prince*, the *Black Princess* and the *Fearnot*. Like the fictional *la Reine Noire*, the *Black Queen*, they were French-owned, but unlike Jean Donet's ship, they had American captains and Irish and American crews.

Privateers—British, French and American—played an important role in America's War for Independence. Unlike pirates, privateers acted under cover of government sanction (a "letter of marque") and generally behaved according to a code of rules. While they often sailed with several sets of false papers and the flags of a half-dozen nations and lied when they spoke to other ships, they were generally civil to the women they captured at sea.

There were many spies in Paris during the time of the American War, including Dr. Edward Bancroft, secretary to the American diplomatic mission, dubbed "the Scribe" in my story. At one time, he had worked for Franklin spying on the British, but when Franklin took up his role in Paris as an American commissioner, the British recruited Bancroft to spy on Franklin, which he did.

Bancroft's missives, written under the name "Edward Edward" using secret ink and transmitted via a bottle left in a tree in Paris, were not discovered until seventy years after his death when the British government provided access to its diplomatic archives. It is said that through his messages, George III knew of the French-American Treaty of Alliance just two days after it was signed. Bancroft's final work as "Edward Edward" lasted from the start of peace negotiations in the spring of 1782 to the signing of the preliminary peace accord on November 30 of that year.

William Eden, another historic figure, was the head of the British spies in Europe during the time of my story, probably overseeing a small group of intelligence collectors for Lord Suffolk. In 1789, Eden, rewarded for his many services to the Crown, was made 1st Baron Auckland.

I chose to begin my story in Saint-Denis, which today is a part of the city of Paris, to tell of the good work of the Ursuline nuns who, in addition to vows of poverty, chastity, and obedience, added a "fourth vow" of dedication to teaching. I knew nothing about them before I began my research but was impressed with all I learned. They became famous for their education of girls, from both noble and poor families. Élise was one of the latter, of course. In Ireland, they also educated boys like the cook McGinnes, who is a young man in this story, but is an older man (and perhaps a better cook) in *Wind Raven.*

Though they generally educated girls younger than the teenaged Claire, by special arrangement, her papa was allowed to leave her in the charge of Sister Augustin until she reached maturity.

Sister Augustin is the Mother Superior in my story, but she would have been more properly called "Sister Saint-Augustin" as was the Ursuline tradition in France at the time. Both Sister Augustin and Sister Angélique were modeled after real Ursuline nuns.

As my story indicates, the students in the Ursuline Convent would have received an excellent education. Though Claire was a wild child at heart, she would one day become the very proper lady she was raised to be, much loved by her English husband. (You may recall the conversation in *Wind Raven* where Nate, thirty-five years later, tells Capt. Jean Nicholas Powell, Claire's oldest son, about his mother.)

I invite you to visit my Pinterest board for *To Tame the Wind*: http://www.pinterest.com/reganwalker123/to-tame-the-wind-by-regan-walker/. There, you can view maps and pictures of the coastal ports, the characters as I see them, and even the convent in Saint-Denis as it is today. It's my research in pictures!

If you want to read the stories of Claire and Simon's sons, you can find them in the Agents of the Crown trilogy. For those of you who have read *Racing with the Wind*, did you note that Lord Ormond's father, the Duke of Albany, was a guest at the soirée Cornelia had for Claire in London in *To Tame the Wind*?

I love to hear from readers. Contact me via my website, www.reganwalkerauthor.com, and I promise to answer. There you can also sign up for my newsletter.

Coming next in 2015... I am going back to the 11th century for *Rogue Knight*, book 2 in the Medieval Warriors series, Sir Geoffroi's story.

Author's Bio

Bestselling author Regan Walker loved to write stories as a child, particularly those about adventure-loving girls, but by the time she got to college more serious pursuits took priority. One of her professors encouraged her to pursue the profession of law, which she did. Years of serving clients in private practice and several stints in high levels of government gave her a love of international travel and a feel for the demands of the "Crown" on its subjects. Hence her romance novels often involve a demanding sovereign who taps his subjects for "special assignments". In each of her novels, there is always real history and real historic figures.

Regan lives in San Diego with her golden retriever, Link, whom she says inspires her every day to relax and smell the roses.

www.reganwalkerauthor.com

CPSIA information can be obtained at www.ICGtesting.com
Printed in the USA
LVOW10s1603010615

440721LV00020B/1271/P